The Wisp

by Pryde Foltz

© Pryde Foltz 2014
All Rights Reserved
Available for sale on Amazon

Part I

The Enemy Within

I

A Dream

Bara walked along the boulevard. Above her head gentle gusts blew through layers of whispering leaves. Those with the lightest grip let go and cut red and gold traces through the air before settling soundlessly on the pavement below. The sun still shone brightly but a pale moon had crested the horizon. It was a lovely evening but Bara walked alone. Not another living soul—an empty town at a time when the residents of Windfall were usually rushing home for dinner. *How strange?*

But then there was a very insistent tug on her sleeve. Bara looked down. A little girl of maybe four or five years old looked back up. She wore a red pea coat with a matching beret. Curls not far off the shade of Bara's own strawberry blonde scooped down and just brushed her collar. Dark glasses with white frames—heart shaped—hid her eyes. The girl said nothing but a tear escaped from below the plastic rims and trailed down a plump cheek.

"Are you lost?" Bara asked. "Do you want me to help find your mommy?"

The little girl nodded and held out her hand. Bara

reached out but was jostled from behind before her fingers could take hold. The street was full now. A steady stream of men and women pushed and shoved as they passed. *Most peculiar.* They all wore sunglasses.

Bara looked down again. The little girl was gone. *Where?* The tot now stood under the shade of an oak tree a few meters away. A tall man, made even taller by a black top hat, had her by the arm and she struggled to get free. Something told Bara he wasn't the girl's father. A protective spirit surged in her. She fought her way through the crowd and threw her slight sixteen-year-old body at his massive frame. The man merely stepped back but he did let go of the girl.

"Run!" Bara said.

The girl didn't hesitate. Her short legs took flight and she disappeared into the crowd. Bara would get no chance for escape. Dark gloved hands reached out and took hold of her shoulders. She looked up, opened her mouth to protest, but never uttered a word. Because under the brim of the man's top hat were two empty black holes where his eyes should have been. Sudden terror squeezed her throat shut and her face screwed up in revulsion. It wasn't just the eyeless sockets. His eyelids quivered and for a moment something—something that shouldn't be there—rolled inside his skull in waves of shiny black.

The man gave a wry smile and let out a chuckle that cracked with charge. His black hands moved up from her shoulders and took hold of her throat. His fingers stiffened.

The realization hit. *He's going to kill me.* Bara struggled, her flailing arms making contact with no one and nothing. The man's smile grew wider. His grip tightened, closing off her windpipe. He lifted her from her feet. Her toes just grazed the ground below and then she was in the air ... only for a moment. His hands loosened from her throat and Bara fell to her knees. And then the man took flight. With her face hidden under red-gold curls a girl about Bara's own shape and size held him aloft with only one arm. Curiously she also wore a red pea coat and beret.

"She is mine," came her hissing voice.

Then as if the man were no more than a rag doll she tossed him aside. Before making contact with the asphalt he exploded in a burst of silver and screams. Charges trailed and sizzled through the air. When the sound and movement finally died down, a silver dust hung for just a second and then dropped with a surprisingly heavy thud. The wind blew away the dust and the man was gone.

Thinking the nightmare over Bara looked to her rescuer. Her rescuer turned to her. The nightmare wasn't over. There stood a mirror image—same shape, size, hair, and face. A doppelganger. Everything was the same, everything but the eyes. They were black and as empty as the man's had been. Slowly she cocked her head to the side. With a hand as gentle as a venomous snake she bent down and reached out for Bara's cheek.

"Hush, hush," she cooed and stroked.

Her youthful mouth turned suddenly down and she began to transform. Two heavy folds grew from her nose, dragging her cheeks until they sagged below her chin. Crow's feet formed around black eyes, spreading until they reached a now grey hairline. Finally deep crevasses pocked and ran across a once-smooth forehead.

Bara stared at herself as an old woman.

"I am here now," her demented double reassured. "Everything will be just fine."

But everything wasn't just fine, not even close.

The doppelganger smiled a very wide smile that grew wider, jaw-cracking wide. Wrinkles bent and twisted under the strain of an ever-increasing black hole of a mouth, a mouth that threatened to erase its face …

Suddenly it closed and returned to normal. She turned her head as though at a sound and then back at Bara.

"Soon," she whispered and then disappeared in a storm

of silver and electricity.

The doppelganger was gone, the man wasn't to be seen, and all the others had disappeared too. But Bara wasn't quite alone. A solitary form approached.

The dark-haired boy!

Everything *would* be alright now. This boy Bara knew well. He was tall and lean with broad shoulders, his strides long. His hair, dark and wavy, shown copper in a sun setting too rapidly to be real. But it didn't matter because Bara forgot about the racing sun, forgot the nightmare that had just occurred. He was so close now …

The sun slipped below the horizon. The sky disappeared into night. Bara heard her own breathing, fast and shallow. His was strong and even. She reached out. Her fingers found his warm cheek. She stepped closer and he opened his arms. Like someone had thrown a switch the moon lit up the sky. Stars burst through the night. His eyes, vibrantly blue, smiled down at her. His lips brushed her mouth. She returned the kiss, wishing it would go on forever. It didn't.

II

"They were tortured until they confessed. For those who continued to deny their guilt there was a test, the water test. A suspected witch was held under water. If she died, she was found innocent and buried in sacred ground. If she lived, she was proven a demon's handmaiden. Death by burning was her fate."

Professor Chestermire paused and sipped at his coffee. The students of St. Catherine's Academy for Girls—St. Cat—were studying the witch trials of Europe. Everyone was too worried about the upcoming exam to give any real thought to what they heard. The only sounds outside Chestermire's voice were the low murmur of clicking keyboards or the even smaller scratch of pen on paper. But Bara remembering something about her own town's history did the unthinkable and raised her hand. Like having just one hair out of place on a thickly-jelled and smoothed head, it instantly caught his attention.

"Yes Miss Cavanagh?"

"Didn't Windfall have its own witch trials?" she asked.

The question wasn't met with any real curiosity from the rest of the class. It wasn't like it was going to be on the test. Keyboards stopped clicking; pens stopped writing.

Most of the girls just phased out, but Cassandra rolled her eyes, Louise snorted, and several other Pops, the most powerful clique at school, followed suit by giggling.

Bara despite her good looks and money wasn't popular. She wasn't counted among the brains and she certainly wasn't a Goth. She had only two real friends: Amy Frank and Colin Van Fitt from the neighboring St. Xavier's Academy for Boys—St. X. With friends like Amy and Colin, Bara told herself she didn't need the rest. *Quality over quantity, right?*

Anyway that's what she told herself.

Chestermire laughed good-naturedly.

"Quite right, quite right, Miss Cavanagh. Salem, Massachusetts is most often remembered for its witch trials of 1692 but Windfall did have its own *Petit Inquisition*."

He paused, taking another sip of coffee. His mug claimed he was the number one teacher. Placing the self-congratulatory cup on his desk he put his hands into the pockets of his sweater vest, puffed out his sizable chest and even bigger belly, and rocked ever so slightly on his heels. This was a sign. He was about to go on and on—and possibly—on some more. Sly smiles crept onto teenage faces. The more time he spent answering Bara's question, the less time everyone else would have to spend memorizing facts. Forbidden cell phones emerged from bags and pockets; browsers opened to banned websites.

"If I remember correctly it was five women and one man found guilty. They were sentenced to burn at the stake, except for one. Her, they intended to bury alive."

The mention of burning flesh and live burials regained the attention of a few others, Patsy Pillanger among them, the only girl less popular than Bara.

"They really *burned* them?"

Patsy hadn't raised her hand. Chestermire narrowed his eyes before answering her.

"There's no record of anyone actually having been burnt or buried. Rumor is some remains were sunk in a lake just north of Windfall, a lake which has since dried up. But I would imagine the townsfolk saw sense before actually putting match to light."

"Did they really believe in witches?" Bara asked.

Most of the other girls realizing no grotesque story of witch burning was to come shifted focus back to where it had been. The tech-inclined texted or surfed, the brains caught up on homework, and most everyone else drifted back into daydreams. Chestermire might as well have been only talking to Bara. She was the only one listening. But then a small, sparking touch on her shoulder split her focus. Assuming it was Amy her first thought was to ignore it but there was a second, more insistent summons.

Bara turned around. A bright glare came through the window. She brought up her hand to shield her face and blinked. The light disappeared. When her vision cleared there was Amy with her head down in a Math textbook. Amy didn't look up. She hadn't tapped her shoulder.

Okay ... maybe someone had thrown a wad of paper? It wouldn't be the first time. The Pops often used Bara as target practice but both Louise and Cassandra had their heads down, their concentration focused on their laps. Their hands moved ever so slightly. Then they both giggled, one after the other, obviously texting each other. It hadn't been them either. Bara continued to look around. No one met her eye and no one seemed to be purposely avoiding it. But there was no way she'd imagined the touch.

Chestermire's sharp voice interrupted her thoughts.

"Really Miss Cavanagh, you asked the question. It is only common courtesy that you await the answer before turning your attention elsewhere."

Bara turned back. Chestermire had grown red in the face and his thick neck bobbed side to side in his starched collar. He resembled a boiling kettle top. It was hard not to laugh.

"I'm sorry," she said, stifling her giggles. "I was distracted. I thought someone tapped me on the shoulder."

"That could only have been Miss Frank."

Amy raised her head.

"Well Miss Frank? Did you tap Miss Cavanagh on the shoulder?"

Amy looked blankly.

Chestermire's voice rose in volume.

"Of course, you didn't."

Somebody quipped, "Barbie was off in her Malibu mansion."

"No," someone else, no doubt a Pop, chimed in. "Her dad lives with Barbie now."

Ouch! Bara's parents were freshly divorced and her father newly married to a much younger and blonder woman. Bara was far from okay with it. There were unkind snickers all around.

Chestermire held up his hand to signal for silence.

"No Miss Frank, your interest was elsewhere as was Miss Cavanagh's." He looked pointedly at Bara. "Would you like me to finish?"

She nodded.

Chestermire scanned the classroom. Those who happened to be looking up nudged those who weren't.

Electronic devices were put away, browsers closed.

All eyes faced forward.

"Well then," he began again. "The women were jailed and tortured. The question is why. Did the townspeople truly believe in witchcraft? Witches? Demons?"

No one responded and he answered his own question.

"They may have practiced ancient ways of healing and non-Christian religion, nature worship and such, but communing with the *dark side?*" Chestermire looked ominously at a few of the Goths, smiled, and shrugged. "I don't think so. It is far more likely that the townsfolk wanted the wealth the women would lose if they were found guilty. They were all without husband, widowed, or orphaned, and all held property. Greed would seem the obvious motive."

He took another sip of coffee and continued on with the lesson. Again keyboards clicked; pens scribbled. With the heat finally off Bara looked back. Amy gave her a sympathetic smile in return.

The bell rang. Chestermire reminded the class of their upcoming exam and dismissed everyone. The girls began to pack up and exit. The Goths all but flew out of the room, their long black hair flapping like crow wings behind them. Everyone else moved at varying but slower speeds. Bara slid her laptop into her bag and was quickly ready to go. Amy taking a little longer had pens, highlighters, and notebooks to put away.

"I have to go to Tech and sign out a computer," she told Bara. "Do you want to come with? Then we can go the library?"

Amy finished packing up and headed for the door. Following behind Bara yawned.

"You know what? I think I need a coffee."

They spoke in hush tones as they walked down the hall. The terrible twins, Cassandra and Louise, watched. They stood near the exit with the other Pops gathered around paying court. It would do no good letting them overhear.

"You dreamed about him again?" Amy asked.

Bara was having a reoccurring dream about a dark-haired boy. The dreams were usually pleasant enough. *Okay, maybe too pleasant.* They left her with a sense of longing when she woke and realized he didn't really exist. But the last dream had been a bit terrifying too—eyeless doppelgangers and mouths threatening to eat their own faces. Not exactly sweet dream material. Getting back to sleep afterward had been a struggle and Bara was exhausted.

"Why don't I go and get us a couple coffees?" she

offered. "Then I'll meet you down in the stacks."

Amy agreed and they separated, going in opposite directions. Bara headed for the exit. *Just ignore them.* She had to pass the Pops. She stumbled and almost fell. Someone had tried to trip her. She didn't stop to identify the culprit. Such occurrences were far too common to bother.

"Say hi to Ken, Bar—beee," Louise taunted.

Mocking titters followed Bara down the hall and out the door. They ended with the slam of wood against a metal door frame.

III

Everything was alive with wind and color. Bara took a deep breath. The air smelled of trees—damp but fresh. A falling leaf settled on her shoulder and worries fled. She paused long enough to wrap her scarf around her neck and then made her way across St. Cat's wooded lawn.

Windfall was surrounded by a forest on three sides with the ocean not far off on the fourth and it wasn't hard to see how the town had gotten its name. As Bara turned onto Windfall Boulevard leaves fell as thick as snow on a winter day. The oaks that lined the street were hundreds of years old. Rather than reaching for sunlight lower branches had grown earthward and now selfless limbs braced the ancient giants against toppling under their own weight.

At one end of the Boulevard was the School District where both St. Cat and St. X could be found and not too far off Windfall High. You could travel from St. Cat and follow the boulevard to Library Square—the heart of the town. Several streets fed off the square.

Maple Avenue ran north and would take you past a middleclass neighborhood. The home Bara sometimes shared with her mother was at the end of the avenue in the Garden District. Anything but middleclass the Garden District had some of the largest homes in North America. Continuing straight through Library Square along the east end of the boulevard, you'd pass through a heavily-wooded park, a forest really, and then finally the Grande Oaks District where her father and his new wife, Courtney, lived. South of the square was the Business District and further south a rundown area known as the Tracks. This was where Amy's family lived. But Amy attended St. Cat on scholarship so most of the time she roomed with Bara on campus.

Before reaching Library Square Bara veered off

Windfall Boulevard and cut across a small park with a fountain—a shortcut. A chestnut fell from the sky and collided with her foot. She watched it skid to a stop at the base of its parent tree. Just then her coat pocket vibrated. She stopped under the shade of the tree and took out her phone. Colin had sent a text.

Help! They're either trying to poison or starve us. Save me! Send food. Colin was forever complaining about the meals at St. X. Day old cat food he called it—spiced with kitty litter. He didn't kid. Bara often took pity and brought him treats from St. Cat's dining hall. *I'll see what I can do* she texted back and continued on her way.

Bara left the park and crossed Main Mall, a street of banks and a supermarket. Rounding a corner she found the south entrance to Windfall Way. It was one of the town's original streets. It wasn't much wider than a single lane of traffic which four hundred years ago served just fine for horse and carriage. But today's large SUV's would have taken out the potted plants and store signs hanging out into the road. So now it was pedestrians only.

Antique and curio shops dominated the lane. There were also two restaurants, French and Italian; a flower shop; a bakery; and the Tragic Sip Café where without a doubt they served the best coffee on the planet.

Windfall stopped an inch past way-too-much when it came to decorating for seasons and holidays. Along the lane every window was filled with strings of fall leaves and pumpkins. There were even a few black cats, skeletons, and other left-over Halloween ornaments. Bara smiled at the festive air and made her way down the cobbles.

The Goths had beaten her to the Tragic Sip. They occupied two tables. For these girls Halloween never ended but under the bright sunlight even their deathly-white faces glowed an almost healthy—if unnatural—pink. They were all but quivering with excitement, not the usual state of being for this gloomy group. Taking no notice of Bara as she passed they spoke excitedly.

"He's so gorgeous," Drusilla, not the name her mother gave her, Barnaby drawled.

Vixen Rose, born Vivian Rothby, returned, "I saw him first."

"Finally a guy worth even thinking about in this stupid town," said a purple-haired girl Bara didn't know. She must have been in a grade below.

"One thing for sure," Drusilla chimed, "we're all going to need *a lot more coffee.*"

"I want a little more than coffee from him," Vixen countered.

There must be a new baristo. Bara was filled with curiosity. She could only imagine what kind of guy would get the Goths all a flutter. Images of tattoos and rings hanging from each and every orifice came to mind. Well she'd soon see *Mr. Dreadfully Wonderful* for herself. She headed for the café door and almost stopped in her tracks.

Ragman, the strangest resident of Windfall, sat at the table closest to the door. He stared at her with a smirk, a way-too-familiar smirk. They'd never spoken. Yet he always managed to irk her. He just gave her the strangest feeling. The way he dressed didn't help. His wardrobe consisted of torn pieces of old clothing tied together to form a kind of mesh. A little more skin than was decent peaked through. He wore sandals even in cold weather. His bald head was covered with a red and black bandana and it wasn't just his head that was hairless. Except for his eyebrows which were exceedingly bushy, he was as smooth as porpoise. He had to wax.

Swallowing her ill-ease Bara passed Ragman—who never broke his glare—and entered the café.

The air rang with the tinkle of door chimes.

Inside was as full as the patio. Bara looked around, trying to pinpoint the object of the Goth's affection. Waiting tables was Mona, a twenty-something pretty brunette. Surly Bob staffed the counter. He wasn't new. No one else seemed to be working. Bara scanned the tables full of housewives taking a break from shopping but whoever had grabbed the Goths' attention had either finished his shift or was on break.

Surly Bob noticed her standing in the middle of the café. He threw her an impatient glare and asked if she needed any *help*. The way he emphasized the word help made her think he meant *mental* help. Bara had been coming to the café since she'd been old enough to drink coffee but he still treated her like a stranger. She ignored his obvious disdain and ordered two Black Mountain Blends and a couple of croissants. While waiting for her order to be filled she watched the backroom door for any sign of the new guy. It remained closed.

None too swiftly and like he was doing her the greatest of favours Surly Bob poured the coffees and bagged the pastry. Bara paid and stepped over to the condiment table. She took her time adding cream and cinnamon, maintaining an eye on the backroom door, hoping to catch a glimpse of the new baristo. Chimes rang again. Drusilla came in and sauntered over to the counter. Incidentally she also watched the backroom door. She hummed and hawed for what felt like a painfully long time, even to Bara, so to Surly Bob it must have been truly excruciating.

Finally she said, "I'll have a chai."

"A chai what?"

Surly Bob rolled his eyes. Drusilla acted confused, thinking her request obvious.

Letting out enough air to inflate a balloon, Surly Bob sighed. "A chai tea? A chai latte? A chai muffin? We *gotta* a lot of chai."

Drusilla pursed her mouth and put one hand on her hip. She'd had this planned.

"Then why don't you *chai* being nicer, dude?"

Then apparently no longer thirsty she turned on her heels and flounced out of the café, leaving Surly Bob with a look on his face that could only be described as priceless. Bara fought not to laugh but couldn't help smiling. Surly Bob shot her a glare. *Time to go.* She took one last look at the backroom door. No dark teenage god appeared. She shrugged and went back out into the bright sunshine. The patio was almost empty. Both the Goths and Ragman had gone. Bara took a left and walked north, heading toward the tall clock tower looming ahead.

She entered Library Square.

In the late afternoon sun Main Hall threw a pretty imposing shadow across the cobbles. Constructed more than a hundred years ago with its marble columns and stone lions, it was a building meant to inspire awe. Two stucco wings built somewhat later weren't as awe-inspiring. Stucco hadn't aged nearly as well as stone. The wings now hung off Main Hall like two unsightly love handles. These were the stacks. Inside they were dusty and at times smelled just a little rank, but it was where Amy and Bara always studied. There, they'd be left alone.

The clock tower chimed as Bara climbed the stone steps. After taking a moment to hide the coffees she pushed open the glass doors and passed through the entry hall and under the portrait of Nelson Sedgewick. A rich coal tycoon, Sedgewick had left his money to the library. His hair was rather on the brighter side of red but he'd been attractive enough. There was a kind look in his warm brown eyes. He seemed to be watching over his beloved library.

Ms. Korey eyed Bara up as she walked by the checkout. Bara smiled back guiltily. It wasn't just the coffee contraband. Ms. Korey always made her feel a little off. Despite her petit frame the librarian was as intimidating as a Rottweiler.

Bara entered the west wing. Finding a rickety old staircase she descended creaky metal rungs and reached into the underground portion of the stacks. Another reason she liked the stacks: they ran deep—deep underground actually. Underneath the three above-ground floors were still another two levels—a cellar of knowledge and fantasy.

She reached the lowest floor. Somewhere down here she and Amy would find each other. They hadn't said exactly where they'd meet. They didn't need to.

Bara headed for the far left corner—their usual spot.

***

An unseen observer had watched Bara leave St. Catherine's and walk down Windfall Boulevard. Its gaze didn't flicker when she cut across the park with the chestnut trees. Patiently it waited while she was in the café. It followed her across the square and watched her enter the library. Unseen by all it pushed through the glass doors and pursued down into the stacks.

It had a plan, a plan for Bara. Shuddering it shook the air with its intent. Bara felt the breeze but saw no one. For the watcher the eternal wait was all but over.

IV

Bara walked past rows of dusty volumes stacked on worm-eaten wooden shelves. She really didn't feel like studying just yet. Amy always took ages in Tech and probably wouldn't arrive for a while. So why not do a little reading? Picking a random row she took a left. Her hand grazed firm backs and metallic emboss. She didn't have a book in mind. The right one would call out. A tingle, maybe a shock of static, bit at her fingertips and Bara stopped to see which book her hand had settled upon.

She found herself in the L's. Taunting her from the shelf, worn and frayed, was an ancient edition of the *Magician's Nephew*.

***

An invisible curtain hung, isolating the diners from one another. They ate in an oak-paneled dining room at a long oak table—a very long oak table. Three of the four middle leaves had been removed but it was still too big for just the three of them. Mr. Cavanagh sat at one end with his new wife to his right, his daughter to his left. To Bara her father felt miles away, her stepmother far too close.

There was only one saving grace—a large centerpiece. If Bara slouched she could almost hide her entire face behind the orange tiger lilies and bright red mums. But there was no real hiding … not really.

Courtney shifted so she could see around the flowers.

"Do you like the roast?" she asked.

Bara nodded but said nothing. Her dislike for Courtney only grew when she was in her presence—with her perfectly-coifed hair and pink cashmere sweater set. *Blah!* Courtney always wore pink. Bara never wore pink and not because she was almost a redhead. She hated what she thought of as an insipid shade of red. Pink—the *girl* color. Why not just wear a sign that said *walk all over me. I'm vulnerable and weak?*

Without a doubt pearls would have suited the pink cashmere. Bara's mother always wore pearls. *Her mother* had a wonderful sense of style but Courtney for some reason had chosen a simple locket. It was dark silver but not actually silver. Maybe iron? Large and heavy, it was clumsy looking on her slender neck.

Courtney looked to her husband and he gave her a reassuring smile. She reached below the table. Her hands reappeared with a pale pink box with a bright fuchsia ribbon. A little too excitedly she pushed the box close to Bara.

"I was shopping this afternoon," she explained, "and I found this wonderful little bookstore."

Bara put down her fork and eyed the box suspiciously. She sighed and removed the lid to reveal a leather-bound edition of the *Magician's Nephew*. She knew the story well.

"I hope you like C.S. Lewis." Courtney chimed happily, sensing her pleasure.

And Bara was pleased but then she remembered how her mother had read the story to her, years ago. No way was she going to accept this book from Courtney, the woman who—as far as Bara was concerned—had broken her family in two. *No way!* Of course Courtney couldn't have known the meaning the book would have for her stepdaughter. She was still smiling when Bara thrust it across the table.

"I already have a copy," Bara said. "Maybe you can get your money back."

Bara returned to eating.

After a moment Courtney got up from the table.

"I think I'll see to dessert," she said and left the room.

Mr. Cavanagh went to scold Bara but *the look in her eyes ...* he softened. *She needs time to get over the whole thing* he thought. *It's just too soon.*

***

Breaking the rules of her own game Bara lifted her hand and reached instead for a copy of the *Hideous Strength* lying a little less mockingly on the same shelf. *So there!* she retorted to no one but herself. Clasping it to her chest she made her way back down the aisle. The *Magician's Nephew* remained untouched on the shelf.

Bara found a termite-eaten study carrel, switched on the reading lamp, and sat down. She took a sip of coffee and opened the *Hideous Strength* to a random page. This wasn't her first reading. She was just looking to pass the time and seconds later she was in pursuit of an immortal Merlin.

The coffee wouldn't be enough. Bara read a page and then realized she had no idea what she'd just read. Her mind drifted. With the written page of C.S. Lewis, dreamy blue eyes fought for her attention. She blinked hard. It was a good fight but then a heavy head drifted down into the crook of her arm. It felt good to be there, so she gave in and surrendered to dreams.

A mist rolled in. Bara might have fallen into a deeper, dreamless rest but the soft whistle of rustling paper filled the air. Books, rusty brown and red, flew from the shelves, performing a strange aerial ballet like that of a troop of jet fighters but at the speed of falling leaves.

They circled around her.

Bara came to her feet and reached out her dream hand. Her fingers grazed a hard cover and soft pages. A book fluttered to the ground, settling on the stone floor soundlessly. A small breeze flipped pages and lifted locks of her hair. She reached out for another but was interrupted by the sound of someone coming down the stairs and passing close by. She looked but saw no one.

The wind picked up then and was now thickly-scented, sweet and floral. It rustled through the alit books. As each was touched by the sickly-smelling zephyr it dropped with a heavy thud. Eventually the air was empty, the floor littered with open spines and fluttering sheets.

As sometimes happens in a dream the place and characters changed. Bara was far from complaining.

The dark-haired boy had joined her.

They sat on a low stone wall under the shade of blossoming cherry tree. Pink petals drifted down. A bloom landed in her hair. He plucked the pink from her red-gold locks and held it up to the blue sky. In his hand the single petal multiplied and darkened. The one cherry blossom became a full red rose.

Delighted Bara took the flower.

"Who are you?" she asked.

The dark-haired boy opened his mouth to speak and dissolved to mist. She was left sitting under the tree, alone. But then there was a touch on her shoulder. It sparked with electricity. Perhaps he'd come back. She opened her eyes.

The stone wall and cherry tree were gone. She was again seated at the study carrel, her head in her arms.

No dark-haired boy.

Still she had the strangest feeling. Had the tap been real? *Yes!* There was a second and another spark of static. She lifted her head and looked for Amy but no one was there. Bara sat up, suddenly remembering where she'd felt that touch before—History class. And just like in History class there'd been no one there. But someone had definitely touched her ... and then there it was—a bright light and a wisp of silvery white wafting through the air like a long flowing scarf. The vision disappeared into the book stacks. Seconds later there it was again, passing between the aisles and moving incredibly fast.

Bara jumped up and pursued, running down the aisle where it had last been. But there was no one there. She ran to the next row and the next and then retraced her steps. Definitely no one and nothing.

Okay... what was going on? There seemed just one likely possibility. *It was just a dream, freak.* Bara laughed at her own silliness and went to return to the carrel but stopped. On a neighbouring shelf one book hung over the ledge, threatening to fall to the ground. She reached out to return it to its proper place but pulled back and stared.

Again in the L's she was in the spot she'd stood before. The book that hung over the edge was the *Magician's Nephew*. But Bara hadn't done this. She'd made a point of not touching it. Could someone else have come down into the stacks and moved it? It seemed too much of a coincidence.

Bara reached out. Her hand just touched the spine and there was that same sickly scent and that same odd breeze. Someone stood just behind her now, breathing thick floral-scented breath upon her neck. She spun around and found herself back in the dream terror of the night before. Strawberry-blond hair streamed over a large black mouth, a mouth that had consumed its own face and now seemed determined to consume her.

The doppelganger had returned. A screamed built up in Bara's throat but it was never released. Behind her there was the thump of a book landing on the floor.

V

"Sorry I didn't mean to scare you."

Amy gave her a confused look. Bara stood up and looked around but there wasn't anyone to see. Except for her and Amy the stacks were deserted.

"Was anyone else down here?" Bara asked. "Maybe they passed you on the stairs or something?"

"No? I think it's just us."

"Wearing silver and white?"

Amy shrugged.

"I didn't see anyone."

"Or someone who maybe looked just like me?"

Amy needed some clarification.

"You mean besides you?"

"Yes."

"What a strange question. What's going on?"

Bara sat back down. She rubbed her aching temples.

"I had the oddest dream. It seemed so real."

"Did you dream about *him* again?"

Bara smiled guilty.

"Yeah … but that wasn't the strange part. It was really weird. I was sleeping and I knew I was sleeping. Someone tapped me on the shoulder. A woman, I think. I remember smelling her perfume. It was very strong. You're sure you didn't smell anything?"

Amy shook her head.

"I only caught a glimpse before she disappeared into the stacks. She was all flowing like—wispy. She had silver hair. I couldn't find her when I followed but a book was moved. Then everything just became a nightmare. I was attacked by someone who looked just like me, only she had this really big mouth. I think she meant to eat me."

"That's freaky!" Amy laughed. "But you want to talk terrifying? I once had a nightmare that I'd married Chestermire and Patsy Pillanger was our daughter."

"Okay." Bara chuckled. "That's worse."

"But what book was moved?"

Bara picked up the *Hideous Strength* from the floor where it had fallen and waved it in front of Amy.

"It was the *Magician's Nephew*. It was next to this."

Amy gave her a look that said *so what*.

"Come on. I'll show you."

Bara got up and led her to the L's. She stopped short. One book—no one had to tell her which—hung off the shelf. Amy came up behind. She looked at Bara who stared agog down the aisle and then noted the dislodged spine.

"You moved it yourself."

"No. No I didn't."

Amy wasn't convinced. She had no reason to be spooked. She hadn't had the dream. Brushing past Bara she grabbed the *Magician's Nephew* and held it out.

"See, just a book."

Thud. The volume that had rested next to it toppled face-down to the floor.

"What's that?"

Amy looked down.

"Another book, so what?"

"No it's something more."

It was a book alright. But what a book! Bara picked it up and wiped away at dust. There were five amber pieces on its leather-bound cover, orange ovals about the size of a sand dollar. They encircled a central golden cross. Technically amber wasn't a gem, rather petrified tree sap, but the sheen and cut of this amber was every bit as fine as any diamond. Bara ran her hand over the amber once again. Her fingers traced the circle, stopping before completing the full arc. It was truly beautiful, almost perfect, except for what must be a missing sixth piece of amber, a break in the circle. She held it out for Amy.

"What do you think?"

"Wow! Let me see."

Bara handed it over. Amy ran her hands over the cover the same way Bara had done. She gave it one more look and handed it back. She picked up the *Magician's Nephew*, returned it to the shelf, and then headed back to the study carrel. With the found book clasped tightly to her chest

Bara followed. They arrived back at the carrel. Amy grabbed a coffee and croissant. She sat down and began to eat and drink.

"Well what's it about? Open it up."

Bara ran her hand along the spine of the closed book and then cracked it open. The first page was yellowed with age. There was no writing, just a drawing of the front cover without the missing stone, a perfect circle of six.

"What's it called?" Amy asked.

"It doesn't seem to have a title."

Bara turned another jaundiced page. She shivered a full body shiver and then held up the book so Amy could see what was drawn on the second page—a five pointed star within a circle. Amy choked on a mouthful of coffee. She looked at Bara wide-eyed.

"No way! Maybe we should just put it back where we found it? This reminds me just a little too much of the start of a horror movie."

Bara gave Amy a blank look.

"The walls are bleeding and the house is screaming *I know what you did last summer*."

Bara shook her head.

"Actually I think the circle and the star are meant to be a protection against evil."

Amy wasn't convinced.

"You know what? It's all a little bit much for me—dreams and black magic books. Leave it on a shelf somewhere and some other sap can find it."

Ignoring the suggestion Bara flipped another stiff page and read out loud.

Dear Clavigen,

If you have found this book you were destined to do so. The responsibility is now yours. You must slay and cage the evil. Beware. She will come in the guise of beauty and kindness. Be not a fool. There is no goodness in her heart. The demon is a trickster, so let her not trick you. The gift of the ages she offers is a living coffin. Put her in hers before she puts you in yours. Should you meet with more success than I.

Nelson Sedgewick

"Nelson Sedgewick? Doesn't he have a portrait upstairs?"

Bara nodded.

"He donated a lot of money to the library. I think this is his diary or something."

"What does he mean Clavigen?"

"Clavigen?" Bara thought. "I think it's French. He says we need to *slay and cage the evil*; maybe that has something to do with it."

"Slay, hey? Well I don't know about you, Buffy, but I don't want to be a slayer or whatever a Clavigen is."

"It doesn't sound like we have a choice."

"Come on!" Amy scoffed. "This guy was just a nutcase."

"Well then I'm nuts too. Something weird is definitely going on. Seriously I think my dream led me to this. No! I know it did."

"Maybe …" Amy took a moment to think. "When did this Sedgewick die?"

Chestermire had talked about the library's history, another example of Bara getting him off topic.

"About thirty years ago," she told Amy.

"Do you really think this book has been lying on the shelf for that long, just waiting for you to dream your dream?"

"How should I know? All I know is he says I was destined to find it. Or we were?"

Amy still looked unconvinced. Bara tried harder.

"*Someone* or *something* led me to it," she insisted.

Amy opened her eyes very wide.

"Maybe it was Sedgewick's ghost?"

"Ghosts?"

"I don't know. Dream visions, so why not ghosts?"

"No. Maybe it was a ghost but not Sedgewick. It was a woman. I could sense that. She was all wispy. A wisp … like a will-o-wisp."

"A wisp?"

"Do you have a better name?"

"No. But there's also your nightmare double."

"Yeah. If dreams say something about your inner psyche I don't want to think about what being eaten by my own face means."

"Maybe you wear too much candied lip-gloss?"

Amy laughed; Bara didn't. After a beat Amy sighed.

"Sometimes dreams are just dreams. You shouldn't always read into them."

Amy was trying to make light but she really didn't have a good feeling. The dream was a little freaky. But the diary? She really wanted to be rid of it and so she convinced herself that everything was normal. An idea came to her head.

"It belongs to the library, right?"

Bara closed the cover and looked at the spine.

"There are no call numbers. I don't think so."

"Maybe it's part of the rare books collection? They don't put call numbers on those."

"It's rare for sure. We should take it back to the dorm."

"We should turn it in to the library. After all we found it on the shelf and then we can be done with this nonsense. Don't you think?"

Bara looked down and thought. *No, I don't think.* She really wanted to keep the diary even if it were part of the rare book collection.

"Let's go!"

Amy grabbed her bag and headed for the stairs. Bara went to argue but Amy had already disappeared into the floor above. So instead Bara put her own bag over her shoulder, grabbed the *Hideous Strength*, and followed reluctantly.

VI

Amy had already joined the back of the checkout line when Bara reached the foyer. At the desk Ms. Korey had her head down, busily signing out books. The streak of silver in her otherwise black hair swayed back and forth in the dim light until, obviously annoyed, she tucked it neatly behind one ear. Bara tried to put Amy off.

"She looks busy. We should show it to her tomorrow."

Amy was firm.

"If the book belongs to the library we can't take it."

An exiting patron in a black hood opened an entrance door and outside came in. A gust of wind along with a few leaves blew across the marble floor. Bara looked out. Gone was the sunny fall day. The sky was now grey and it had begun to rain. The door opened and closed again, more wind, more leaves. Looking back at Ms. Korey and then down at the diary, Bara felt an increased unwillingness to give it up. She actually thought about making a run for it but it was too late. The last remaining patron was served.

It was her turn.

Amy pushed Bara toward the counter. Ms. Korey put out her hand. Bara placed the diary cover down in her open palm. Ms. Korey took the book automatically and scanned the spine. There was no telltale beep. She turned it over and looked at the cover. Her grey eyes widened.

"Where did you find this?"

Amy went to speak but before she could utter a word Bara broke in. Her glance had stolen to the portrait of Nelson Sedgewick and inspiration hit.

"Oops! That's one of my dad's books. I meant to take

out this."

Bara placed the *Hideous Strength* on the counter. Then a little too eagerly she took the diary from Ms. Korey's loose grip and slipped it into her bag. Amy made to protest but was stopped by the weight of Bara's foot landing on her own. Ms. Korey stared at her empty hand. Bara waited for her to challenge the lie but she didn't. Instead she reached for the *Hideous Strength*

"It really is a beautiful book," she said. "It would be a tragedy if it were lost."

Ms. Korey finished signing out the *Hideous Strength* and placed it on the counter. Bara put it in her bag alongside the diary. She mumbled a thank you and motioned to Amy that they should go. They almost reached the glass doors.

"Oh, Bara," Ms. Korey called. "What's the book about?"

There was a long pause as Bara thought up another lie.

"Gemstones," she finally said.

"Of course, that makes sense with the stones on the cover. They must be Topaz?"

Eager to just get away Bara agreed, "Yeah, topaz."

Her hand was on the door when Ms. Korey stopped her with yet another question.

"You're sure they aren't amber?"

Bara said nothing.

"But no," Ms. Korey answered her own question. "That can't be. Amber isn't really a gemstone."

"No." Bara returned, "They're topaz like you said."

"Well take care it isn't stolen. There are a lot of people who would love to get hold of it for the amber alone."

"Right. Let's go Amy."

"Be careful girls."

"Careful? Yeah, you said that."

Ms. Korey motioned to the outside.

"I meant the weather. It's turned into a real storm out there."

Bara tried to open the door but it resisted.

"Good night!" Ms. Korey said. "I'll see you both soon."

Bara took one last look back. Ms. Korey still watched. Bara pushed at the door all the harder and broke through the wind resistance. Followed by Amy she went out onto the stone steps. A cold wind hit her full on, giving a mouthful of unwanted air and almost sending her reeling back in. Ms. Korey was right. There was a storm coming and it was robbing the day the last of its light. Bara caught her breath and ran down the steps and into the square.

"Why did you lie?" Amy called after her.

Bara wasn't stopping. She barreled across the square. Amy ran to catch up.

"Why did you have to lie?" she repeated.

"Lay off," Bara threw over her shoulder. "If the book isn't part of the collection what does it matter?"

Bara continued across the square and then started down Windfall Boulevard, still rushing but no longer running.

Amy caught up again.

"I just don't see why you couldn't have told the truth."

Bara stopped and rounded. The cold wind whipped through her hair and wisps of red-gold fell on her face.

"Tell Ms. Korey about my dreams and how they led me to the diary? Seriously? She'd have thought we were lying, on drugs, or just plain crazy."

"Okay, maybe not the dream part."

"She'd have claimed the diary!"

"No."

"If we told her we'd found it in the library, she'd have said it *belonged* to the library."

"I don't think she'd have done that. You're paranoid."

"I'm not!" Bara insisted. "Besides it's mine. Sedgewick said it himself. I found it. It's mine."

Amy looked unconvinced and Bara's frustration grew. She reached into her bag and brought out the diary, gesturing it roughly.

"I get it. You want it for yourself? Here! It's yours!"

Amy actually took a step back.

"I don't want it." she said quite firmly.

Seeing Amy's obvious reluctance to have anything to do with the diary Bara relaxed and her sanity returned. She put the diary back into her bag and looked at Amy. Amy was shivering, her coat too thin and worn for the weather. Amy didn't have a large wardrobe. Back when they were still preteens, growing spits and spurts, she'd been forced to wear pants torn at the knee and short at the hem. The terrible twins had a habit of asking her when the flood was coming.

Bara gave her a guilty smile

"I'm sorry. I'm a total loser. It's cold. Let's go back to the dorm. We'll see what the diary has to say together." Trying to lighten the mood she added, "For all we know it's some mushy romance."

Amy agreed and they made their way back to St. Cat. Along the dark boulevard and into the darker School District, they walked. Their fight was over but neither felt any better. There wasn't much light coming from the cloudy sky and what little made it through was pretty much blocked out by the trees above. The presence of others hurrying home might have helped but the streets were empty. Foul weather made sure of that. After they left the square they didn't see another soul. Yet they were filled with the oddest sense. One didn't tell the other but they both felt there was someone else out there. They took turns looking back, peering into black shadows.

St. Cat's gates were closed. They paused to unlock a side door before passing through. The school was dark, all the teachers and students gone home. The stone gargoyles that perched on the upper towers were just barely visible, shadowy outlines in the last specks of day. Not bothering with the winding path that ran from the gate they cut across the lawn. They rounded the school and the dorms came into view. It was ablaze with light. Most of the girls were already in the dining hall but many had left on their room lights. The glow guided the last few meters home.

Amy opened the heavy door. She and Bara passed through and it closed behind them with a reassuringly sturdy thud. The click of the lock echoed through the stairway. They were safe from the prying eyes of twilight but still there was that *feeling*. They climbed the wooden stairs to their second floor room. Bara opened the door and turned on the light. The room was empty. Amy crossed to the window and closed the curtains.

Finally they were alone.

VII

It was dinnertime. Stomachs grumbled but food would have to wait. Soaked from the rain Bara and Amy needed to change. Amy peeled off her coat and hung it on the back of a chair. It was far too wet to go in the closet. Her argyle sweater was damp through. Bara hung her own coat on another chair, crossed the room, and opened her closet. She pulled out a pink coat Courtney had given her. Even she had to admit it was beautiful. She took in the size. Amy was a bit taller but it should fit her just as well.

"Ugh," Bara faked disgust. "Courtney picked this out."

"It's not that bad. I kind of like it."

"You like it; you wear it."

Bara threw the coat on Amy's bed.

"I can't take your clothes."

"Please—take it. You'd be doing me a favor."

Amy stroked the soft wool. She did need a new coat.

"You're sure?"

Bara waved it off

"I'll never wear it. I think it cost a bundle ... probably.

Courtney doesn't buy anything unless it's expensive. Someone should wear it."

"Won't your stepmother be angry?"

"I have *like* half a dozen coats. It won't be missed. Besides it's pink. Everyone but Courtney gets the fact I don't like pink. But you do. You should have it."

Amy immediately hung up her new treasure. She smiled, feeling the soft wool one last time before closing the closet door. By far it would be the nicest thing in her wardrobe. Seeing the pleasure her friend took in the gift Bara smiled too. They finished changing. Bara was done first. Her book bag was on the bed. She crossed the room and sat down next to it. While Amy was distracted with her unruly hair Bara reached in and took out the diary.

Amy finished.

"Let's go," she said brightly.

"I'm not really hungry," Bara countered. "I might skip it. Maybe you could just bring me back a sandwich."

"That thing can wait," Amy chuckled. "Dinner—now!"

Bara still didn't move. Amy crossed the room, took the diary from her grip, and placed it on her desk. She pulled Bara up from the bed and pushed her out of the room. Amy turned out the light, closed the door, and locked it. Delicious smells wafted up from the dining hall below.

Bara was reminded of her hunger and forgot at least momentarily about the diary. She and Amy followed their noses down the stairs and to the dining room. A near-deafening cacophony of adolescent chatter greeted them.

Most St. Cat residents were already at dinner and the huge dining hall was full. In a situation like this they had their routine. Bara joined the food line. She'd get the food. Amy would look for two seats together.

Bara could have lived at home. Her mother still stayed in the house but Bara spent most of the school year in the dorms. The decision had been made during the divorce. There'd been too much fighting. It was supposed to be a short-term fix but once installed in a room with Amy she'd wanted to stay.

Life wasn't perfect at St. Cat—Louise and Cassandra saw to that. But even with the terrible twins school was relatively carefree. Bara could be happy, pretend things hadn't changed. She could almost forget the divorce

Tonight there were two choices for dinner—pasta shells stuffed with spinach and cheese for the vegetarians and for the more adventurous, chicken curry. Bara took an order of each. She and Amy would split the meals. Lemon meringue pie was for dessert. She grabbed three slices—one for Colin—and went looking for Amy.

Finding two seats together had been a challenge. There was some space at the terrible twin's table but that would have been social suicide. Sitting with the Pops would have meant spending the entire meal at the mercy of Cassandra and Louise's taunts. The only other option was at Patsy Pillanger's table. She sat alone. Social Siberia was far preferable to social suicide and Amy claimed two seats across from Patsy.

With no real friends Patsy spent most of her time with books. Not taking her eyes from the page she shoveled pasta into her mouth. Spinach fell onto a crisp page. She took no notice of Amy sitting across the table but when Bara sat down with her overloaded tray, she looked up and smiled a very large smile, too large and too teethy to be attractive, but genuine, almost endearing.

"Hi, Bara," Patsy chirped.

Her smile actually grew wider. For some reason Patsy really liked Bara.

"Hey, Pats," Bara returned through a yawn.

The lack of sleep from the night before was really catching up to her and Patsy was partly to blame. Bara had woken early from her dreams and gone to bed late because of Patsy. Bara and Amy were in the room next door. It wasn't unusual to be woken up by loud banging and odd smells. They'd run next door. There'd be Patsy, loopy as all, her current roommate cowering in the corner looking for a chance to make a break for it.

Uncharacteristically Den Mother had recently admitted defeat and allowed Patsy to bunk alone. But as it turned out Patsy didn't need an audience.

"What were you doing last night?" Bara asked.

"Calling on the spirits of the forest!"

Patsy's voice easily carried to the terrible twin's table—with predictable results. Pop entourage in tow, Cassandra and Louise stood up and sauntered over. Cassandra disliked Bara but she hated Patsy. And because Cassandra hated Patsy, Louise detested her.

"The spirits of the forest?" Cassandra taunted. "Is that why you smell like a toad?"

The entourage tittered.

Even Bara had to admit Cassandra had a point. It wasn't that Patsy smelled bad exactly, just strange, like flowers left a little too long in a vase.

"You know the difference between toads and spoiled princesses?" Patsy returned. "The warts are hidden on the inside." Her eyes widened and she added mockingly, "But then I can see a wart now. It's on your snout. Oh no, don't worry. It's just a hideous zit."

Cassandra's hand flew to her nose. There was a blemish, a small one, but she reacted as though it were a volcano ready to blow. She was sorely outmatched and so Louise took over, giving Patsy—and Bara just because—a look that would have withered an oak tree.

"Let's go, Cas-Cas" Louise said.

"Yeah, Lou-Lou," Cassandra agreed, her voice muffled behind her hand. "The smell's getting to me."

Louise took Cassandra's free hand. Cassandra's other hand still hid the pimple. The terrible twins and the Pops returned to their table.

"Cas-Cas Banks and Lou-Lou Bellevue! *Love it!*" Patsy taunted as they left. "But I'm surprised you can smell anything with that on your nose."

The Pops glared, promising revenge. Bara and Amy tried to ignore the threatening stares and returned to eating.

"What a storm, hey!" Patsy marveled. "Do you think we'll lose power?"

Anxious to get back to the diary Bara shook her head and shoveled another forkful into her mouth.

"I think the school has a backup generator," Amy reassured.

"That's right," Patsy said with a mouth full of spinach.

Amy looked away.

"You know why they had to do that, don't you?"

Bara continued to eat. Amy shook her head.

"There was a girl who died." Patsy paused for another mouthful of food. "It was years ago, during a black out."

Amy and Bara didn't respond. They were kind of hoping Patsy might drop the subject. She was always telling shocking stories at the worse times. They were trying to eat and didn't feel up to a tale of blood and gore, death and mayhem. But Patsy had no sense of what was appropriate or the ability to read her audience.

"Yeah," she continued on. "The girl fell down the stairs. They found her in the morning with her neck broke"

Patsy let her head loll to the side and her spinach-specked tongue hang out. Bara and Amy fought not to react. Patsy shrugged. She straightened up and pushed her finished meal aside. She reached for her pie.

Amy bit.

"Patsy, that's not true!"

"Sure it is. My dad told me."

Patsy's dad was Windfall's sheriff. The Pillangers weren't wealthy. Her enrollment at St. Cat was a work benefit.

"The girl was in her nightgown. No one knows where she was going. Her roommate said she'd gotten out of bed and opened the window. Then she left. The roommate thought she was going to the can or something."

Patsy paused to gauge reaction. She wasn't getting the response she wanted, so she added, "Spooky, hey?"

Bara and Amy exchanged a knowing look. They both concluded there was only one option open to them.

"I think I'll have nightmares," Bara offered.

"It gives me shivers up my spine," Amy agreed.

Finally satisfied Patsy smiled and began to eat her dessert with gusto. It was a tragic choice. Just as she'd been about to heap a rather large fork-full into her mouth, Louise and Cassandra, entourage in tow, passed the table.

Louise made a great show of tripping. "Whoops!" she said loud enough for the entire hall to hear. She fell into Patsy, sending Patsy careening into her dessert. Patsy lifted her head. She had meringue on her face, clothes, and hair. There were the clicks of a dozen or so camera phones taking focus and shooting. Her humiliation would be online in short order.

"Soooo, sorry Pat—zee," Louise drawled.

Everyone but Amy and Bara laughed. The Pops led by the terrible twins exited the room, leaving Patsy to clean up the mess. Patsy didn't say anything but wiped at her face with her sleeve. Amy handed her a napkin. She and Bara were embarrassed for her but Patsy seemed only subdued.

"I'm going to get those two," she hissed.

"Here. Have one of these and don't worry about the Pops. They're total jerks."

Bara pushed a slice of pie in her direction. Bara and Amy, still uncomfortable, rushed through the remainder of their food. They shared a dessert and then left Patsy still eating and no doubt planning revenge.

VIII

Bara raced ahead and was first to reach the room. She had the remaining piece of pie in one hand and had to fiddle with her key to get the door open. Amy had just crested the stairs and Bara was inside. *Odd?* Amy had turned out the light but everything was ablaze. And the curtains were open again. They flapped in the wind. *The diary!* Bara ran to her desk and threw down the pie. It slid half-off the plate and onto an unfinished Shakespeare essay.

"What's wrong?" Amy asked from the doorway.

"The diary! It's gone!"

Amy closed the door and joined her at the desk. She moved a few papers aside but there was no doubt. The diary definitely wasn't there.

"I left it here. I know I did."

Bara looked through the pile of papers one last time and then plopped herself on her bed in frustration.

"Somebody stole it!"

"Who'd have done that?"

"Ms. Korey was the only one who knew we had it. It had to be her. She took it?"

"I don't think Ms. Korey would break into our room and steal anything. Maybe it fell on the floor."

Amy went down on her knees and began to search around. She was under the desk when a crash sounded. Startled she bumped her head and let out a gasp of pain. Bara shushed her and then helped her up.

"Someone's in there," she whispered, pointing to the closet.

"The thief?" Amy mouthed.

Bara nodded.

"Let's get help!"

Bara shook her head and took Amy's hand, stopping her from leaving the room. She grabbed a hockey stick from where it leaned against the wall and crept toward the closet door. She put her hand on the handle. Amy looked around the room for something with which to arm herself.

She settled on an empty vase and came up beside Bara. Slowly Bara turned the knob. She lifted the hockey stick into the air, ready to strike, and threw open the door … her arm froze.

"It's me! "It's me!

Colin Van Fitt cowered in the closet, one arm protecting his face. The other hand held the diary. It was obvious what had happened. He'd snuck into their room, something he did on a regular basis, scaling the wall outside the window. Hearing a noise in the hallway he'd hidden. Boys no matter how innocent their intent were not allowed in St. Cat dorm rooms. Bara dropped the hockey stick and grabbed the diary. Amy replaced the vase and put her hand out to Colin. He accepted the help.

"You're going to get caught one of these days, Col," Amy warned. "And then we'll all be in trouble. Couldn't you've waited until tomorrow?"

"I was bored."

"Won't they miss you at your dorm?"

"*Nah* my roommate's gone home early for Thanksgiving. I have the place to myself."

Colin eyed the pie, expectantly, perhaps pleadingly. No one knows hunger like a growing teenage boy and *boy* was Colin growing.

"Bored?" Amy chuckled. "Hungry more like it."

Colin grinned. His smile was his best feature. Actually with his auburn hair and warm brown eyes he was kind of good-looking but one had to look up—way up—to notice. Colin was probably closer to seven than six-feet-tall. He scooped up the pie and threw himself onto Amy's bed, stretching out his long and painfully lean frame. His feet hung more than a foot off the end. Taking large ravenous bites he set upon devouring the dessert.

"Don't get food on my bed, you big slob."

Amy brushed at a few crumbs that had already fallen. Colin sat up and ate more carefully.

"Where'd you get the book, Barbie doll?" he mumbled with his mouth full of pie.

Bara didn't like to be called anything but Bara, not Bar, not Bar Bar and certainly not Barbie doll, but she'd known Colin since she was five. She loved him like a brother. She had no actual siblings and so put up with it. But still focused on the diary she didn't answer him. She sat down on her bed. Amy shook her head.

"You wouldn't believe it if we told you."

"Did you get it from your dad?"

Colin continued to focus on Bara. Bara didn't even look up. Colin shoveled one last forkful of pie into his mouth.

He placed the empty plate back on the desk, reached over with his extraordinarily long arms, and grabbed the diary.

"Hey!"

He ignored the protest.

"Won't he be miffed when he finds it missing? It looks like it's worth a mint. I'd keep it under lock and key."

"Maybe it should be if only to keep it out of *your* mitts. And no I didn't get it from my dad."

She got up from her bed and went to reclaim the diary. Colin jumped to his feet and held it above her head. Bara made a jump but gave up quickly. Even standing on a chair there was no way she could have reached it.

"Give it back!"

Colin gave a challenging smile. Bara would never retrieve it from his airy reach. A firmer approach was needed. She elbowed him in the ribs. He buckled over and collapsed like a folding chair, laughing and moaning at the same time. Amy grabbed the diary and returned it to Bara. Bara sat back down on her bed, clutching it to her chest. Defeated Colin rolled over on his side and propped his head on his arm, quite at home on Amy's bed. Amy not entirely sure where she should sit eventually chose the floor.

Colin tried again. "If you didn't get it from your dad where did you get it?"

"Like Amy said you wouldn't believe it."

"Try me."

Bara looked at Amy. Amy nodded.

"Okay then ... we found it at the library."

"The library! Oh, of course, where else would you get a book. Come on, no library would let you take that out."

"We didn't check it out," Amy told him.

Bara shot her a warning glance.

"You mean you stole it!" Colin said with mock intensity. "You did. You stole it. Did Amy drive the getaway car while you in your best blacks pulled off the heist of the century?" Colin, and no one else, was finding himself quite entertaining. Chuckling away, he added, "I'm shocked ladies but don't worry. I won't turn you into the Sheriff—for a price anyways."

"Lame!" Bara shot back.

She stood and went to put the diary away.

"Okay ... okay. I'll be serious. Just tell me."

Bara didn't look convinced but she sat back down.

"I think we should tell him," Amy urged. "Maybe he can help."

"Help with more dumb jokes?"

"I'll be nice. I promise."

Colin knelt and struck a beggar's stance, hands clasped

together. Bara couldn't help herself. She smiled. Amy was right. Even if Colin found humor in just about everything, often at her expense, she could always count on him to have her back.

"Okay then," she relented. "We found it at the library. A dream led me to it."

Like a confused puppy Colin cocked his head to the side. "A dream? Really?" Then he just couldn't help himself. "Was I in it?"

Bara threw up her hands.

"I told you. He can't be serious. Unbelievable! Just forget it. Forget we said anything. You were right the first time. We got it from my dad. That's all. So just for—get—about—it!"

Colin realizing he'd pushed too far tried to sound staid. "Okay tell me about the dream?"

"Do I smell like a lollipop?" Bara sniffed her sweater. "Nope not a sucker."

She grabbed another book that happened to be handy. It was the Plays of William Shakespeare. Not even noting the page she pretended to read. Colin looked at Amy. Amy shrugged. Colin crawled to the side of Bara's bed.

Poking his head above the edge, he said, faking a lisp, "Barbie, will you tell me, pretty please."

She put down the book. He smiled victoriously—a premature celebration. She grabbed a pillow and threw it at his head, hitting him square on.

"Alright! Alright!" he pleaded. "I give up!"

Bara threw another pillow. It hit as well.

"Cease fire! Really, I believe you."

She'd grabbed a stuffed bear and was about to throw it too. Colin held up his hands in surrender.

"Peace!"

Bara didn't look convinced.

"Honest?"

He nodded. She put down the bear and pretended to read again. Colin crawled up onto the bed and perched on the edge. He wasn't going to give up.

"But seriously how did you find the book?"

Bara sighed.

"Okay fine, but you have to promise not to laugh."

IX

Colin read from his phone.

"There isn't any dictionary entries for Clavigen. In French *Claviger* means keeper of keys. And there's a mining company that uses the name, but yeah, that's it."

"So we still don't have the foggiest what a Clavigen is," Amy said. "Or why the diary was in the library."

Colin turned off the screen.

"Why don't we look at our cast of characters? We got Sedgewick, the diary author, this wisp-being, and some creature that looks just like Bara but without eyes."

"I think the Wisp wanted me to find the diary and the evil me, well maybe she didn't want me to, or maybe she was only a nightmare. I don't know. But I'm almost certain the Wisp is real. I could smell her and everything."

Bara had chosen not to tell Colin about the dark-haired boy. No doubt he'd have teased the stuffing out of her if she'd told him some mysterious boy—a boy she'd never met—visited her dreams on a nightly basis. Besides she wasn't certain the dark-haired boy had anything to do with the Wisp and the doppelganger. She'd been dreaming about him for a long time. So for the time being she kept his *nonexistence* a secret.

"Let me take another look at the diary."

Colin held out his hand and Bara passed it over. He opened it and read aloud.

Guenevere arrived in Windfall, dressed in dusty rose

velvet, a feather waving from her hat. Her hair was truly golden and her eyes the deepest blue.

I fell instantly and hopelessly in love.

Some said she'd been born in Europe, orphaned when she was just a babe and then raised by nuns until she came into her inheritance. Less generous gossips suggested her wealth had come from shadier sources and even then there were whispers of witchcraft. But I shut my ears to this kind of talk. Guenevere was alone and I was certain in need of my protection. I knew she'd choose me. Wooing women was a talent I counted as mine.

Alas courting my lady love wouldn't prove easy. Guenevere moved into a cottage in the wood—deep, deep in the wood, said to be surrounded by a hedge maze. She obviously wanted to be left alone. Such was my arrogance I didn't include myself among those she wished to avoid. She may have wanted a quiet life but neither I— nor the Slip spirits—was about to grant her wish. I told myself if she were but to meet me ...

Colin paused. A look of alarm overwhelmed his face.

"Why did you stop?"

"Shh ... someone's coming!"

Someone or something was indeed coming. Barely heard footsteps approached in the hall. The lightness of foot and the time in between steps suggested that whoever it was, he or she didn't want to be heard—a footstep and then silence ... a footstep ... then silence. But the wooden boards of the dorms were telling, betraying the stalker with every creaking step.

Slip Spirits? No, not spirits, but no less terrifying.

"Ladies!" A shrill English accent carried down the hall, piercing through the closed dorm door.

"It's Den Mother!"

Having announced herself at full volume Den Mother gave up any further attempt at stealth. Her footfalls were now as heavy as a linebacker on egg shells and they were coming fast. Amy threw Colin's bag at him. Bara was pushing him to move.

"You have to get gone—now."

Colin sprang to his feet, diary still in hand, and headed to the window. No one thought his escape route too dangerous. They were on the second floor, not an impossible jump or climb. After all it was how he'd gained access to the room in the first place.

He was at the open window. He had one foot out. Bara

pointed at the diary.

"Leave that here."

"Right. Let me know how it ends."

He tossed it to her. She slid it under her bed.

"Lights out ladies!"

Den Mother was doing bed checks. Doors could be heard opening and closing all along the hall. The door knob to their room rattled but didn't open. Amy had locked it.

"Bara!" came Den Mother's sharp tones. "You open this door instantly!"

"Coming, Den Mother!"

Den Mother had a name but no one used it.

Keys rattled. In seconds she'd be in the room. Colin disappeared from the window frame just as the knob turned. The door flew open and an enormous shadow fell across the room. With her heavily-muscled hands on her broad sturdy hips Den Mother did a very thorough job of filling the doorway. She had the gait and physique of a tank and was as well-armed. Only the extraordinarily simple or suicidal ever crossed her.

"Are you girls alone?" she asked Bara pointedly.

Den Mother didn't like Bara, not in the least. She liked few of the students at St. Catherine's—*spoiled princesses* she thought—but *this one* she held in special disdain. Bara was far too headstrong for her own good, or rather for Den Mother's comfort.

"Yes Den Mother," Bara answered with her best imitation of meekness.

"I heard a third voice ... a *boy's* voice."

"That's impossible."

"I know what I heard."

Den Mother stepped into the room and peered around. Bara looked at Amy who looked as guilty as one could look. It would be up to her. Bara thought up a lie, quick.

"We were practicing," she said.

One heavy eyebrow lifted.

"*Practicing*? What were you *practicing*?"

Den Mother bore her gaze into Amy—the weak link. Amy remained silent. She looked down, refusing to meet Den Mother's stare. Bara rolled her eyes and handed over the book she'd been pretending to read to avoid Colin's questions. Den Mother read from the page.

"Macbeth?"

Macbeth it is. Bara's mind continued to race to make the lie more believable.

"Amy was playing the three witches and I was Macbeth and Banquo. *So fair and foul a day I have not seen*" she said in a grasped-for-baritone.

Den mother studied her.

"Impressive performance, Miss Cavanagh."

She wasn't buying it. Her narrow eyes focused on the open window. She crossed the room and looked out. Thankfully Colin had completed his escape.

"Why in this weather would you have the window open?" Den Mother demanded.

"To add mood to the scene." Bara quoted Macbeth once again. *"In lightening, thunder, and rain."*

"The weather certainly is being accommodating to your studies now, isn't it? But let's keep nature outside where it belongs, shall we?"

Den Mother closed the window with a little more force than necessary. She had no way of proving her suspicion and so she had to let it go. But she knew—as sure as raccoons like to eat garbage by the pale light of the moon—she'd been deceived. She vowed to keep a closer eye on this little snippet.

"Lights out in five minutes and I'll be back to check."

After throwing Bara one last glare Den Mother exited the room. Amy and Bara knew she'd be true to her word. They wouldn't be surprised if the old bat was listening just outside. Amy jumped up and closed the door but a closed door was little defense against her prying. It would be best to do as directed and go to bed. Further reading of the diary would have to wait. Bara slipped it out from under the bed and placed it in the top drawer of her desk. She locked the desk and placed the key under her pillow. Then she and Amy got ready for bed.

Five minutes later, probably to the second, Den Mother opened their door. Amy and Bara had turned out the lights. They were deep under the covers, pretending to be asleep, fooling no one. "Hmmphf!" Den Mother sniffed like she smelled something rotten and closed the door.

X

A Dream

The room was dark. Amy's breathing told Bara she was in her dorm room but Amy hadn't woken her. There'd been a sound. Now there was only silence, silence and the low hum of Amy's snores. Bara closed her eyes but there it was again, a tapping, something tapping very insistently against the window. There'd be no sleep, not until she figured out what it was.

Colin, if that's you ... I'm going to murder you.

Bara lifted her sleep-heavy body and rested on her elbows. The blanket fell from her shoulders and the cold bit at her bare skin. She was tempted to lay back down, pull the covers up, and ignore whatever was outside. Instead she slipped from beneath the blankets and came to standing. The wooden boards were ice slats on her bare soles and the air revealed her breath on the exhale.

Dragon's breath her mother called it.

Ignoring the cold Bara fumbled through the darkness to the window, drew back the curtains, and peered into the night. Outside the storm still raged. The heavy weeping of rain had stopped but the wind was still angry, picking up fallen leaves and branches and throwing them at the window. *Tap tap tap.* The fury reached through the glass pane with invisible, icy hands and Bara shivered as though shaken. The cold almost pushed her to return to bed but something held her back. As she looked out into the storm she felt someone was watching.

And someone was.

Bara was right. It had been a woman in the library and that woman now stood on the edge of the forest, looking up at the window. Tall and thin with long limbs, the Wisp could only be called elegant. Her skin was ivory pale and glowing. Even from a hundred yards away it glistened like waves in the moonlight. Her hair was long and silver, not grey, but metallic silver. She stood motionless but then like an iridescent dove taking flight turned into a blur of silver and white. She disappeared into the woods ... only to reappear seconds later.

Amy stirred, breaking Bara's attention from what was outside. Bara went to the bed.

"Amy, Wake up!"

Amy had no intention of doing any such thing. She lay still, seemingly able to sleep through a hurricane in a drum shop. Bara tried again, shaking her this time.

"Go back to bed," Amy said groggily. "Tell me in the morning."

"There's someone outside the window."

Bara met with silence and then Amy answered with a snore. There was another tap. Bara went back to the window. The Wisp was still there but when Bara reappeared, she re-entered the woods. Bara waited. Seconds passed. *No Wisp.* Bara wouldn't lose this chance. She grabbed her housecoat from the back of the door and fled the room. The corridor was deserted. She ran down the hall to the stairs but then stopped.

It suddenly occurred to her that Patsy's story from dinner sounded a lot like what was happening now. Would morning come to find her lifeless at the foot of the stairs? *No.* Patsy was always telling those stories. The one at dinner was no different. *But still* ... Bara descended the stairs at a very cautious pace.

Slowly she drew back the lock on the outside door. There was a small click heard only by her. She pushed open the door, stepped through, and carefully guided it closed. And then she almost went right back in. The wind lifted the hem of her pajamas and the icy ground reminded her quite sharply she didn't wear any shoes. It was then she realized the major flaw in her hastily-made plan. Her keys were in her coat—in her dorm room. She couldn't go back in.

Okay, what now? Lacking Colin's superhuman climbing ability she could have thrown rocks at her window. Still there was a good chance Amy wouldn't wake up. A dim light framed the curtains of Patsy's window. She was still awake. Bara groaned at thought of having to explain why she was outside in the middle of the night without any shoes or coat.

But Patsy was better than Den Mother.

Bara shrugged. She'd figure a way back in later. Instead she crossed the wet grass and stopped at the forest edge. She peered through the dark night and into the darker still woods, looking for a telltale flash of silver. At first, nothing. Then the clouds cleared from the moon. Bright beams from the midnight orb lit up the lawn, reaching into the black abyss of the woods. Fallen rain reflected back like shards of a broken mirror.

Was something moving through the dark? *Yes* it was warm white, almost golden and glowing, floating through the trees at an unbelievable speed.

Again not giving it proper thought Bara pursued. But catching her quarry wouldn't be easy. Her steps covered far less ground than what she chased. She sped up, but the faster she went, the farther the light seemed to get. The earth tore at her feet and she stubbed her toe with enough force to make it bleed. Rough branches slapped at her face and shredded her pajamas and robe. Her lungs burned; her muscles ached. Still she kept at it, cringing with each new bruise or cut ... and then the trees no longer blocked the way and she was out of the scraping reach of their pitiless limbs. Most glorious of all the ground below had changed. Soft moss now soothed her mistreated feet.

She'd entered a clearing.

The sudden easing of demands, rather than giving her the strength to go on, brought on surrender. The soft earth called to her. Bara collapsed to her knees. The moss was every bit as soothing to her knees as it had been to her feet.

She sank further down until she was on her back, looking up at the moon. She didn't care anymore if she caught the Wisp. She rested and even slept.

A small sound woke her. A boy had come into the clearing. He was tall and lean with broad shoulders and long limbs. His face was broad but not round. He had a strong nose, slightly hawkish. Dark wavy hair gave him the look of a young Roman god. *But his eyes.* Against the almost glowing white of his skin, his eyes shimmered as though made of cut blue glass.

It wasn't the Wisp. It was the dark-haired boy.

Bara realized she was dreaming and then forgot just as fast. She came to her feet.

"Who are you?"

The dark-haired boy said nothing, shaking his head and putting a finger to his mouth.

"You can't talk?"

He nodded and held out his hand. Bara took hold and was instantly filled with a pleasant heat. He helped her to her feet. Together they moved out of the clearing and into the trees, into the darkness. No branch scratched her skin and her feet no longer hurt. The moss continued on like someone had laid out a green carpet for visiting royalty. As they traveled through the velvet black it was just Bara and the dark-haired boy. Nothing else mattered.

XI

A Dream

They came out of the darkness and onto the shore of a small lake. *How strange?* Bara knew of no lake nearby. They could no longer be in the forest surrounding Windfall. She looked up at a foreign starscape of constellations and planets, unnaturally bright. They'd moved into another world. It was the only answer.

And then the stars began to fall …

Light blazed down from the sky and hovered before piercing through the lake surface. Radiant rapiers cut down through watery volumes, trailing down into the depths. The last shimmering trail disappeared and Bara was standing alone. Her eyes searched the beach and the little she could see into the forest. She saw nothing.

A large wave hit and shattered the silence. Bara gave up looking for the dark-haired boy and turned back to the water. A rush invaded the shore, quickly followed by another. She stepped back. The lake bubbled and surged.

Moonlight reflected off the splash seemingly as steam.

A glow appeared beneath the waves and lifted from the water. The glow was a woman. Her arms and legs unfolded. Her hair was full and thick and rode upon a wind of its own. Her long robes, her eyes, and even her skin were gold. It was as though she'd been dipped in melted ore.

As she glided across the lake her feet just grazed the water below, creating trails of spray.

She stopped and hovered a few meters from shore.

All beauty is not beauty she sang.

"Who are you?" Bara asked.

I am the messenger. All beauty is not beauty.

The Messenger opened her mouth to sing again but stopped. There was a snarl. A wolf, larger than any wolf Bara had ever seen, came out from the woods, belly low to the ground. Its fur was silver, not grey, but silver. Another snarl revealed sharp and long canines. Metallic foam flowed from a jagged mouth. As it neared it grew in size. Its teeth lengthened and sharpened.

Its intent was clear—attack.

The Wolf sprang. The distance was great, too great for any wolf to cover with one leap, but this one flew through the air with ease. Bara ducked and her hands flew to cover her head. She waited to feel sharp jaws and heavy claws pierce her tender skin. She felt only the weight of a shadow as it soared above and over her head.

There was the splash of water.

The Wolf jumped with such power it positively flew. It sprang once more and covered the remaining distance, barreling into the Messenger. Gold and silver entwined a foot or two above the water and did battle. The Wolf pulled the Messenger down to the surface. They splashed ferociously in the shallows. The Messenger fought back but the Wolf was too strong, too quick. Its teeth took hold of her throat and bit. Thick trails of red ran down her golden skin. The Wolf didn't give up its bite and eventually the messenger stopped struggling.

Still in the creature's jaws she turned her head to look at Bara. Her mouth opened and closed. No sound. Vocal chords were cut. Satisfied the wolf released its jaws from her bloody neck and backed off just an inch.

It watched and waited.

The Messenger touched her throat. Her skin glowed beneath her hand. When she removed her fingers the glow died down. Miraculously she was healed and so once again she opened her mouth to speak. She tried again and again. Her eyes brimmed with tears of frustration but only silent air passed between her lips. Finally she gave up and hung her head. The depth of the water grew then and she sank beneath the waves. An instant later a large globe of light rose from the lake. Like a reverse comet it soared into the dark sky and the Messenger was gone.

Bara looked at the Wolf now approaching menacingly slow through the water. She backed away but her foot caught on a rock and land gave way. She fell. With a single bound the Wolf cleared the space between them. Bara found herself eye-to-eye with the feral creature. Her tranquil green battled its stormy silver. She smelled its breath. It was warm and metallic. It smelled of blood.

Not wanting to witness her own end Bara went to close her eyes but stopped and opened them wide again. Flickering like the glow of the predator's eyes a locket hung from its thickly-furred neck—an odd collar for such a ferocious beast. The Wolf gnashed its teeth and lifted a heavy and sharp paw …

A blur of warm light prevented sharp nails from slicing soft skin. Appearing from mist the dark-haired boy threw himself into the Wolf. It sounded as though a boulder had collided with a granite cliff. The Wolf should have flown through the air but its silver fur merely shook. Then like an icicle falling up, the locket rose above and over its head and into the dark-haired boy's grip.

The dark-haired boy didn't hang around. On the fleetest of feet he stole into the trees. His glowing white dimmed—from a blaze, to a spark, to a pinpoint, to nothing. The Wolf growled and shot Bara a glare and then tore off after the dark-haired boy and the locket.

Her shock faded and Bara came to sitting. *Follow* she told her weary body. She brought herself to wobbly legs and began to run clumsily through the woods. Pain quickly reminded her she wore no shoes. The moss had disappeared. The ground was rough and sharp. Wounds tore open but the way was clear—a path of broken branches and trampled earth she need only follow.

XII

A Dream

Bara should have come upon the Wolf and the dark-haired boy, heard them up ahead, but she'd seen and heard nothing. And the path was now overgrown. No it wasn't a path at all. She'd lost them. But things were worse than that. Bara looked around; she was lost too.

A cold wind reached deep into the forest and the wood

shook in its frigid grasp. Being lost wasn't her only problem. It was move or freeze to death. So ignoring the cold and the pain in her feet she carried on. Oddly her feet didn't hurt as much as they had before. The cold had numbed them. It was a blight disguised as a blessing.

As she limped along the woods lightened, stars dimmed, and the sky got brighter. Bara couldn't see but sensed the horizon had taken on the rosy hue of early morning. Amy would be up soon. She'd raise an alarm. People would be searching. Trouble is would they know where to look? *Unlikely.*

No one was going to find her. This Bara knew. But she wasn't exactly alone. An owl announced it presence with a hoot and then soared low and over her head, guiding her glance where she needed to look. *A cross!* It had to be the cross of St. Cat's Chapel. A few more yards and she'd be in the school clearing.

The trees and the bushes stopped and Bara did indeed enter a clearing. But St. Cat was nowhere to be found. She stood before a maze, about ten-feet-high and who knew how deep. Sedgewick's Guenevere had lived within a maze in the woods? It had to be the same one. *Great!* Bara had battled her way through the woods and now she'd have to figure her way through a maze. But the steeple she'd mistaken for St. Cat's still stood. It would offer shelter, perhaps warmth. *Survival.*

A little wisp of a cloud floated up and above the cross and disappeared into the twilight. It was soon replaced by another curlicue of grey. The cloud had to be smoke, smoke from a fireplace. Perhaps it was only wishful thinking but it was all she had. Imagined heat unthawed her muscles and Bara entered the maze. She didn't get far.

Just past the entrance the locket hung from the hedges. There was no wolf and no dark-haired boy. Disturbingly the locket dripped with blood. Still there seemed just one thing to do. Bara took hold of the chain. One drop of red landed on her hand. It burnt and she drew back. The blood bubbled and sizzled with silver and then dissolved to nothing. She held up her hand and flexed it. It seemed okay. She reached out again ...

The dream let go and the maze disappeared to mist. Bara wasn't in the forest any more but back in her own bed.

"Why did you wake me?" she demanded of Amy.

"You cried out in your sleep. I thought you were having a nightmare."

"You don't understand. I almost had it."

"Had what?"

Bara looked around. No locket. Just a headache.

"I had another one of those dreams," she told Amy.

Not again. Amy had been thinking it over. The dreams were no doubt brought on by exposure to mold. They were probably spending a little too much time in the stacks. And the diary? *Well, so what. It's just a book.* Anyway mold poisoning was a lot more likely than spirits, dream visions, and haunted books.

Amy strove for her most convincing tone.

"It was a just dream, or a delusion. Just like the one yesterday. Either way, let it go."

"A *delusion*?" Bara echoed. "You really believe that? I'm just imagining things?"

Bara threw off the covers, hitting Amy in the face with the blanket. Amy got out of the way before she was hit with something heavier—like Bara's feet as they flew past her face. Bara came to sitting on the edge of the bed and Amy gasped. Muddy feet were covered in dried blood and scratches. Amy was pretty certain Bara had never left her bed. Yet her feet definitely confirmed a rough night.

Amy sat back down on the bed.

"Okay, maybe it wasn't the mold.

XIII

A strong breeze rattled the leaves above. Several shook free, landing on Bara and Amy and the stone bench they sat upon. The maple still held onto most of its color but the underside of wet dark limbs stood bare thanks to the strong winds the night before. Colin stood a few feet away, drinking from his stainless steel cup. Bara was retelling her dream if that was what it was. He listened without comment. She finished and waited for him to respond.

A moment passed and Colin remained silent. A red leaf drifted down and landed on his green scarf. He didn't bother to brush it away. As though she hadn't said anything out of the ordinary he took another sip of his Earl Grey.

"Well?" Bara finally prompted.

Colin raised an eyebrow but still said nothing. Another leaf fell, this time landing in his auburn hair lit ginger by the bright fall sunlight. He remained mute and Bara lost it.

"Say something!"

Colin blew on his tea.

"It's weak. I know all you St. Cat girls think the new coffee guy is *so hot* but he can't make tea to save his life."

Bara had yet to see the new *baristo* at the Tragic Sip and at that moment she really didn't care. Colin's response was too much, or rather too little. She'd had enough. She jumped up and grabbed the cup from his hand.

"About the dream!" she demanded.

Without changing his easy tone he said, "It seems pretty obvious to me, Barbie."

"Obvious how?"

He looked at her solemnly.

"You're haunted."

Colin continued to look at her gravely but then broke into a gigantic toothy grin. Bara was fast. The poor boy didn't see it coming. With a fluid movement of her arm she hit him upside the head, removing the leaf that had taken up residence.

"Thanks for nothing."

"Hey, that hurt!"

"It was supposed to."

Bara removed the lid from his cup and took a sip. She winced. It was indeed weak and in need of lemon. Bara had learned from Betty, her mother's maid; unlike orange pekoe, Earl Gray took lemon and not milk.

Colin rubbed his head.

"The question is what to do about it. Can I have my tea back?"

Amy broke in. "It's the Diary. It has to be. If we put it

back all of this will stop."

Bara gave Colin back his tea and Amy a look of warning.

"My thoughts exactly," agreed Colin. "If we put it back maybe some other sucker will find it. All this will stop being our problem. He'll become the chosen one, Obi Wan Kenobi and all that, but there is …"

"We can't do that."

"But it all started with that stupid diary," Amy insisted. "This is getting really weird and not to mention dangerous. You could have been seriously hurt out there in the woods … or wherever you were. I mean look at your feet."

Bara's feet were in pretty bad shape. Amy had tended to them. They were covered in gauze and antiseptic but it had still hurt to walk in her saddle shoes. She was wearing a pair of red rubber boots which were larger and slightly more comfortable.

"The thing is did it really start with the diary?"

Amy glared at Colin, sensing a mutiny.

"I thought you said putting it back was a good idea?"

"I wasn't allowed to finish." Colin took another sip of tea. " Now it's cold."

"Forget the tea!" Bara barked.

"You didn't find the diary so much as it found you."

Colin pointed out. "And it all started with the dreams, not the diary. Chances are if you put it back it won't do any good. The dreams might even get worse. It seems this wisp-woman was pretty determined to get you involved. And then there's the dream-you with no eyes and a big mouth. That has to mean something."

Bara had decided yet again to leave out the dark-haired boy's part in the tale. Amy was being pretty judgmental and Bara found herself wanting to spare him her disdain. It was irrational. She knew. But there was no way she was telling Colin about him anyway, at least not until she really had to. When she'd come to the part where she found the dark-haired boy, she claimed it was the Wisp. The tale had just rolled on from there. So as far as her friends knew the Wisp had led her through the woods to the lake and saved her from the Wolf.

"There's no guarantee putting the diary back would accomplish anything." Colin continued. "The Wisp would probably keep haunting you. There's obviously something she's trying to tell you."

"What do we do then?" Amy asked. "Do we just let Bara go crazy?"

"I'm not crazy!"

"I didn't say you *are* crazy. But come on, going out into

the forest, coming back with torn up feet, but not actually having left your bed. All this stuff about a messenger and a silver wolf? A wisp? I mean what the hell is a wisp? *Slip spirits*? It's just too much to believe. You must have been sleepwalking or something. Maybe I just didn't hear you. I'm a pretty deep sleeper."

"I'm not going crazy. I don't walk in my sleep. It all happened. You said you believed me."

"Will you two stop?!" Colin snapped.

Both Bara and Amy gave him a sharp look.

"If we're going to figure this out," he said in a much softer tone, "we need to stick together."

Amy and Bara stopped arguing but they were still angry. Everyone was angry. Bara was angry with Amy and Colin, Amy with Colin and Bara. Colin however was only irked that his tea had gone cold and it was weak. *Stupid coffee guy!* He dumped what was left into a planter and put his cup away. He looked at Amy apologetically.

"I hate to say it but we have to keep reading the diary. Maybe it'll give us some answers."

"We don't know it is actually a true story," Amy pointed out but neither Colin nor Bara took note.

Bara took the diary from her bag. The amber was blinding in the bright sunshine. She and Colin joined Amy on the bench. Colin read.

XIV

The Diary

I waited for Guenevere to come to town. She didn't. I had to go to her. Fortunately the forest surrounding Windfall was a place I knew well. Unfortunately I entered it to find everything had changed. Clearings had disappeared and new ones formed. A lake had sprung up overnight. Worse of all I found myself in a fight for my life with a wolf too large to be of our world, its teeth and claws like blades. Armed only with a pen knife I fended it off, but it was a battle I was likely to lose.

My throat was all but in the creatures jaws when a glowing sight appeared. It challenged the wolf and led it on a chase. Seeing my chance I ran—ran for my life.

I would eventually find what I sought. The maze. But what a sight I was. Bloodied and battered I now wore rags. My clothing was in such a state I was almost tempted to go back. But then the day's heat was slipping away and the night's cold rolling in. The desire for warmth overcame my vanity. Comforting myself with the thought of taking shelter with Guenevere I entered the maze. I didn't dally. A wolf howl urged me on.

The maze wasn't more than thirty yards deep. Its twists and turns should have been few. Yet night fell and still I didn't find its centre. The cross and its steeple remained in sight but gave no clue of what direction I should go. I was lost, hopelessly so.

The hours passed. The air became colder, the wind sharper, and I eventually gave up. My real defeat came when I realized I couldn't find my way out either. I was trapped and in all likelihood about to freeze to death.

Finding a sheltered corner to settle in I pulled my wolf-tattered cloak around my legs. The cacophony of my chattering teeth broke the silence of the night. I wanted now only to wait out the hours before dawn. Deep down inside I knew I had little hope of doing so.

Black and enormous ... I felt its shadow first. The wolf had returned. I heard its snarl and in my mind's eye remembered its teeth before I saw the pearly glint in the scant light. I was exhausted, hungry, and very cold. I knew there'd be no way to fight it off. Still I raised my little blade. It had once seemed so dangerous but now I knew I should have brought a pistol.

I readied myself for the coming of canines and claws. I waited … I waited … nothing. The wolf did not attack. As though struck by a daze it was stopped. Its paw hung suspended. I turned to what had its eye. She held a lantern. In the glow her hair flowed like liquid gold. Rays of light shown through the pale pink of her billowing skirt, outlining her slender long legs. Her face was a pearl under moonlit water. It was Guenevere.

I yelled out a warning. For certain the wolf wouldn't hesitate to kill us both. But Guenevere came ever closer, not stopping until she was at my side. The wolf snarled again. She wasn't frightened.

"This man is not for you, Brynndalin," her musical voice sounded in the savage night. "You belong to me. I will not let you have him."

It seemed the wolf was her pet, but a disobedient one

at that. It snarled yet again. Guenevere brought from beneath her cloak a metal locket. It opened to reveal a large piece of amber. As the amber swayed the wolf stopped its snarls and began to whimper. The clouds were cut in two and the moon shone down. The amber caught the moonlight, magnifying it. Bright yellow and orange flashed and reflected onto the silver of the wolf. The light spread, gaining heat and intensity. The wolf backed away to avoid the glare.

"Be gone this night," Guenevere said. "Do not come again, not until I call you."

The Wolf snarled one last empty snarl and then turned on its heels. It disappeared into the shadows of the hedges.

I rejoiced. I was saved … or so I thought.

Guenevere looked to me. Anger flashed behind her blue eyes. "Come!" she ordered.

I followed, though what else could I do. The wolf no doubt still lurked within the maze, the most savage of watch dogs.

A small white cottage with red trim soon came into view, a fairy-tale cottage. Most peculiarly a tall steeple and a cross grew from its squatness. There was a light in the window, the glow of the fireplace. My heart lifted. At least I'd soon be warm. The door opened. Martha, Guenevere's lady's maid, stood in the frame, candle in hand. She couldn't have been much older than Guenevere, maybe even younger, but she spoke like an old woman.

"And where did you find him?"

Her accent was hard to place. It definitely wasn't local, some odd combination of English, Irish, and something more familiar, but I wasn't able to place it. She moved her small frame aside to allow us entry.

"He somehow found his way into Brynndalin's grasp," Guenevere told her.

Martha snorted and motioned to a hard stool where I was meant to sit. I settled. I'd have preferred one of the wing chairs that sat on either side of the fire, but after hours in the cold I was very pleased to warm myself.

"I think he was pursuing me."

Guenevere looked at me like one surveying an ant that has found its way into one's lunch. I was filled with a heat that had nothing to do with the fire. She definitely did not return my tender feelings. On the contrary she seemed to find me an annoyance. She crossed to the one of the wing chairs and sat down wearily.

"The question is what to do with him now." She turned to me. "Did you tell anyone you were coming here?"

I tried to answer but found my tongue lay paralyzed on a sticky palate. And there was an odd lump in my throat that I hadn't felt since I was a lad in short pants. Indeed, sitting next to Guenevere on her comfortable chair, with Martha looming above, I felt a child on my low stool. It was all I could do to shake my head like some sort of mute imbecile.

"Well, that's something."

Guenevere poured tea from a pot that sat on a table next to the chair and took a sip. I was reminded of my own dry throat. I may have licked my lips.

"We can't let him go," Martha said. "Not after what he's seen."

Guenevere let out a heavy sigh.

"No ... no, we can't."

A strange look came over Martha's face. Her grey eyes

glinted with an odd light. My embarrassment was soon replaced by fear. It was becoming clear Guenevere had saved me from the wolf only to make me HER victim.

ESCAPE. I lifted myself from the stool and made for the door. It wasn't locked and it opened with ease. I had one foot outside when an unknown force pushed me back into the room. I took flight and would have crashed to the ground had not the stool, which I'd knocked over, righted itself and slid across the floor. My bottom landed squarely on the seat as the door slammed shut and bolted itself.

Still not quite understanding the power of the women, I tried again to come to standing. I tried with all my might, but I'd somehow lost the ability to perform such an everyday task. I was secured to the stool and it to the floor—floor, stool, man—all one. I looked to Guenevere. Her hand glowed with its own light. She'd prevented my escape without even leaving her chair.

Martha gave out a low mocking chuckle.

"The last thing we need is you telling anyone who'll listen what you've seen and heard. I, for one, do not plan on being burned at the stake."

The glow in Guenevere's hand dimmed.

"They don't burn witches anymore," she reassured. "No one believes these days. This isn't the 1600's. Windfall has changed. Besides I kept you safe then. I will do so now."

Witches—the word rung in my head. What else could explain these events but witchcraft? It wasn't true that no one believed in witches anymore. I definitely did. But witches were old and ugly. I looked at my captors, their smooth faces. Not even a wrinkle. They had the skin of infants. Yet to me they seemed as old as crones. Still what had Guenevere said—this was not the 1600's—she'd kept Martha safe then. Oh, of course, they'd lived these some three hundred years, maybe more. After all I'd seen immortality seemed but a small thing.

"Do you think we should take the chance?" demanded Martha.

"Really you could easily defend yourself."

"All the same he'll need to be dealt with—permanently."

Martha hand glowed with power.

XV

"Girl!"

He stood not so tall but seemingly gigantic to the teenagers. Even Den Mother would have been more welcomed. Colin, Bara, and Amy were startled by the appearance of Amy's stepfather.

"Girl!" he barked again.

Mr. Frank rarely called Amy by her name. As though ordered to attention by an army sergeant she jumped to her feet. Bara didn't like Mr. Frank, not at all. There was no way she wanted him to know about the diary. She slipped it into her bag. Mr. Frank didn't bother with Bara. To Colin he gave a look that could only be described as threatening.

"You were supposed to meet us five minutes ago," he snapped. "I've better things to do than wait for you."

Amy looked down.

"I'm sorry. I forgot."

"Sorry isn't good enough. You be on time."

Colin had never met Mr. Frank but the look he passed Bara confirmed he shared her feelings about him.

"Get a move on," Mr. Frank said and stalked away.

Embarrassed Amy couldn't even look at her friends.

"Bye," she said, head still lowered. "Have a happy

holiday."

Happy holiday?

Bara had been so caught up in the diary and the dreams that she'd forgotten it was the start of Thanksgiving break.

***

Bara lay across the four-poster bed, flipping through a magazine, her sock feet crossed behind her head.

"Where are you going?" she asked her mother.

Ms. Cavanagh was choosing clothing. She took a sip of wine before answering.

"I've decided to take a vacation, refresh my batteries."

She held out her glass. Betty, rushing about, placing chosen pieces in trunks and suitcases, paused and refilled the glass.

"I'll take the flat shoes," Ms. Cavanagh told her.

"No heels, madam?"

Ms. Cavanagh sipped from her glass again.

"I don't think I'll need them."

Bara threw the magazine aside and jumped up from the bed. She grabbed the shoes and so Betty couldn't put them in the suitcase, hugged them to her chest.

"Where are you going?" she asked again.

Betty winked and waited patiently. Ms. Cavanagh let out a bothered sigh.

"Just to a spa a friend from the club suggested. She said her cousin went and came back looking ten years younger. Now will you give me my shoes?"

Ms. Cavanagh drained what was left of her wine and held out the glass again. Betty immediately stopped what she was doing and refilled it. Bara cringed. Her mother had never cared much about getting older before Courtney. Now she seemed obsessed with shedding the years.

Bara gave up the shoes.

"You look fine, Mom. You don't need to look younger."

"You're so sweet. What a sweet child I have, Betty."

Ms. Cavanagh cusped Bara's heart-shaped face. She kissed her forehead and then continued to go through her clothes. Betty ruffled Bara's curls

"That you do, ma'am. Never met a nicer child."

Ms. Cavanagh began to instruct the packing of a third suitcase.

"You're taking a lot. How long are you going for?"

"A month or so."

"A month! But that means you'll be gone for Thanksgiving."

"You're meant to spend the time with your father. You won't even miss me."

"Yes, I will."

Ms. Cavanagh studied an array of sweaters.

"I'll take the blue set. It's in third guest room. Fetch it, will you, and bring another bottle of chardonnay."

"Another bottle, ma'am?"

"Yes Betty. Another bottle … from Napa."

Betty gave Bara a sympathetic smile and went in search of the sweater set and wine. Bara waited for her to leave and then leapt from the bed. She grabbed hold of her mother's sleeve and tugged like a toddler.

"You can't go!"

Ms. Cavanagh pulled from her grasp.

"Bara, really."

"I *will* miss you, Mom."

"And I'll miss you. But it's all been decided. You can spend most of time at the dorms but you'll go to your father's for Thanksgiving."

"I could just stay here?"

"By yourself?"

"Betty will be here. She'll keep me company."

"I've given Betty the month off. It won't do. I'm thinking of redecorating."

"Redecorating? Why are you redecorating?"

"The house could use a freshening up, some new drapes

and paint. The place will smell of fumes. You need to go to your father's."

Ms. Cavanagh swallowed what was left of her wine.

"Betty, where's that bottle?" she hollered.

***

As Bara watched Amy scurry after Mr. Frank, she didn't know who she felt sorrier for—Amy, who'd have to avoid the anger of her stepfather—or herself, who'd be dodging the supposed goodwill of her stepmother.

Okay she felt sorrier for Amy.

Bara could see the Frank family car, a run-down sedan, parked on the edge of the square. She watched Amy get into the back seat. Amy looked so sad. It broke her heart. Bara didn't know exactly what went on in the Frank home. She didn't like to think about it. But she knew one thing. Amy was a lot happier living in the dorms. Bara would be relieved when they were both back at school.

Colin interrupted her thoughts.

"It's getting dark. Don't you have to be somewhere?"

He knew she'd be spending the holidays with her father. He'd been invited for Thanksgiving dinner. His own parents were out of the country.

"Come on," he grinned. "I'll walk you home."

Mr. Cavanagh's new home, the Lavender House, was in

the Grande Oaks District, so named for its Oak-lined streets. It was but a mile from the library. Bara wished it was farther. They left the square and walked along the east end of Windfall Boulevard, cutting through the forest which flanked it. They raced a setting sun; the sun was winning. Colin prattled on about some sporting event and Bara pretended to be interested. They were purposely not mentioning the diary and her strange dreams, trying to make as though everything was normal. It would have been a lovely walk if they both hadn't been preoccupied with what they refused to discuss.

Finally Bara couldn't stand it. Colin asked her who she thought would win some game or other, the Lions or the Bears, and she responded with a question of her own.

"What do you think the Messenger meant by *all beauty is not beauty*? Sedgewick talked about evil coming as beauty. There has to be a connection."

Colin wasn't bothered by the change in topic.

"I've been thinking. It has to be the witches, right? Guenevere was supposed to be some great looker. Sedgewick and the Messenger must have meant her."

"Maybe, but why do they want me to know about her now? All this happened over a hundred years ago."

"Assuming what's in the diary actually happened and

that's a big *if*. But if it's a real telling Guenevere may still be alive. She was immortal or something, remember?"

"And the maze? Do you think it's real?"

"I don't know. But with the similarities to your dreams it can't all be a coincidence."

"So witches and witchcraft, you think it's all real?"

"It's that or you're crazy and I know that's not true."

"You really believe me?"

He gave her a smile and shrugged.

"But what I really want to know is how the Wisp fits in. Why did she want you to have the diary? And why did she lead you into the woods? Even if it was just a dream it all has to mean something. What is she trying to tell you?"

"I'd like to know that too. But I'm glad about one thing."

"What's that?"

"At least the *eyeless-me* has taken a breather."

"Yeah." He grinned. "There's that."

They arrived at the Lavender House. The iron gates of the Victorian mansion were shut tight. Dusk had settled and a gray slate roof was silhouetted against a purple sky. The arched and gabled windows of the second floor were dark. It wasn't an inviting sight. Bara lifted the lid to the security box and punched in the code—her birthday. The gate clicked and swung open an inch. She paused before slipping inside and looked back.

"I guess I'll see you for Thanksgiving. I'm glad you're coming for dinner. I'm happy for the backup."

Colin chuckled.

"She's not that bad."

"She's not *your* stepmother. Courtney won't stop hovering."

"I think she just wants to get to know you?"

Bara felt like a whiner. Colin's parents always left him on his own. He had no choice but to live in the dorms. She often wondered if it didn't hurt him to see them so little. If it did he never let on. But then he rarely complained about anything. Always joking that was Colin. Still his parents paid him next to no attention and here she was harping on having too much.

"Yeah, maybe you're right."

Bara turned to go but Colin stopped her again.

"Hey, Barbie! Do me a favor. Don't read anymore of the diary, not until I'm with you. I don't think it's a good idea to read on your own"

"Alright I'll wait until tomorrow."

He didn't seem to believe her.

"Promise," he said with an odd gentleness.

"Okay, Dad!"

She gave him a playful punch. He smiled and rubbed his arm.

"Oh and I'd wear shoes to bed."

She laughed.

"Good idea!"

Putting on a Texan accent he drawled, "Until tomorrow then, ma'am."

Not waiting for a response he turned and walked away, whistling. Bara watched him round the corner and waited for the sound of his whistle to die in the distance before slipping through the gates.

XVI

In the dusk the Lavender House had dimmed to gray. Odd shadows played across marble Greek Gods in various states of undress lining its circular drive. The statues were no doubt Courtney's idea. Bara couldn't decide if they were spooky with their shadow-veiled eyes, or just plain tacky. Either way she wasn't a fan.

Across town her mother's drive was lined with cherry trees, pink in the spring, mauve in the fall. Gravel crunched under her feet as she passed the stone army. It stopped when she stepped onto the marble entryway and disappeared into the shadow of the portico.

Not having a key she rang the bell and waited. Seconds later one of the heavy black doors opened.

Thank God—no Courtney.

"Oh hello, Miss Bara," Gloria drawled in her deep-southern tones. It was a little like having Scarlet O' Hara for a maid. "Won't you come in?"

Bara went inside.

"Give me you things, girl."

Gloria held out her arms. Bara handed over her coat but kept her bag and the treasured diary inside.

"Where's my father?" she asked.

"He's still at the office but he rang that he'll be home for dinner." Then Gloria answered the question Bara hadn't asked, "Mrs. Cavanagh's in the study with a friend. She said you should join her for tea."

It took Bara a moment to realize Gloria wasn't talking about her mother but Courtney. She was definitely *not* going to join her stepmother for tea.

Faking a yawn she made an excuse.

"I'm really tired. I think I'll take a nap."

"I'll tell Mrs. Cavanagh."

Gloria headed to the study. Taking two steps at a time just in case Courtney decided to come say hello Bara raced up the stairs. She was almost at the top when voices from the open study door reached her. There were the musical tones of her stepmother and another speaker with an odd accent. *British perhaps?* The voice sounded strangely familiar. Bara almost went back downstairs to see who it was but her white lie was quickly becoming the truth. All of a sudden she was very tired. She shrugged off any interest and continued on her way.

The room set aside as *hers* was being redecorated the last timed she'd been at the house. Mr. Cavanagh had suggested she and Courtney decorate it together. Bara had refused, sullenly telling her stepmother to do whatever she wanted with the room. *Bad move!* Bara opened the door and almost fell backwards. It was a Pink Palace—the palest pink wallpaper with white and silver roses, a dusty rose bedspread, and a carpet displaying every shade of pink from petal to bright fuchsia. The only other color was white. All the rich wooden furniture had been white washed. A pink and white palace for a Barbie doll—*Yuck*.

Bara made a face of disgust and then went inside.

She kicked off her boots, forgetting Colin's suggestion she sleep with her shoes on, dropped her bag on a chair, and plopped herself down on the bed. She might have had a full nine hours the night before but it was hardly a restful sleep. She climbed under the blankets and laid her head on a fluffy and very frilly, pink pillow. The ache returned to her feet now that her boots were off. But she didn't ponder her *poor dawgs* for long. She quickly fell into the early stages of sleep.

A tired mind went over recent events. Bara thought about the diary. She imagined what the beautiful golden-haired witch, Guenevere, must have looked like to have inspired so much passion. Her thoughts drifted to the dream of the night before and she re-imagined the hideous Wolf, with its glorious silver coat, and the mysterious Wisp. Tears came to her eyes when she recalled the Messenger and her silent mouth opening and closing. And the dark-haired boy. He'd stolen the locket from the Wolf. *The locket!* Her eyes flew open. *It's too ridiculous. What are the odds?* There'd definitely be no sleeping now.

Bara rose from bed and left the Pink Palace. She crept down the hall to the top of the stairs but stopped before going down. Her stepmother and her guest were at the door. Courtney blocked the other woman but Bara caught just a glimpse of dark hair, before hiding behind the corner. She strained to hear what the two women were saying.

"You're certain she still has the diary?"

"They were reading it today in the square."

That voice? It was so familiar.

"I guess there's little we can do if she's been chosen," Courtney said. "I do wish it could be otherwise"

"We should confront her," the other woman urged.

"No we'll keep an eye on her for now. We still may be able to get the diary back."

Courtney opened the heavy oak door and the crackle of leaves in the wind muffled the end of the conversation. There was the *thump* of the closing door and then the *clip-clop* of footsteps retreating into the study.

Bara ran back to the Pink Palace for her boots and bag. She'd go to Colin. Together they'd decide what to do. Intent on escape she didn't hear the approaching footsteps.

"Are you going somewhere?"

Bara turned around and there was Courtney. Courtney's skin and hair were golden and her beauty timeless. But the *clincher* ... the locket hung from her throat, the dream locket, the one the dark-haired boy had stolen from the Wolf. If Bara hadn't been sure before she was now. Her new stepmother was Sedgewick's witch. She had to be.

Courtney took a few steps forward and asked again, "Are you going somewhere?"

"I ... I thought I'd go for a walk."

"Do you think that's a good idea? It's dark. You shouldn't be out alone. It isn't safe."

She crossed the room and took the book bag.

"Please give me my bag?" Bara croaked.

Courtney gave her the oddest look and Bara lost the power to close her eyes or open her mouth. *For real!* She tried to do both. She really couldn't. She couldn't move. Fortunately the spell didn't last long. Welcomed noises flowed into the room. There were footsteps on the stairs. They were still facing each other when a cheerful Mr. Cavanagh appeared in the doorway.

"Hey, you two!" he almost chirped. "Can I cut in on the *girl* talk?"

Suddenly free to move again Bara fell into his arms. He kissed her on the cheek and then wrapped an arm around Courtney's shoulder.

"What's for dinner?" he asked. "It smells delicious."

"Pot roast. I'll go see to it."

Courtney peeled her eyes from Bara and went to leave, the bag—and the diary within—still in her grip. Summoning her courage Bara held out her hand.

"Courtney? My bag?"

Bara waited, not sure what Courtney would do. She was

pretty confident she was safe with her father there but then she wasn't used to dealing with a witch. Courtney didn't look very happy but handed the bag over.

"I'll see you both downstairs," she said and exited through the open door.

"I'm so glad you're here, Daddy," Bara sobbed into his sleeve.

XVII

They sat as they had the other night at one end of the large table, Mr. Cavanagh at the head, his wife and daughter to either side. But this time there was only a low centerpiece of miniature pumpkins. Bara wished ruefully for something larger to hide behind. As it was Courtney had a clear view.

"Is your dinner okay?" she asked.

"It's good."

Bara did not lift her eyes from her plate. Dutifully she ate but she could have been eating paper. Her taste buds didn't seem to be working. Mr. Cavanagh sensed something was wrong.

"Are you feeling alright?" he asked.

Bara snuck a glance at her stepmother. Courtney wasn't

all that interested in her food either. She was studying Bara through narrowed eyes, her mouth drawn in a grim line.

Get Away! Get away! her thoughts screamed. "Could I be excused?" Bara asked instead.

"Don't you want to finish your dinner?"

"I'm not that hungry. I really am tired. I didn't sleep well last night."

Mr. Cavanagh put down his fork.

"You know, Bara, I don't think ..."

Support came from an unlikely corner.

"She does look pale," Courtney said.

Mr. Cavanagh was quiet for a moment.

"Courtney went to a lot of trouble so we could have a nice dinner," he finally said. "The least we can do is eat it together."

"I think we should let her rest," Courtney urged.

Mr. Cavanagh looked at Bara and then Courtney. He let out a surrendering sigh.

"Alright then. But we *will* see you for breakfast."

Bara got up from the table. Not looking in Courtney's direction she wished her a good evening. She kissed her father on the cheek and left the dining room. She walked slowly until out of sight and then ran up the stairs, down the hall, and to her room.

The Pink Palace was waiting. Bara crossed to the dresser. It wasn't the best hiding place but it would have at least slowed Courtney down. She moved some pink argyle socks aside. *Where on earth did Courtney find pink argyles*? The diary was still there. Bara grabbed her bag from the chair, slipped it inside, and turned to leave. This time she heard the footsteps coming down the hall. Quickly she removed the diary from the bag and put it back in the drawer. When Courtney entered the room Bara was in the next drawer down. She pulled out some pajamas at random. They were of course pink.

Courtney took but one step inside.

"Your father asked me to check in on you. Can I get you anything?"

Bara held up the pajamas.

"I think I'll just have a shower and go to bed."

"Just the same, I'll get you some tea with honey."

Bara thanked her stepmother and *thankfully* she left. Figuring Courtney would be listening for the sound of running water Bara then took a shower and redressed. The pajamas were quite roomy. She put them on over her clothes. The diary she removed from its hiding place and put it back in her bag. All was ready to go. She thought about reading more of the diary but stopped herself, remembering her promise to Colin. With no computer in the room there really was nothing to do but wait.

Strangely there was the smell of baking. Bara noticed for the first time the bedside table held the tea Courtney had promised along with a plate of cookies. Suspicious of the food Bara dumped the tea down the toilet. The cookies she wrapped in tissue and placed in the garbage. Then she lay down on the bed and stared at the ceiling. At times her fatigue was stronger than fear. Heavy lids dropped several times. Each time she willed them to re-open but despite herself she slept.

***

Someone called her name. Bara opened her eyes, expecting to see the dark-haired boy who seconds before she'd been walking hand-in-hand through a dream meadow. He'd stopped, caressed her cheek, and leaned in like he meant to kiss her. Gently he lifted a lock of hair and whispered into her ear. She felt his breath but heard nothing and then she'd woken. Had someone actually called her? She stilled her breath and listened. *Not a sound.*

The bedside table said it was well after eleven. Her father always went to bed early. Would Courtney be with him? There was no way of knowing. All Bara knew was the house was quiet. She got out of bed and took off the pajamas. An empty stomach rumbled and she almost grabbed the cookies from the waste basket. Instead she slipped on her rubber boots and wrapped her scarf around her neck. From the closet she grabbed a hooded pea coat. Bought by her mother it wasn't pink but red. Lastly and most importantly she grabbed her bag with the diary inside and left the Pink Palace. She crept down the hall and stairs and out the front door, undiscovered.

With shoulders up and ears down Bara hurried past the dark statues and slipped through the iron gates. Her hands were shoved deep into pockets. Her unbuttoned coat flapped in the wind. The air was angry and it only seemed to increase its rage as she made her way through the darkened streets and past the lightless mansions. Enormous blustering flurries grasped leaves, sticks, and other debris, whipping them through the air and at dark windows.

In its fit the tempest wanted in.

Hanging miles above her head, heavily-soiled cotton clouds held suspended torrents. Before long the wind would wring out the wet. Bara gave a silent prayer the rain would hold off long enough for her to reach Colin and his dry dorm room and entered the parkland. She passed through a thick set of trees into greater darkness. Strangely she only felt all the more exposed.

XVIII

St. Xavier's gates were closed tight, the grounds surrounded by a ten foot brick wall. The message was clear—keep out. Bara was about to give up when she remembered something Colin had told her. There was a place along the wall where a couple missing bricks and a plum tree on the other side gave nightly access in and out of the grounds. About fifty feet from the gate a tree just skimmed the top of the wall. Its mauve leaves, onyx in the night, were nearly gone but dried fruit remained. She went to the tree. Running her hand over the brick she found the first chink and then the second. It was the spot.

Like she was mounting a horse Bara fixed a foot in the lowest ledge and propelled herself up. *Seriously how does Colin do this?* Her hands sought holds that weren't there but somehow she clung to the wall. Her other foot found the second ledge. A push and her open palms found the top. One leg swung over and then the other.

The mortar tore at her tights but she managed, just barely, to clamber atop the wall.

Now the tree. Colin had neglected to mention it was a good six feet away, not much of a jump for him, a serious challenge for her. But the tree was closer than the ground.

Bara crouched, gave a silent prayer, and literally took a leap of faith. She fell upon a thick branch like the largest and clumsiest of squirrels and held tight. Then came her descent which compared to the stunt she'd just performed was a relatively easy one. But it would be the end of her tights. She dusted herself off and set out to find Colin.

The wind picked up as Bara made her way across the grounds, rattling noisily through the trees, and so she didn't hear the following footsteps, not until she also felt a rasping breath upon her neck. Her scream was muffled when a hand covered her mouth. Using the little judo she knew, she flipped her attacker and *thud*—a tall thin figure hit the ground. It wasn't Courtney. Had a stick insect and a scarecrow made a baby? Long wiry limbs, topped with a big mop of red hair, lay splayed out on the lawn.

The stick insect spoke.

"Holy Fuzz, Bara!"

Fear unclouded from her eyes.

"Why did you sneak up on me?"

Colin rubbed his mistreated rear-end.

"I was coming to see you when I saw you on the lawn. I'd have called out but I didn't want to wake up Weasley."

Bara laughed. She sat down next to Colin on the lawn, threw back her head, and gave into a fit of giggles. The stress of the night had been so intense and laughter went a long way in breaking it. Colin laughed too. They both lay down on the grass and howled until the first raindrop fell. Colin stopped and looked at Bara. A smile that had nothing to do with what had just happened stole over his face. With her green eyes pools of emerald in the night Bara really was quite pretty.

Actually he thought *she's pretty all the time.*

Something about his gaze made her feel just a little self-conscious and Bara stopped laughing too. She pulled her coat closer and not because she was cold. She stood.

"Come on. Take me to your lair."

Colin continued to look up at her.

"What are you waiting for? It's cold out here and it's starting to rain."

Dutifully he came to his feet.

"Follow me, my lady."

He gave a bow and led the way.

Bara watched as Colin scaled the dorm wall and disappeared through a window. Alone on the lawn again she felt watched. Fortunately she didn't have wait too long. He opened the front door and she rushed in. They crept up to the second floor to his empty room. His roommate was still away and they'd have the place to themselves.

She'd never been in his room before. It was neater than she expected. Actually it was neater than her own—well her side at least. Amy was neat but Bara always had books and clothes littering her desk and floor. She often had to kick a path from the door to bed. Colin also had quite a few books but his were placed neatly in a bookcase or in an orderly pile on his desk. The absent roommate obviously shared her slovenly habits. Random pieces of clothing loafed on his bed but Colin's steel grey bed spread didn't have a wrinkle, never mind any dirty clothes.

Embarrassed Colin grabbed a pair of boxers from the other bed and threw them in the closet. Bara chuckled and then like she owned the place she crossed from the door to his bed and plopped herself down. Colin stood awkwardly. Should he join her or sit on the bed opposite? He chose instead his desk chair and pulled it close.

"So why did you risk coming here tonight?" he asked.

"Why were you coming to see me?" she countered.

Colin hesitated. He obviously had a lot to say but didn't quite have the courage to say it, not just yet.

"You first," he insisted.

Yeah, about that. Now that she thought about it Bara wasn't certain he'd believe her. But she did need to tell someone. She took a deep breath and just let it come out.

"Courtney is Sedgewick's witch. She's Guenevere."

And then she waited. She'd expected Colin to howl, to make light of her accusation. He didn't even seem surprised. He only nodded and waited for her to go on.

"You believe me? Why do you believe me?"

"I had a dream."

It was her turn to say nothing. She must have looked doubtful.

"Apparently whatever's going on … it's contagious."

Bara leaned up against the wall and shook her head.

"You had a Wisp dream too? Really? What happened?"

Colin didn't want to tell her his whole dream and so he lied. Well he didn't really lie but he didn't tell her everything. He phrased his words carefully.

"I don't remember it all."

Okay, that was a lie. He remembered everything.

"But Courtney was in the maze. She was standing over you. She had this strange green dagger. It all seemed so real. When I woke up I had this really strong feeling you were in danger. That's why I was coming to find you."

What Colin didn't tell her was that the Wisp had been in the dream too. She'd led him to the maze and told him he'd find Bara inside and that Bara needed his help. Once inside he got lost. He kept catching glimpses of the Wisp and then Bara but couldn't catch up to either. Eventually he'd turned a corner and there was Courtney. She was dressed in clothes from the nineteenth century. Only her arms were bare. She held the dagger above her head.

At her knees was Bara.

Colin had acted without thinking, propelling himself forward and knocking Courtney to the ground. The dagger flew from her grip and landed on the other side of the hedge. Delivered from danger Bara fell into his arms. Colin lifted her chin and without hesitation kissed her and she'd kissed him back. The kiss was reason enough for him not to tell her everything but what happened next was all the more disturbing. As the kiss increased in passion Bara transformed in his arms. Her lips became thinner and colder and she grew tall, almost as tall as him. He opened his eyes to discover he was no longer kissing Bara but the Wisp.

Then he'd woken up.

Kissing the Wisp had made Colin feel he'd betrayed Bara. And kissing Bara? Well that had made him feel something entirely different. He'd tell her how he felt, eventually, but not now and not because he had some stupid dream. *No way!* What mattered was that he knew Courtney's secret identity. *Right?*

Bara was watching him. There was heat in his cheeks,

the color of which no doubt matched his hair.

"Did you bring the diary?" he asked.

Bara handed over her bag. Colin took out the diary, found where they'd left off, and read.

XIX

"I think we should deal with him now," Martha said.

A slow smile crept onto her face. The glow in her hand grew in intensity. I could only suppose how she meant to DEAL with me. I feared for my life.

"Brynndalin has some interest in him," countered Guenevere. "We should hold onto him for a while."

Martha didn't argue and her hand returned to normal.

No I didn't meet my end that day. Instead these two mystics kept me prisoner locked in a separate room. I saw them only at meal times. Brought out to my little stool where I again became rooted I was fed my dinner. Surprisingly the meals were tasty. I wondered if I were not being fattened for dinner. Witches ate children, didn't they? At least they did in fairy tales. I was no child I reminded myself and they ate along with me. Both as slim as reeds, where would they have found the room?

When I'd had my full I was led back to my small cell. The door would open on its own and close behind me the same way. I'd tried to open it but it would only open for the witches. One small window let in some light but was made of a material much stronger than any glass. I'd tried to smash it but with no success.

There was no escape and little to do and so I spent my days listening at the door. Martha often spoke of the fear of being burned or buried alive. Such was her distress, I, her prisoner, actually felt sorry for her.

"I cannot go through that again."

"No one is going to hurt you." Guenevere reassured.

"You may have saved my life but you didn't save me from the pain, the fear. They buried me alive."

"They had to think you were dead so we could make our escape."

"But the others, their deaths were real," Martha sobbed.

Or at least I thought she sobbed. It was hard to tell

through the closed door. And other than carefully controlled anger I hadn't seen her express any real emotion.

"Chained like animals ... crushed beneath the weight of all those stones ... burnt alive. You may be able to forget the screams. I cannot."

I knew something of Windfall's history. They could have only been talking about the witch trials of the 1600's. If what I was hearing was true this made Martha over three hundred years old...

Bara and Colin could clearly see Sedgewick crouched next to the door. Light would have flickered around the frame, taunting him with the promise of freedom, but the door wouldn't open. His only hope—something he might learn from behind it. Caught up in the tale Bara and Colin failed to worry that someone might actually be listening in on them as well. They should have paid more attention. The door knob clicked as it turned. Colin expecting some kind of danger threw himself on the bed, pushing Bara behind him. This was a truly an unfortunate choice. It made them look guilty of something they were not.

The door swung open and Den Mother stood in the

open frame. She'd obviously come straight from bed, not bothering to dress. In her green housecoat she resembled an avocado-colored refrigerator from the fifties, rounded at the edges but basically rectangular, her head a canister on top. She stood motionless, a supremely satisfied look on her portly face. Her eyes narrowed, slanting upwards into a smile, but it wasn't a happy smile.

Behind her was the broom handle of man that was Dorm Master Weasley. He looked very ill-at-ease, nerves causing him to jump around as he tried to get a look into the room from behind her bulk.

"Oh my, Mr. Van Fitt," he croaked. "When you parents hear of this, they will be most displeased. And I shudder when I think of what the Head Master will say. I absolutely shudder."

"It's not what you think Dorm Master Weasley," Colin protested.

"Real-lee?" Weasley mocked.

Den Mother stepped into the room, allowing him to do the same. Unlike Den Mother, Weasley had dressed, dressed well in fact. His black suit hadn't a wrinkle. He'd obviously come from a night on the town.

"Just what is it then? Because what I see is a young lady in your room, in the middle of the night, and upon your bed, I might add."

"Never mind your worthless excuses," Den Mother shot. Then she spoke over her shoulder to an unseen individual. "Here they are, just like I said they'd be."

Bara's heart dropped. Her father came into to the room. From the look on his face it was obvious he'd also jumped to the wrong conclusion. Bara, even though she'd not done, or even been about to do, what they all thought was so obvious, blushed. Den Mother took in her red cheeks and the state of her stockings. There was no doubt in her mind.

"Shameful girl!"

Bara made to protest. She may have been guilty of many things but not *that*. Silenced with a look from her father she never uttered a word.

"Thank you for your concern in this matter," Mr. Cavanagh said in a tone that ended any discussion.

"I …" Den Mother stopped midstream, rethinking the wisdom of continuing.

Mr. Cavanagh turned to Bara.

"Get your coat."

"Dad …"

He wasn't having any of her excuses either.

"Now, Bara!"

Colin rose to her defense

"Mr. Cavanagh ..." he started; he didn't finish.

"I'll be discussing this matter with your parents."

Mr. Cavanagh made a fist. It was obvious he was working hard at controlling his temper. Bara could only hope Colin had the sense to remain silent.

Weasley was almost gleeful.

"You can rest assured his parents will hear of this. Oh yes *indeed* they will hear."

Bara hadn't made a move.

"Where's your coat?" Mr. Cavanagh shouted. "We're going!"

Colin jump into action. He rummaged around on his bed and grabbed her coat and bag which Bara noted was heavy with the weight of the diary. He handed it over.

"I'm sorry," she whispered.

"Be careful," he countered.

Den Mother had stood, ham-hock arms folded over an enormous bread-basket chest, silently protesting, but she couldn't contain herself.

"I should think it's a little late for that."

Mr. Cavanagh looked sternly. Weasley nervously smoothed his already smooth hair.

"I think, Penelope, we should let Mr. Cavanagh deal with his daughter."

Den Mother's breast and arms lifted with the strength of her breath. She let out a little snort but said nothing else.

With her coat in hand Bara was ushered out into the hallway. She tried to stop and put it on but Mr. Cavanagh continued to push her along. The clucking and harping of Den Mother and Weasley followed them down the stairs. Poor Colin was getting an earful. Bara didn't envy him. But then as she looked at the stern set in her father's eyes she began to worry for herself. He paused at the foot of the stairs just long enough for her to finally put on her coat. Then an enraged father and an anxious daughter went out into the tempestuous night.

XX

There was no conversation in the car. Bara tried several times to talk it out but her father said nothing. She quickly realized there was no point in trying to explain. What could she say anyway? *Dad, your wife's a witch.* It wasn't like he was going to believe her. So instead she turned her head to the window and waited out the ride home.

Mr. Cavanagh wasn't purposely trying to make Bara suffer. He was just too furious. It wouldn't serve to simply yell. He had to make her understand. It was too soon. She wasn't ready to date, never mind … he didn't finish the thought. For the first time in a long time he actually missed his ex-wife. Despite *her problem* he had to admit Beth knew Bara better. They had a better relationship. It hadn't been the same since he'd left the house. He doubted things would ever be the same again.

The car pulled up to the house. Courtney waited at the open door. Bara got out of the passenger side and Courtney rushed at her. Bara thought Courtney might actually attack but Courtney stopped suddenly and regained control.

"Is she okay?" she asked.

"She's fine."

They all made their way back into the house and stood in the foyer. Mr. Cavanagh told Bara to go to her room. He needed time to think. Bara did as she was told but stole one last glance at Courtney before going up the stairs. She swore there was nothing short of satisfaction on her stepmother's face.

Bara returned to her pink catastrophe of a room, took off her coat, and threw it on a chair. It occurred to her that the carelessly discarded coat was out of place in the spotless room. The Pink Palace had been tidied. She'd half expected to find it ransacked. Or maybe it had been and then Courtney had tidied up afterward. It hardly mattered. Courtney wouldn't have found what she was looking for—the diary.

There were footsteps outside the door. Next came a knock. Bara told the knocker to come in and then working at some avoidance grabbed her coat and went into the closet. When she came back out her father took a seat on the bed and motioned for her to join him. Dreading what was to come she crossed the room and sat.

"I'm worried about you, Bara Evelyn."

Evelyn—her middle name, her grandmother's name. He only used it when she'd really put him at wit's end.

"I'm okay, Daddy."

It was a shameless ploy calling him daddy. Bara knew. But it was worth a try. Her father didn't soften, not at all.

"I'd have liked to have talked this matter over with your mother but as she seems to be out of reach of any communication." He paused and took a deep breath. "Well in the absence of your mother, I've talked with Courtney and we …"

"You talked about me with *her*! How could you?"

"I needed another opinion."

"What do really know about Courtney?" Bara countered. "You married so quickly. You and Mom hadn't even been divorced a year. For all you know Courtney could be a ... a murderer or something."

"A murderer?" Mr. Cavanaugh mocked. "Really Bara? That's what you're going with. Courtney didn't sneak out of this house and worry everyone. You did. I didn't find her in a strange boy's room doing God knows what!"

"Colin's not strange. I've known him since I was five."

"All boys are strange at his age. They *all* want the same thing."

"Colin's my friend. He'd never try anything on me."

Her naiveté was too much and after finding her in Colin's room, on his bed. She couldn't be that dense. Mr. Cavanagh couldn't contain himself any longer. He lost it.

He came to his feet and hollered, "*Oh, yes he would*! I was a boy once. Believe me, *I know*."

Anger is contagious and Bara lost it too.

"Colin isn't anything like you," she fired back ... and then they ceased to fight about Colin. "He's loyal. He'd never leave his family. Never! Not like you."

Bara had finally said it, what she'd been thinking all these months. But looking at her father she wished now she hadn't it. His pain was clear. Mr. Cavanagh took in a deep breath to regain control.

"Be that as it may my shortcomings are not the issue

here. Your behaviour is. You're grounded. There's no question about that. And I don't want you seeing Colin, not until I've had a chance to talk this over with your mother."

Bara tried to backtrack.

"Dad, I'm sorry."

"I know you are."

At a loss Mr. Cavanagh left the room.

***

Bara lay in bed until the clock by the bedside said it was 4:30 am. Her father would be in bed, most likely Courtney with him. It was becoming obvious there'd be no sleep for her, not until she talked this out with someone. Unfortunately her phone was still in her other coat, downstairs. Treading through the dark house would likely wake someone. After her last escape act her father had armed the security motion sensors in the entryway.

There was also a landline down the hall. But then getting caught talking to Colin would only rev things up again. If she did get discovered Mr. Cavanagh would go a lot easier if it were Amy—a nice, safe—female friend.

The decision made Bara got out of bed and crept down the hall. Conscious of every creak of the floor boards she hoped she was the only one.

The phone was on a table across from a guest room.

She picked up the receiver. To her mind the click sounded as loud as thunderbolt. She listened. The house remained silent. She dialed and prayed Amy and not someone else, especially Mr. Frank, answered. There was only one ring. A familiar alto sounded on the other line. Mr. Cavanagh and Courtney's room wasn't ten meters away. Talking in the hall wasn't the best idea. Hoping to muffle the conversation Bara took the phone into the guest room.

"Amy," she whispered. "I know it's late. I'm sorry if I've gotten you into trouble."

"It's okay. I knew you'd be calling."

They continued to speak in hushed tones.

"Amy ..." Bara paused not sure of her reaction. "I think ... no, I *know* my stepmother is Sedgewick's witch. She's Guenevere."

Predictably Amy reacted with disbelief but then she took a moment to think.

"How can you be sure?"

Bara went over the events of the night.

If it had only been Bara having these weird dreams Amy would have clung to her doubt. But if Colin was having the dreams too something was definitely going on. Besides Amy'd had her own weird experience of late. They couldn't all be crazy? And so Amy listened and then agreed. It seemed in all likelihood the Wisp really existed, the diary was a telling of real events, and yes, Courtney was Sedgewick's witch. Too much had happened for her to continue to doubt.

"Does Courtney know that you know?" Amy asked.

"I don't think so. She'd have tried to do something to me, wouldn't she? All she's done is to try to get the diary."

"Try not to be alone with her. Can you lock your door?"

"There's no lock but I can push a chair in front of it."

There was silence on the other end.

"Amy?"

Still no response.

"Amy!"

A moment passed and then Amy spoke in a whisper.

"He's awake—*he* meant Mr. Frank—I should go."

"Wait, you knew I'd be calling. How did you know?"

"I had a dream. The Wisp told me."

"What? First me, then Colin, and now you?"

"It wasn't like your dream or even Colin's. I'm not even sure it was a dream. I wasn't in the woods. I was in my room and she came in. It was really weird. I couldn't move or speak or anything. She stood over of my bed and whispered I should wake up. That you'd be calling. When I opened my eyes she was gone. I snuck out to the hall and sat down next to the phone. A minute later you called."

"She must be watching me ... and you."

"That's good, isn't it? If she's watching she might be able to protect you from your stepmother."

"Do you think she can do that?"

"I don't know. I have to go. He's in the kitchen. I'll call you tomorrow. Be careful."

Click.

Bara crept out of the guest room and hung up the phone. She listened to the house for any sign that someone had overheard the conversation. Everything was still. She retreated down the hall and into the Pink Palace. Keeping her promise she pushed a chair in front of the door. It was hard work. The chair was heavy and Bara was trying not to make any noise. But if she found the chair heavy so would her stepmother. Mission accomplished she settled on the window seat and looked down at the lawn statues—an army of silent watchers.

Odd under the circumstances with a real-life witch just down the hall but Bara felt somehow safe. It made her feel better to think the Wisp might be watching too. At the thought she got up and crossed to the bed. It was comfy even if it was pink. Something told her Courtney was sleeping and wouldn't bother her until morning. The witch was sleeping and so should she. Dreams were calling. Bara hoped they'd be of the normal kind. Better yet she hoped she wouldn't dream at all. There was no rest with the dreams. They only tired her all the more. She closed her eyes. Her mind finally quieted and she drifted off. Blessed day her sleep was a restful one—at first.

XXI

A Dream

Someone was playing an accordion. Bara was at the circus. The stands were full of a large and rowdy crowd. Her father and Colin were in the center ring, only Colin was a kangaroo, Mr. Cavanagh a circus ringleader. They circled each other. Both wore boxing gloves and their dukes were up. Bara was off to the side, wearing a pink baby doll dress with lace and puffy sleeves. The dress was too much, or rather too little, and she wanted to change. But when she turned to go the crowd—the Pops, the Goths, and the other girls of St Cat—roared with amusement. They were laughing at the frilly underpants that went with the dress.

Trying to shield her rear end Bara backed up against a

platform, the kind a circus elephant might balance upon. She jumped up and sat down. Her long legs dangled. She looked down on pink bobby socks and pink Mary Jane's. *Yuck!* Why had she allowed herself to be dressed this way? Everyone knew she hated pink. Still things were a bit better on the platform. Her dress covered to the knees and the scandalous underpants were out of sight.

Just then a supremely satisfied Amy entered the ring. The crowd roared its approval. The cheers were deafening. Flowers flew through the air. Amy picked up a red rose and clenched it between her teeth. She danced a mix between the Mexican hat dance and the twist. Finishing up she threw the rose into the crowd.

Drusilla caught the flower and swooned.

Bara stared enviously. No one had dressed Amy like a baby. She wore her school uniform. But instead of the customary tights she had on fishnets over neon fuchsia leggings. On her feet were black military boots with enormous heels and somehow she'd managed to shellac her long black hair into a purple-tinted Mohawk. With the combined height of shoes and hair she stood even taller than Colin. She crossed the ring in a single bound and handed Bara a large silver bell and spoon.

"Rock n' roll!" she hooted, made the sign of heavy

metal horns, and stuck out her tongue.

Amy then proceeded to play a little air guitar. The crowd couldn't get enough. They went wild. It occurred to Bara that maybe she'd enjoy a little crowd adoration. She jumped down, her mind on a duet, but everyone laughed at her frilly underpants again. As quick as she might she scooted back on top of her platform. Amy finished her solo. The crowd jumped to their feet shouting *encore.* Amy threw her hands into the air and screamed *Thank you, Windfall!* Fever-pitched applause continued long after she'd loped out of the ring.

Everyone turned to Bara then. They looked at her like she'd picked her nose in public. It was as if she were in a play and had forgotten her lines. She lifted her hands and shoulders in a sign of helplessness.

"The bell, stupid!" Louise shouted. "Ring the bell!"

Of course! Raising the large silver spoon above her head Bara rang the bell. The fight began.

Mr. Cavanagh went on the offensive first. He snapped his long lion tamer's whip, connecting with Colin's humongous kangaroo feet. Considering he wore boxing gloves Mr. Cavanagh handled the whip with skill. Colin leapt around the ring, trying to avoid the snapping lash. He aimed a kick at Mr. Cavanagh but the older man easily avoided the impact. Colin fell on his backside. He struggled like an upturned beetle-kangaroo, legs moving frantically in the air. Mocking Colin's predicament Mr. Cavanagh waved his arms in front of him. He turned to the audience and got them involved. They began to jeer at the unfortunate kangaroo and throw things—rotten fruit and insults. Colin tried but not used to his gigantic feet and large round rump—and of course his small, spindly arms were of no help—he couldn't right himself.

Mr. Cavanagh put the whip between his teeth and threw his boxing gloves to the ground. Like a pro-wrestler he tore open his shirt. The crowd chanted *Cavanagh! Cavanagh! Cavanagh!* He went to one side of the ring and put his hand to his ear. The chant grew louder. He crossed the ring again and repeated the action. The crowd grew positively frantic with bloodthirsty excitement.

Somehow Colin managed to return to his feet. He saw the murderous glint in his opponent's eyes. He heard the bloodlust in the crowd's chant. The musty scent of fear rose from his kangaroo coat. *Fight or Flight?* Colin chose flight. He headed for the edge of the ring, managing it in two hops. On the third he bounded for freedom. Only the ring had other ideas. Colliding midair with an invisible wall he was thrown back into the center, again landing on his backside. Mr. Cavanagh approached, whip in hand.

Bara didn't know what to do. She had to help Kangaroo Colin. She looked at her hands. She still held the bell and spoon. *Of course, end the round.* She rang the bell. The round was over, the fighting stopped, but as the bell's echo died things changed. Her father transformed, shrinking in width except at the shoulders and growing in height. When his face came into view he'd grown young. His grey hair was now dark, thick, and wavy. Mr. Cavanagh was gone. A teenage boy stood in his place. He had the most piercing blue eyes. *The dark-haired boy!*

The dark-haired boy looked down at the whip and grew disgusted. He threw it to the ground. Colin who was suddenly no longer a kangaroo came to his feet. He stood taller than the dark-haired boy. But while Colin still had to grow into his height, the dark-haired boy owned every inch of his. Alas it really didn't matter what Colin looked like. Since the dark-haired boy had appeared Bara hadn't even glanced his way.

Colin looked at Bara and saw the way she looked at the dark-haired boy, the way the dark-haired boy looked at her, and was filled with rage. He bent down and grabbed the discarded whip. His arm rose in the air and he cracked it. The light cotton of the dark-haired boy's shirt was sliced through and a thin line of red formed on his bared skin.

The sight of blood only seemed to grow his anger. Colin raised the whip again. Bara reached out and pulled back his arm. The whip flew from his hand and fell to the ground just outside of the ring. The dark-haired boy looked at Bara with obvious meaning and then fled. Unlike Colin he had no difficulty leaving the ring. The force field disappeared and he was gone. Bara knew she was meant to follow but she paused to look at Colin.

"How could you?" he accused. "After all we've been to each other."

Colin went for the whip again. He was going after the dark-haired boy. Wasting not a second longer Bara fled the ring and out of the circus tent. Her heart caught in her throat. She was back in the woods. The circus tent was in a clearing, meters from the maze. *Not again!* She felt like dropping to the ground and throwing a good ole-fashioned temper tantrum which would have almost been appropriate considering she still wore the hideous baby doll dress. The sound of rushing feet brought her to her senses. It was Colin. Anxious to find the dark-haired boy before he did, she entered the hedges.

Bara turned but one corner and there she was—the little girl from her dream two nights before. The doppelganger.

She wore the same red coat and the same heart-shaped glasses. Bara knew that under those glasses was only black. She opened her mouth to scream. The little girl reached up and put a finger to Bara's mouth. "Shush!" she said with a sharpness that demanded obedience.

There was a terrible moment as Bara waited for the little girl to transform but the little girl stayed a little girl. She cocked her head to the side and gestured that Bara should follow. Then she turned and began running through the hedges, taking its turns and twists at top speed. What else could Bara do? She followed. It didn't take long. No more than half a dozen turns and they were in the heart of the maze in front of the cottage. Vines and moss covered most of the outside, working their way up to the very top of the steeple, reaching out to the cross that stood at the tip.

The little girl stopped and stood for just a moment at the door and then began running again. The cottage wasn't their final destination. Bara took a deep breath and continued to follow. She rounded to the back and immediately wished she'd stayed in the clearing.

At the best of times one doesn't like to be in a graveyard, let alone in the middle of the night in a strange wood. Unfortunately, there, only a few yards away were three graves each marked with a cross. Two small wooden crosses flanked a larger metal one. In the moonlight the trio cast long shadows over the graves they guarded.

The little girl stood upon the center mound. She gave Bara a toothy grin and then dissolved to mist. If she'd been thinking clearly Bara would have taken that very moment to make a brisk retreat. But she didn't. She remained were she was. The crosses mesmerized her. She crossed to the center mound, reached out, and touched the cold metal. Like it had been hit with a steel rod and not the flesh of her hand, the cross rang through the night. *Not ordinary metal.*

A strange desire overtook her then, to dig up whatever lay beneath the iron cross. She'd have fallen to her knees and begun the grisly task with the same gusto as eating an ice-cream cake after a day in the desert without water. But on a windless night she was suddenly shaken from the top of her pink-beribboned head to the tip of her bobby sock wearing feet. It wasn't just being in a graveyard at night, thinking about grave robbing, and it wasn't the cold. The hairs on the back of her neck stood up.

Someone or something was watching.

Bara turned toward the cottage. Through the one and only window Courtney Cavanagh's lovely face stared back … it was just for a second and then it faded and the window was black. Her stepmother was gone. But the terror of the night only mounted because now there was a loud banging coming from the grave below, shaking the earth with its strength. Something was trying to unearth itself. A little plump hand reached up through the dirt, grabbed hold of Bara's ankle, and pulled.

XXII

Waking up didn't ease her fright. There was a banging here too, coming from the blocked door. Someone was trying to get into the Pink Palace but couldn't because of the chair barring the way. Mr. Cavanagh had heard screaming and come running.

"Why can't I open this door?" he called.

Bara sprang from bed and pushed the chair away. Her father stumbled in. He wasn't alone. Courtney was with him. Seeing Courtney there Bara screamed once more. It came into her mind she might still be sleeping. Delirium took over and her dream world melded with the real one. In the confusion she forgot that one should behave differently in real life.

"Get her out of here!"

Mr. Cavanagh looked at his wife pleadingly.

"I'll leave you two alone," Courtney murmured.

She left the room. Bara waited for her footsteps to fade and then went to the door and closed it. She made to pull the chair in front again. Mr. Cavanagh took her from the chair. She pulled from his grip and crossed the room to her boots. Mr. Cavanagh led her boots in hand to the bed and sat her down.

"It was only a nightmare," he reassured. "We're not going anywhere."

Bara slipped on her boots as they spoke and still gripped by the dream said what she hadn't in the car, "You don't understand. Courtney's a witch."

"That's enough. I know you don't like Courtney but calling her names is not okay."

"I'm not calling her names. I mean it. She's not just mean or evil. I'm saying she's a *bonafide* witch. Witches are real, Dad. Courtney is immortal or something. And there's the Wisp, at least that's what we call her. She's a spirit or something. I've seen her a couple times. Amy and Colin have too."

Bara finally stopped and waited for him to say something. His face said it all. He didn't believe her.

"You're too old for this fantasy."

"There's this too ..."

Not quite ready to give up Bara rose from the bed. She was about show him the diary but stopped. He might take it. He might give it to Courtney.

"What else?" he said. "What else is there?"

No she definitely couldn't tell him about the diary. She sat back down in frustration.

There was a knock. The door opened and Gloria came in carrying a tray.

"Mrs. Cavanagh thought you might be in need of some breakfast and tea," she twanged in way of an excuse.

"Thank you, Gloria. Just put it down there."

Mr. Cavanagh motioned to the bedside table. Gloria did as directed. After giving him a sympathetic smile she exited the room and closed the door.

Bara tried once more.

"Say you believe me, Dad!"

Mr. Cavanagh looked at her strained face and realized Bara wasn't just having a go at Courtney. She believed what she was saying ... and so at a loss he lied.

"Okay I do. But you need something in your stomach. Then we can do what needs to be done."

Mr. Cavanagh held out the tea. Bara believed the lie. She calmed and took the cup. Mr. Cavanagh returned the chair to its place by the window and sat. Resting his head in his hand he watched her eat and drink. When he'd found her in Colin's room he thought the obvious. Now it seemed he had so much more to worry about. What was going on with Bara and her friends? A cult, drugs ... worse? Beth had a sister in an asylum. She saw things that weren't there. Everyone knew insanity could be genetic.

But no. That can't be the case with Bara.

Mr. Cavanagh thought many things. But never, not for one second, did he believe any of what Bara had said was true. Thankfully she'd fallen asleep, the empty cup in her hand. Reluctantly he rose from the chair and went to the bedside. He took the cup and placed it on the tray. She still had her boots on. He wouldn't wake her to remove them. He pulled up the blanket and tucked her in like he had when she was little. Despite everything that had happened he looked down at her with love and pride.

There'd be no more sleep for him. It was already dawn. He closed the curtains and left, leaving the door ajar should she cry out again. Mr. Cavanagh couldn't be blamed for what he did next. He wasn't choosing a new wife over a daughter. He was turning to his wife for help and he told Courtney everything.

Bara slept soundly, completely unaware of what was going on in the house below. Her dreams would be of the usual sort. The sun would rise and set again.

In a drugged coma her tired mind reordered itself.

XXIII

The chiming of grandfather clock reached into her sleeping mind and slowly Bara woke. Her eyes fluttered open as gently as a butterfly might take flight. She stretched and yawned. It had been a truly wonderful sleep and for a short moment she forgot everything—the dreams, the Wisp, and even her stepmother. The curtains were pulled and the room was dark. Tempted just to go back to sleep Bara closed her eyes but it was no use. She was utterly rested. The bliss was short-lived. Somewhere a phone rang.

Bara had thought she was in her dorm room but there was no land line on her floor. No she was in the Pink Palace at her father's new house. Like a tsunami everything came flooding back, washing away that little butterfly, washing away the calm and leaving behind confusion and fear. *Light!* She needed to see. Fumbling in the darkness Bara clicked on the bedside lamp and looked around. There wasn't much new about the room. It was as pink as ever. The only addition was the tea set and half-eaten muffin on the bedside table. Gloria had brought them up on Courtney's orders. The remains looked so harmless lying there, so homey. Bara picked up the muffin and sniffed. *Nothing.* She dropped it back onto the plate and lifted the rim of the tea cup to her nose. It smelled of chamomile and something else, something bitter, something it shouldn't smell of. Normally it took her awhile to fall asleep. She'd been tired but not that tired.

Had Courtney *drugged* her?

There was a melodic rap on the door. *Courtney!* Bara thought about pretending she was still sleeping to stall. But there was a second knock, this time more insistent, and then a soft voice spoke through the door.

"Can I come in?" Courtney called.

Escape. There was the window. The Pink Palace was only on the second floor but the double ceilings of the first made it more like the third. Colin probably wouldn't have had a problem scaling down but Bara didn't like her chances. A fall would mean a hard landing on a stone patio, a broken leg if she were lucky, a broken neck if she weren't.

Courtney came again.

"Bara!"

There was no escape. Her stepmother wasn't going

away. Bara faced the inevitable.

"Come in," she returned.

The door swung open and Courtney entered, carrying another tray of food. She placed the tray on the bed and removed the tea cup to the bedside table. She took a seat next to the bed and set about readying the tea.

"Good morning or should I say good evening," she chimed as she stirred. "You slept the whole day away. I thought you might be hungry."

"More tea? So thoughtful. How long will I sleep for this time. Or maybe I won't wake up at all?"

In an instant Bara had decided the best defense was a good offence. Courtney looked alarmed but recovered quickly. Her face changed into something else, something harder to read. Taking the spoon from the tea she placed it on the saucer and then with great ceremony took a sip. A steady hand replaced the cup next to the spoon.

"You know," she said in a flat tone.

"About you drugging me? Yeah."

"Your father told me everything and …"

Dad told her everything! How could he?

Bara started … but then the shock left. Of course her father hadn't believed her. Seriously why would he? None of this had happened to him. If she hadn't been so deliriously tired she wouldn't have told him anything. But there was no going back, not now.

Courtney was still talking.

"I just thought with all the *goings on* you needed an undisturbed sleep. You did sleep? You weren't bothered with anymore nightmares?"

"*Nightmares,*" Bara echoed. "I may be a teenager but I'm not stupid, Courtney."

"I don't think you're stupid."

"I know things!"

Courtney raised an eyebrow.

"Perhaps, but you're just a girl. Stay out of this. You're dealing with forces far stronger than you."

"I guess you'd like that, wouldn't you?"

"Yes. Very much."

Courtney was calm, her voice so soft it all but caressed the listener. *She shouldn't sound like that!* Bara silently screamed. She should sound like an old woman, hoarse and rough. Her eyes were round and looked as gentle as her voice sounded. Her skin was flawless, her mouth youthful and full. *No she shouldn't look like that either.* She should be old and ugly. Courtney was neither and Bara's anger grew because of it.

"I don't care that my dad doesn't believe me. I know

you're a witch. I know the truth."

Courtney took another sip of tea. She put the cup down on the saucer, this time with a clink. She took a deep breath and looked Bara in the eye. "There seems no point in denying anything, is there? Yes, my dear, you could most definitely call me a witch."

Bara backed up against the headboard.

"Now I want you to stay calm," Courtney said. "We're all alone and we need to talk."

"What do you mean we're all alone?"

Bara jumped up from the bed, upending the food tray. She ran to the door and called for her father.

"Your father's working late."

Dad's gone. She couldn't be alone with Courtney. *Maybe the maid?*

"Gloria! Can you come up here?" Bara called.

The house was silent.

"She's gone too." Courtney confirmed.

Courtney rose and crossed the room to Bara. She touched her shoulder. The touch was no heavier than a falling snowflake but it made Bara feel she'd been doused with wet cement. She was stuck to the spot.

"It's just the two of us," Courtney continued. "I didn't want to risk being overheard."

Run, run down the hall and stairs and out the door Bara's instincts insisted. But could she get away? The wet cement feeling was still with her. *No* running away would mean she'd never know what Courtney had to say. She needed to know more.

"Okay," Bara said. "I'm listening."

"You have Nelson's diary. How much have you read? I think it's best that we're honest with each other. Tell me everything you know."

Her tongue unraveled itself.

"I know you're a witch and that you're immortal or something. You lived in a maze with someone named Martha. She was a witch too."

Why am I telling her this?

"Yes." Courtney prodded.

She has me under a spell Bara thought; she said, "And I know that you kept Nelson Sedgewick prisoner and I *know* you're evil!"

"I'm evil?"

"You drugged me, for crying out loud. Stop trying to confuse me."

"You're already confused. Give me the diary. It's not for you."

Not the diary! Bara suddenly snapped out of the trance.

"No! You can't have it!"

Courtney's voice was sharp

"I need the diary. Where is it?"

Bara stood firm but her eyes betrayed. Her glance wavered to the bag hanging on the back of the chair. It was only for a split second but Courtney saw it. Suddenly free of the psychic cement Bara sprang. Courtney did the same. Courtney was much closer to the chair, closer to the bag. She had the strap in her grip before Bara reached the chair. Desperation took over and Bara grabbed ferociously, pushing Courtney away at the same time. Like a deathly battle over a turkey wishbone the strap broke in two. Bara held the favored piece but the force of her push and the give-way of the cotton bag would have disastrous results.

There was the sound of breaking glass. Bara looked up to see as in slow motion the falling body of her stepmother, as first her arms and torso, followed by her waist and legs, went through the jagged mouth of the broken window. Last were the red soles of her size-eight pink pumps. Bara reached out but it was too late. Courtney was gone.

Like they were applauding the pink curtains flapped in the tumult.

Bara stood next to the broken window with the torn bag in her hands. She'd been intent on keeping the diary. This she'd done but at what cost? What should she do now? Somewhere inside came the answer. *Help your stepmother!* She broke from her shock and stepped closer to the window. She pushed through the clapping curtains and past the broken glass. Shuddering she noted the blood on the jagged shard ends. Courtney had been cut on the way through. Expecting to see her stepmother's body broken and bent, Bara looked down. There were the lawn statues, mute and motionless witnesses to her crime. There were the pink pumps, now empty of her stepmother's lovely legs. But that was it. Shards of broken glass littered the path but Courtney definitely wasn't there.

In an instant her view of the ground was blocked. Something large, something far too immense to be a bird, had dropped in front of Bara and now hung suspended. Bloodied with her usual neat hair loose and blowing in the wind was Courtney Cavanagh. She floated in the midair. Attached to no rope she'd flown.

Any concern for her stepmother dissolved into fright. Bara backed away from the window. Courtney still hovered, looking back. Adrenalin coursed through her veins and Bara had no trouble pushing the chair in front of the window before bolting. Her hand a claw around the torn strap of the bag she fled the room. Just as she reached the stairs a loud crash came from the Pink Palace.

Courtney had re-entered the house.

Down the stairs Bara ran. But running was pointless. Courtney could fly. Bara stopped in the foyer. She had to outthink her stepmother. She opened the front door but didn't go though. She darted into the study, hid behind a large chaise lounge, held her breath, and waited. She didn't hear any footsteps but rather sensed her stepmother's descent. The reason for the lack of footfalls became obvious. Courtney hadn't run down the stairs but flown. She soared out the door in pursuit.

All that was missing was a broom.

Bara ran for her coat. She fled to the back of the house. Leaving through the rear door she prayed she'd be long gone before Courtney figured out what had happened. She'd bought herself some time. Enough time to escape, she didn't know.

XXIV

The Grande Oaks went by in a blur. There was the parkland up ahead with its thick canopy of leaves. Ten more steps and Bara would be hidden in the shadows. She slipped into those trees like one rushing through a closing subway door. Collapsing under the cover of a large maple she lay still. Only her lungs moved as they fought to take in owed air.

Her breathing eventually slowed and moving without pain was possible. Bara shifted her weight and felt something poke into her side. *Thank you, God!* She pulled her phone from her pocket. The screen said it was 7:30 in the evening, later than she thought. *That must have been some drug.* She scrolled down her list of numbers and pushed the send button, praying Colin would answer and he'd be alone. He picked up on the first ring and didn't give her a chance to respond.

"Your father just called. He said you're missing. Are you okay?"

"I'm as well as can be expected."

"What happened?"

"I'll tell you later. What did you tell my Dad?"

"Nothing. What did I have to tell?"

"I can't go back there."

"What happened?" he repeated.

Bara didn't give him an answer. It would take too long.

"Can you meet me?" she asked instead.

"After last night they locked me in but that's never stopped me before. Give me thirty minutes."

"Meet me behind St. Cat."

"They'll be looking for you there."

"I'll be careful and you too, Colin. She's a lot more powerful than we thought."

There was no need to explain who *she* was.

"Right back at you, Barbie."

Colin hung up. Bara tied the ends of her bag together, slung it over her shoulder, and set out.

***

From just inside the woods that backed onto St. Cat, Bara wouldn't be sighted. She looked up at the massive stone building. Most everyone had gone home for Thanksgiving. There were only three rooms alit—Den Mother's, Patsy's, and her own. A dark form stood in the open doorway of her room. Mr. Cavanagh had called the Sheriff. Having not found who he was looking for, Bara, Pillanger left. He didn't turn out the light. *That's wasteful* Bara thought. Then she reminded herself she had more pressing things to worry about than saving electricity.

She was about to turn her focus back to watching for Colin when movement in the room stopped her.

A smaller frame, a female, was there. She'd gone to the door to lock it. Bara shivered at the thought of Courtney going through her things but then there was something comfortingly familiar about the shape. *Amy.* She'd come back early. Amy didn't have a cell phone. She didn't have the money. There was no phone on the floor and Bara couldn't go inside—too risky. The dim sound of crunching gravel echoed, Pillanger's car pulling away.

There was only one way.

Bara came out of hiding and crept across the lawn. She grabbed a small pebble and tossed it at the closed window. Startled by the noise Amy turned her head but didn't move. Bara threw another pebble and readied herself to throw a third. Amy figured it out. She came to the window, lifted the pane, and stuck her head through.

"Bara," she whispered into the night.

"Over here. Come down and bring a warm coat."

***

Colin, Bara, and Amy stood on the edge of the woods. Bara had shared her tale and they were debating their next step.

"I know you think we should go into the forest but maybe we should finish reading the diary," Amy said.

"Yeah, it's cold out here," Colin added.

Bara raised her eyebrows.

"Okay, where do we go where no one will see us?"

Windfall was a small town. Wherever they went needed to be bright enough so they could see to read. Their dorm rooms were off limits. The library was closed. There was one all-night diner—a favorite hangout for Pillanger and his two deputies. They could have sat under a street light but that would have left them too exposed, soon to be discovered by a passing patrol car.

"No," Bara urged. "It's the woods. The dreams have been pointing to the woods." Colin opened his mouth to argue but she talked over him. "Yours too, Colin. We need to find the maze. I think it exists in real life, not just dreams. There's something there for us. I know it."

Amy and Colin finally agreed but Colin had a point. It was definitely cold. Her pajamas were warm even if they were pink and her coat was thick. But Bara had been outside for a while and her hands and ears were freezing.

"Here."

Amy produced a scarf with a matching hat and gloves. Bara gave her a grateful smile that grew into a large smile. Amy had also brought snacks and water.

XXV

It was a clear, cold night. The forest smelled of moist earth and leaves. Soft soil clung to increasingly muddy soles.

Bara was reminded she'd entered these woods in her dream without shoes. But this time she was shod, the one blessing from being drugged. And *this time* she wasn't alone. Colin and Amy were with her.

The forest was eerie enough but so far no mystical being had appeared to guide or bar the way. Colin led them down a well-worn deer path. Amy yawned. Bara answered in kind. They'd been walking for more than an hour and everyone was tired. A determined Colin kept up a breakneck speed. But as the night wore on it was becoming clear raw determination wouldn't be enough.

"Colin, stop!" Bara urged.

He halted and turned around.

"Why did you stop me?"

"I think we're going the wrong way."

"You said you didn't know which way to go."

"I know but ..."

"Then how do you know we're going the wrong way? You said you came to a lake. It makes sense. If we follow a deer path we should come to a source of water. Deer need to drink."

Nothing Colin said came as news. They'd all agreed on a plan of action. Since they had no idea where to look for the maze it made sense to look for the lake first.

"I know that's what we thought …"

"It's all we have to go on," Amy added.

"The thing is I don't think the lake exists … or not anymore. I think it existed in the past."

"This is just getting better and better," Colin scoffed. "It doesn't exist anymore. Only in the past. So now we have to time travel too?"

"No!"

"Then how in the name of *Doctor Who* are we going to find it?"

"Either it existed in the past or only in my dream."

Colin threw up his hands and sat down on a log that littered the path.

"In your dream? That's even better. So what do we do now? Take a nap?"

Amy suddenly remembered something.

"Didn't Professor Chestermire say there'd been a lake near Windfall once?"

Bara looked at her blankly.

"You know? Where they sunk the witches' remains?"

"Don't you do your extra credit Math in History?"

Amy grinned.

"I multitask. Do you remember where he said it was?"

"North of the town."

"The town's behind us."

This new piece of information invigorated Colin.

"There's a compass on my phone."

He pulled it out and pushed a few buttons. The screen's blue light gave his face an odd glow.

"It's this way."

Colin jumped up and without waiting for any response started walking again. Amy and Bara looked at each other and rolled their eyes. They were thinking the same thing. *What a dork!* But then they followed the dork. It didn't take them long to rue the decision. Going north meant leaving the easy-to-follow path and heading into thick underbrush. The canopy although thinned by fall still blocked out most of the moonlight and it was very dark. Colin, cursing every time he stubbed a toe, continued to lead the way. Bara brought up the rear with Amy in the middle. Bara fought to make out Amy's shadowy form passing through the trees. Eventually she gave up and just followed the sound of breaking underbrush and Colin's constant complaining.

They struggled along for some time and Bara was again losing heart. They didn't seem to be having any more luck among the trees than they'd had on the path. Maybe trying to find the lake hadn't been such a good idea after all. Up ahead Colin and Amy continued to break through the bush. She'd count to hundred and then if they hadn't found anything she'd suggest they come up with another plan. *One ... two ...*

Ninety ... ninety-one ... the trees thinned. Sporadic beams of moonlight cut through the canopy above, lighting up a patchwork on the forest floor. Amy's shadowy outline was easier to spy now. Something told Bara their luck had changed. And finally ... *finally* Colin had stopped griping.

"I think we're close to something!" she called out.

No one responded.

The trees were even thinner now. Amy's shadow disappeared not into darkness but light. Bara stumbled out of the trees and entered a clearing.

What she saw surpassed hopes—the maze.

"We found it!"

Bara looked around for her friends. Someone was standing not far off under the shadow of a tree. Was it Colin or Amy? She couldn't tell.

"We found it!" she repeated.

The tall shadowy outline said nothing.

"Amy?"

No answer.

"Colin?"

The wind picked up and there was the familiar scent of flowers. *No* this being wasn't one of her friends. Moonlight hit the shadow, lighting it up seemingly from within. How could she have thought it was Amy or Colin? Long white robes and silver hair whipped in the wind. *The Wisp.* She stared at Bara for a second longer and then dissolved to nothingness.

XXVI

Bara stood as rooted as the trees, listening, watching, and hoping for some sign of her friends. The forest was dark, cold, and soundless. The wind didn't rustle a leaf and there were no rummaging night creatures. She was truly alone. *What to do now?* There seemed only one option but her legs refused to move. A second later the decision was taken from her. The leaner trees bent in a gusty grasp. A cold wind weaved its way through the dark fabric of the forest and found its way to her shadowy back. Bara felt herself moving, propelled forward by the hand of nature. She made a silent wish that Colin and Amy were safe, relented, and entered the maze.

Dimmed by the shadows of looming shrubs the maze was darker than the clearing. Her eyes adjusted slowly but soon she could see to go forward. *But which way?* Details from her dream returned. Bara could almost see the little girl in her red pea coat. She was relieved she didn't.

Turn left and then right and then right again, just keep going. Bara made one last turn and there it was, just as it had been in her dream—the cottage and the tower. A bell barely seen in the night hung motionless. Its marble tower cast a long shadow; that of the cross disappeared into the darkness of the hedges. Thick ivy lit burgundy by the autumn moon covered most of the stonework and the windows. Only the door was bare. *Oh!*

Someone had been inside and recently.

But Bara wouldn't bother with the door. She ignored the windows. It didn't matter what was inside the cottage. As she had in her dream she went around to the back, heading for what had been her goal all along.

And there they were—three crosses, two wooden and one iron. In her dream she'd wanted to dig up the middle grave. Now the same yearning. The wind was in agreement. *Dig* it whispered. Bara wasn't keen on unearthing the remains of God knows who or what but she'd do it all the same. Still clawing at cemetery dirt with one's bare hands was just a little too revolting.

A large rhododendron bush sat to the left of the cottage. Her eyes focused on something stashed between the house and the bush. Bara went closer. It was an ancient wheel barrel. A collection of wooden handles emerged from the body of the barrel, a rusty pair of pruning shears and—*score*—a small earth-worn spade. The spade would do just fine. She went to the center grave to dig.

The spade made its first pass into the soil. Loose earth gave way with ease. The ground was too soft. The soil should have been solid, hardened by time and the cold night. Yet it was no firmer than sawdust. Natural earth was never so porous. Bara had been to cemeteries before. The untended graves those not mowed and weeded by caretakers and loved ones were always covered with growth. *From death comes life* her mother had said. All around the cottage were signs of life. The grounds could have used a gardener to cut back some of the greenery. The maze hedges grew as tall as tress. But on the three grave mounds it was different. Something had reacted with the soil, eaten away its substance.

Nothing grew. Most unnatural.

Nothing is natural about any of this Bara reminded herself. Then she quieted her thoughts and returned to digging. She made two more passes before the spade hit something hard and its head came off. She'd dig with her hands after all. Fortunately the job was near done. Bara smoothed away the last of the dirt to reveal a metal box the size of a shoe box. A raised cross spanned its length and width. She traced her finger over the cold metal, gripped the sides, and pulled. And pulled. The box wouldn't budge. Somehow it had found an iron grip in the Styrofoam soil.

Bara sat back and thought. *It's only a box, meant to hold something. It's not the box I need but what's inside.* All it took was a gentle tug. The lid gave way and landed with a soft plop in the earth. There wasn't much light, only that of the moon, but it was enough—a dagger lay within. Hilt to tip it was the length of her forearm. The handle was the same iron as the box but the blade was made of some odd metal. It was green, not the green of rusty copper, but a metallic green that glinted in the moonlight. *How strange?*

An ill wind as they say began to blow. The hairs on the back of her neck and arms suddenly stood on end. The blood rushed from her head and into her limbs. *Someone's watching.* Bara knew it. She came to her feet and grasped the dagger in both hands. At least she had a weapon.

Movement through the cottage window stole her

glance. *The window! Of course.* Her dream memory had been incomplete. Bara had remembered her way through the maze, she'd remembered the desire to dig up the grave, but she hadn't remembered the window. Not until it was too late. A pale face formed out of the darkness.

Not possible!

It wasn't Courtney who stared back. It was the dark-haired boy. Had Bara been pulled from reality into dreams?

There was the sound of rushing feet. Colin and Amy came around the cottage. Instantly Colin was at her side. He held her for an unnaturally long time.

Bara pulled away and pointed at the cottage.

"In there!"

Amy and Colin looked but there was nothing to see.

"The dark …" Bara trailed off when she looked at Colin and rephrased. "The Wisp was there just a second ago."

"We believe you," Amy said. "But let's not stick around to find out where she's gone. We need to get out of here."

Colin took Bara's arm and noticed for the first time the dagger. "Where did you get that?"

He quickly lost interest in his own question. A long powerful howl tore through the night air.

The Wolf was near.

"Forget it! Tell me later."

They ran around to the front of the cottage, heading for the hedges. Bara stopped.

"Wait! I don't know if I remember the way."

Colin propelled her forward.

"It's okay. We made a trail."

Colin and Amy had broken off branches as they'd made their way through the maze, clearing them away each time they'd had to backtrack. It had worked wonderfully and would do so in reverse. A trail of debris led them out in only moments.

"Now what?"

Amy pointed to a piece of fabric hanging off a branch at the entrance to the forest. It was her pink scarf.

"There it is. Let's go!"

With the help of Colin's compass they traveled the path they'd beaten to get to the maze. Eventually they came to a well-worn and familiar trail. They were back in the real-world forest of Windfall. With dawn not far off they tumbled onto the grounds of St. Catherine's.

XXVII

Under a sky streaked with red on a palette of the palest blue Bara stood alone and shivering in Library Square. Amy and Colin had already gone inside. After spending the night out in the cold they'd needed to find shelter and fast. There were few places to go. They couldn't go back to the house, not until they had a plan. Discovery would have been all-too-likely in their dorm rooms.

The library had seemed the only option.

And so under the filmy cover of twilight they'd slipped through the maples and oaks of Windfall, hoping to be inside and down in the stacks before the sun rose and they'd be clearly visible to anyone looking. Fortunately at the early hour the town was all but empty. Bara saw but one other person while she waited in the square, a tall teenage boy. At least she assumed he was a teenager. His face and hair were hidden under a hood. He passed the clock tower and took a left onto Windfall Way. Bara didn't recognize him. She assumed he didn't know her either. There was something familiar about him but they lived in the same town. She'd probably seen him around.

A student at Windfall High after a coffee. Whatever the case he didn't even look her way.

***

Of course it was Ms. Korey at the counter. Amy almost lost her nerve. She took a step back, bumping into Colin. He pushed her forward and then seated himself on a couch. He took out his cell and made a call.

Ms. Korey smiled at Amy. Like someone who'd mistaken a flea farm for talcum powder, Amy fidgeted. Anyone who knew her well would have known she was up to something. But Ms. Korey didn't seem to catch on. She nodded and then started typing away on the computer, looking for some rare book Amy had no doubt said she needed. Things were unlikely to get much better.

"Come on in now." Colin whispered into the phone. "Make it quick."

***

Bara hung up and tore herself free of the bush she'd taken cover behind. She rushed up the library steps, through the doors, and passed the front desk. Colin watched Ms. Korey. She never looked up. Bara was down the stairs and Ms. Korey was none the wiser. Colin returned his phone to his pocket. He crossed the foyer whistling a nonsense tune, the signal to Amy their plan had been a success. Finishing on a long high note he went down and joined Bara in the lower stacks. Amy should have followed closely on their heels.

She didn't. Bara was worried.

"You should go up and check it out," she told Colin.

He was already half-way up the staircase when an out-of-breath Amy came up from behind. He retraced his steps.

"What took you so long?" he asked. "Why didn't you use the stairs?"

"I tried but Ms. Korey stopped me. She pointed out that all the books I'd asked about were on the third floor. Go figure. She even came with me to find them. I had to wait for her to go back down. Then I took the elevator."

"You took the elevator!"

Almost no one ever used the old iron-caged elevator that stood like a geriatric dragon in the back corner of the library. It hissed and rattled and *yes* even smoked whenever it was used. Only those with a heavy load ever used the damnable thing. Original to Main Hall it was far from being up to code. Yet somehow it managed to jar itself between the floors without claiming lives or burning the place down. Still it wasn't wise to tempt fate.

"I had to or she'd have seen me come down," Amy explained.

Colin shrugged.

"Let's find somewhere to sit."

They settled at a study carrel in their favorite corner.

Colin and Amy grabbed two chairs and formed a human shield around Bara. It was time to talk. Faced with confessing she'd dug up a grave Bara felt ashamed. She looked to stall and so put the spotlight on her friends.

"What happened to you guys?" she asked.

"When we realized you were gone we tried to retrace our steps. We weren't alone." Colin squinted as though in pain. "We had the pleasure of dealing with your sharp-toothed furry friend."

"The Wolf? No!"

"I guess it exists in real life as well as your dreams and it must be immortal too."

"How did you get away?" Bara asked.

"That's the thing. We figured after we ran for *like* eons it didn't actually want to catch us."

"We think it was toying with us," Amy told her.

"Why would it bother to do that?"

"Who knows," Colin said. "But when we figured it out we stopped running. We were right. It charged us a couple more times, always stopping a few meters away."

"The next time it came at us Colin charged back."

"That was brave," Bara marveled. "And stupid."

"I thought it might run the other way."

"Did it?"

Colin gave a nervous laugh.

"No! It came at me and knocked me to the ground. I thought I was a slice of Sunday bacon. I told Amy to run but she didn't. Thank God! She picked up a stick and started whacking away."

"But it didn't matter how hard I hit the thing. It acted like I was stroking it with a feather."

Bara pointed out the obvious.

"You're not torn to shreds, so what happened?"

"It was the strangest thing. The Wolf gave me this queer look. I'd have sworn it was smiling at me. Then the damnable thing licked me. From chin to forehead."

"It licked you?"

"Like a pet dog," Amy said.

She giggled. Bara laughed too. Colin didn't. He spoke over their giggles.

"It finally got off me. Amy was still hitting away but it moved like it had all the time in the world."

"It got off Colin, looked me in the eye, and growled. I got so scared I dropped the stick. I thought it would kill me but it only sniffed like I'd hurt its feelings or something and then walked away. We started looking for you and there was the maze. Only it was in a place we'd already looked. It was like it had moved or something."

"And that's it?"

"That's it," Colin confirmed. "Your turn. How did you find the maze?"

There'd be no more stalling. Bara took a deep breath and began her side of the tale.

"I lost you guys in the dark. I didn't even realize I was alone, not until I'd found the maze. I thought I was following Amy. But when I came into the clearing the Wisp was there. I guess she led the way."

"The Wisp? Again? But how did you get through so fast? It took us forever."

"I remembered from my dream."

"What happened when you got to the center?"

"How did you find the dagger?"

"I … I dug it up."

"You dug it up?" Amy echoed. "You mean you unearthed it? From the graves?"

"I know it's kind of gross."

"No it's *seriously* gross," Amy corrected. "What if it'd been a dead body?"

"But it wasn't. It was this."

Bara reached into her bag and took out the dagger. The light of the library turned the green blade almost neon. Colin held out his hand and she handed it over. He lightly touched the tip. It was definitely sharp. A small bead of blood formed on his fingertip. Oddly the blood sparked with silver and then dissolved to nothing. Colin looked at his finger, not even a mark. He dropped the dagger to the desktop.

"What the hell are we supposed to do with that?"

Bara hesitated to share her thoughts. Killing her stepmother, as evil as she might be, wasn't really something Bara wanted to do. Digging up a grave at midnight was bad enough. But killing another human being? Was her stepmother human? *Are witches human?* Colin and Amy were waiting for her say something.

"I don't know but it must have some purpose. Maybe there's something in the diary."

It was a possibility. Bara took the diary from her bag and placed it on the table next to the dagger. She opened to a random page. Way too quickly to be natural the air in the library changed. As though someone had opened a door in a storm a current traveled down the stairs, through the stacks, and found its way to their secluded corner. It worked on the open diary. Pages flipped by an invisible hand and then stopped. Creating a small vacuum in its wake the supernatural wind then backed away from the book, retreating through the stacks, row after row, and finally up the stairs. Eventually everything was still again.

Before them was a sketch of the dagger. It lay horizontally. On the next page was a drawing of an amber stone. The dagger seemed to be piercing it. They looked closer. This amber was different from those on the cover. There was what looked like an insect embedded within. They all knew that sometimes insects could get caught in tree sap and then be preserved over the millenniums as the sap turned to amber.

Amy narrowed her eyes.

"I don't think it's an insect. Wait here."

She retreated from the table and disappeared into the stacks. Colin and Bara continued to look down at the diary. Running over both pages was some very ornate calligraphy. Colin read.

"*Mucro Libertas ac Ligatio* ... it's Latin."

They both attended Catholic schools. Along with Mass and Religion they took Latin.

"*Libertas* that's liberty, right?"

"Liberty or freedom and *ligatio* means imprisonment." Bara put the words together. "The dagger of freedom and imprisonment."

Just then Amy returned. She had a magnifying glass. Amy brought it to the book. She gasped and handed the lens to Colin.

"It's not a bug," he said. "It's a woman!"

Bara took the glass. She peered through to the page and saw long hair, long graceful limbs, and pale, pale skin.

"It's not a woman," she told them. "It's the Wisp."

"Are you certain?"

Colin looked again. Bara didn't need a second look.

"Yes! Absolutely!"

"What does it mean?"

Courtney wore a locket, the locket the dark-haired boy had taken from the Wolf. Sedgewick had said that Guenevere had worn amber around her neck contained in a locket. It had to be the same piece.

"Courtney has trapped the Wisp in amber," Bara said. "The Wisp wants to be set free."

"The dagger of freedom and imprisonment," Colin read again. "If the Wisp is your stepmother's prisoner I guess it makes sense she'd come to you for help, since you can get close to the amber. The dagger must be able to free her somehow." He continued to stare down at the diary. "The way it's drawn it's kind of stabbing the amber. You stab the amber and it frees the Wisp?"

They fell silent. It seemed a likely possibility. Bara was relieved. At least she wouldn't have to stab her stepmother.

"But are we sure we should set the Wisp free?" Amy asked. "I mean what is she? A ghost? A spirit? A *Slip* Spirit that Sedgewick talked about? What's a Slip? We have no idea. We should wait, read more of the diary."

"The Wisp did save Bara from the Wolf," Colin argued.

Bara still hadn't told them it had been the dark-haired boy who'd actually saved her from the Wolf. And she hadn't told them about seeing his face in the cottage window. She wrote that off as a slip of a tired mind—or the circus dream. That one was just too weird—but if there were a time to talk now was it. She looked at Colin and he was looking at her and ... she chickened out. Besides did it really matter? Bara knew deep down that her stepmother was evil. She had to be. Courtney was the problem.

"All we know is my stepmother is a witch. She drugged me and kept an innocent man prisoner and talked about killing him. And the Wolf is her pet or something, remember? She controls it. I don't know what the Wisp is but without her we'd never have found out about Courtney."

Amy still looked unconvinced.

"But yeah," Bara relented. "We should read more of the diary. Make sure."

There was a low rumbling sound—Amy's stomach.

"First I think we need some coffee and food."

Colin volunteered.

"I'll go."

"They're probably looking for you too," Amy said. "They'll have noticed you missing. You're grounded, remember? No one will be looking for me. Why don't you two read ahead? See what else you can find out."

Amy stood and put on her coat. Colin handed over some money. He and Bara watched her leave and then turned back to the diary. Bara flipped to where they'd ended off but they'd have no chance to read.

Bara heard them first. Colin noted her tense and then he too heard the footfalls. There were two sets. One was very heavy. It wasn't Amy returning. Bara pushed the diary into the bottom shelf of the study carrel and then handed Colin the dagger. He placed it in the inside pocket of his coat. The dagger disappeared only seconds before Courtney came upon them.

XXVIII

Courtney wasn't alone. She'd brought muscle—a large serious looking man in a dark suit. She rushed at Bara.

Colin took hold of her hand and pulled. They ran down the nearest aisle. As they rounded the end Bara looked behind to see how close Courtney was in pursuit. *Strange!* Courtney and her muscle weren't following.

Bara and Colin skidded to a stop in front of the ancient elevator. Colin pushed the button insistently. He needn't have. It was just arriving. It jerked loudly to a stop and a rusty door slid open with complaint.

Oh, my God! There are two of them! From the elevator stepped the identical twin to the man who'd come with Courtney. Without hesitation he took each of their collars in his gargantuan hands. Bara and Colin struggled in his grip but with no success. He led, slash, carried them back to where Courtney calmly waited. Letting go none too gently he shoved them at the study carrel. He then stood protectively next to Courtney. His twin stood on her other side. Colin and Bara were blocked from fleeing.

Where had Courtney found these men? *1-800-dial-a-goon?* For certain they weren't residents of Windfall. These men Bara would have remembered seeing. They wore all black and had identical cookie-cutter hair—short, light brown, and parted on the side. Their eyes were hidden behind dark glasses. Colin was as tall but he didn't come close to either's bulk, a bamboo among oaks. They were at least a foot taller than Courtney. They showed no emotion but a warning was clearly given. *We can and will hurt you.*

Courtney wore her customary pink, a long coat and silk scarf. Underneath no doubt was the metal locket containing the amber. Despite her fine clothes she seemed worn and tired. She didn't look bad. Courtney was far too beautiful to actually look bad but she definitely didn't look her best. She wore no makeup. Her hair was un-styled, pulled back in a simple ponytail, and her blue eyes were rimmed with the bruises of fatigue.

Black magic must being tiring Bara thought ruefully.

Courtney took a step forward and made to touch Bara but Colin positioned his body between the two, preventing any physical contact. Courtney stepped back again.

"You need to come home," she said in a too-sweet voice. "Your father's very worried. He has the entire Sheriff's Office looking for you."

"What's with these guys, then?" Colin asked. "Since when do cops come in matching pairs?"

Courtney narrowed her eyes and studied him. Her mouth formed a small smile. At first Colin flushed but then he gathered his courage and met her gaze. He was defiant.

"Maybe you should come with us too," she said, still *so* sweet, sweet as honey, thick as tar.

Colin straightened his normally bent shoulders and came to his full height which under other circumstances would have been impressive.

"We aren't going anywhere with you."

There was a low rumble. The sound had come from the two men. They'd stood like zombies Courtney had conjured to do her bidding. But now tree trunk arms, which had been folded across barrel chests, were hanging freely, fists clenched. Neither man would have had a problem folding Colin up like an ironing board and—with as much ease—toting him out of the library.

One thing was certain. They were definitely outmatched. Bara felt the same defiance as Colin but with the physical strength of the men, not to mention Courtney's powers, it would have been like doing battle with a jet fighter and two tanks armed with only a well-meaning garden rake. And wasn't that was what they needed anyway, to get Courtney on her own, to somehow get the locket from her neck? They had the dagger. Once the goons were gone they might be able to use it.

Colin with more courage than sense stepped forward, ready to challenge the world. Bara put out an arm to stop him. She shot him a meaningful look. Her hand rested on the dagger in his inner pocket.

"I think we should go. We need to talk this out with my stepmother *alone*. We can do that back at my Dad's."

Colin felt the blade next to his torso. He understood. Trying not to grow suspicion he shot the muscle one last threatening look.

"Are you sure?"

Bara nodded and turned to her stepmother.

"We'll go with you."

One of the men motioned that they should start walking. Bara and Colin did as he wanted. Courtney and her entourage followed. They left the stacks and started up the stairs. The rungs creaked from strain, threatening to give way under the mass of the men. Bara was more than a little relieved when they reached the top and entered the foyer. They passed an empty front desk. *No Ms. Korey.* Where had the librarian gone? Bara shrugged. It hardly mattered now. One of the men opened a door and waited for everyone to pass through.

The sun was completely up but thick clouds shut out most of the light. Parked by the doors was a black SUV with tinted windows into which they were ushered without protest. It seemed Courtney hadn't hired twins but triplets. Another giant sat in the driver's seat. How many of them were there? Bara shivered at the thought of an army of thickly-muscled zombies existing just to do her stepmother's bidding. Courtney joined the driver in the front seat. Bara and Colin were sandwiched between the other two in the back. It was a tight fit to say the least.

As the SUV pulled away from the library Bara looked back. Amy hadn't returned from the food run. Unless Amy saw them get into the car and drive away she'd never know what had happened. There may have been a flash of pink—Amy's coat—disappear behind a bush. Perhaps Bara had seen Amy; perhaps it was only wishful thinking. The SUV drove out of the square and joined the light morning traffic of Windfall Boulevard. Bara sat back on the leather seat to wait out the drive. Moving like an oil spill on a woodland pond, the shiny black car made its way through the autumn leaves and past the mansion of the Grande Oaks District.

XXIX

Despite the heavy feeling in her gut Bara was relieved when they finally pulled up in front of the Lavender House. The goons exited the SUV in unison and held open the car doors. The driver opened the front passenger side for Courtney. Bara stepped out onto the gravel. There were the marble cherubs and Greek gods, no help as usual. Bara was on the far side and had to come around the car, her arm in the grasp of a goon. She joined Colin and the other monstrosity of a man. The driver returned to the car and drove away. Bara and Colin were led, that is to say dragged, into the house. Courtney followed.

Gloria didn't come to the door. *No maid, no witness.* Courtney took off her coat and hung it on the antique rack. Her arms were heavily bandaged. Bara winced. The trip through the window had not left Courtney unscathed. But Bara quickly forgot her stepmother's pain. The locket lay on Courtney's chest, glittering on a dusty rose sweater set.

"Take him up to the room I showed you," she told the muscle. "And lock the door. My stepdaughter and I will talk in the study."

That wasn't the plan! Colin had the dagger.

"You can't separate us!" Bara said.

The goons hesitated but Courtney waved them off.

"Lock the boy in and then you are free."

One of the men grabbed Colin, a little too roughly. He resisted but with no success. Bara watched Colin and the hidden dagger disappear up the stairs. The look he threw over his bony shoulder told Bara he shared her distress.

"Shall we?"

Courtney didn't wait for a response but went into the study. As long as Colin was locked up she knew Bara wouldn't run. The study was neat and orderly. Antique books lined the walls and their embossing glinted in the dim light. Heavy drapes were partly drawn, allowing yellow sheers to let in a muted glow. A fire blazed in the fireplace. The study was comfortable and warm. Bara felt neither. There was the large chaise she'd taken cover behind earlier. Courtney had already settled in a matching wing chair.

"Close the door and sit down."

Bara did as she was told. She sat on the chaise, choosing the side farthest away from her stepmother and closest to the door. Anxiously she waited for what was to come. Courtney drummed her fingernails in her lap

"What are we to do now?" she finally asked.

Bara didn't have an answer.

"Where's my father?" she countered.

"Out looking for you, my dear. Needless to say he's quite worried."

"Then call him and let him know I'm home."

Courtney actually chuckled like Bara had told a joke.

"In good time. First we need to get a few things

straight."

"Are you going to kill me?"

"Kill you?" Courtney echoed.

"I know your secret."

"I think there's still much you don't know."

Bara was finding it hard to think. Her focus was split. How could she get Colin downstairs?

"Like what? I know plenty already."

Courtney lifted a single immaculately-plucked eyebrow. "Tell me just how much you do know and then I'll fill in the blanks?"

"I know you're a witch. I know that you've lived a very long time. You're immortal or something and I know you're *evil*." Bara all but screamed the evil part.

Courtney gave a long sigh. "You've said all this before." And then she asked what she really wanted to know. "Where is the diary?"

The heart of the matter Bara thought. She said with far more bravado than she felt, "Where you'll never find it. You can do whatever you like to me but I'll never tell. Colin won't talk either. People will come looking. He has parents too. You won't get away with it. People will eventually figure you out. You and your partner."

"My partner?"

"Martha ... your fellow witch. Where's she now?"

Bara suddenly remembered the woman at the door the day before. The other witch? The dark hair, the familiar voice, the interest she'd taken in the diary ... *oh my God, Amy* ... the other witch was Ms. Korey. She had to be.

Bara's defiance dissolved in the rush of fear.

"Please don't hurt Amy. Call Ms. Korey. Tell her not to hurt her. I'll tell you anything you want to know."

"Bara, I won't ..."

Smash! Something very solid hurdled through the bay window, landing with a decided thump on the Persian rug. Someone had thrown one of the smaller lawn statues through the glass. It was a cherub, now with a broken wing. Both Bara and Courtney sprang. Courtney was faster. She was at the window first. She was knocked off her feet as something long and thin flew through the broken glass and tackled her to the ground. Colin had escaped. Of course he'd escaped. Courtney had locked him in an upstairs room and let the goons go. She'd made a foolish mistake. Colin would have simply climbed down, scaling the side of the mansion as easily as he did the dorm buildings.

"Catch!"

The dagger came hurdling across the room, fortunately hilt first. Bara caught it but it flipped in her grip. The blade just grazed her arm, cutting a thin red line of blood. She winced and studied the wound. It wasn't deep. Dismissing the pain she returned her attention to the struggle going on between Colin and Courtney.

Colin despite his lean build was strong, not as strong as the goons but certainly stronger than Courtney. But it appeared Courtney would make short work of him. She was on top and he was fighting with all he had. His hands were around her throat but this seemed not to affect her. Alarmingly there was a pool of blood forming. Colin had been cut from his trip through the broken window and was bleeding pretty badly.

Dagger in hand Bara approached the wriggling mass of arms and legs. She stopped There was a snapping sound. She realized now why Colin'd had his hands around Courtney's neck. He'd been after the locket which he now clutched in his hand. Courtney screamed and tried to retrieve it. Using his length to advantage Colin held the chain out of her reach.

"Bara!"

Courtney watched wide-eyed as the locket slid into Bara's waiting hands. "No!" she shouted. "You don't know what you're doing!"

Bara didn't hesitate. She opened the locket. There was

the amber as she knew it would be. To keep it still she gripped it between her knees and raised the dagger above her head. With full force she brought the blade down. Like it was cutting through something much softer than the petrified sap, metal pierced amber. *Like flesh.* As though it were as soft as skin the blade plunged into the amber, disappearing somehow to its hilt.

Tiny fault lines spread throughout the amber. There was a sound like the breaking of an ice sheet and it shattered into countless pieces. The fracture gave off a blinding light and a force pushed out. The air cracked with sound and strength. Thrown from the blast Bara slid into the chaise. Colin and Courtney were flung to the opposite wall. Heavy furniture moved about on its own. Dislodged books threatened to brain the unsuspecting. Bara covered her head. Colin and Courtney, possibly unconscious, did not.

Flashes of silver surged through the air. Bara lost sight of the other two. She lost sight of everything. She blinked, trying to clear her vision but saw only light, no form. Then came the noise. The strength of it moved the floor beneath in waves. Different from the sound of the first explosion it was high pitched. A shriek? No, a siren. It grew louder and higher, threatening to pierce eardrums.

Bara put her hands to her head and tried to hang on.

Part II

The Enemy

I

The house shook one last time and then slowly the noise lessened, dying down until no longer strong enough to do physical damage. Only one sound continued, sharp and loud. Someone was screaming, not in pain or anger, but triumph. The screech became staccato and turned into hard laughter. After a moment it stopped and the room was silent. Bara took her hands from her ears and looked around. Everything was turned upside down—furniture toppled and shattered, paintings shredded, her father's precious library piles of broken spines and torn pages.

But despite the chaos the room was eerily beautiful.

It was as though a nuclear winter had fallen, radiant and cold. Silver hung in the air, slowly descending, settling like snow. The study was covered in a blanket of silver but there was no warmth. The fire continued to blaze in the fireplace but somehow it burned frigid.

And the smell? Had a flower found a way to bloom in the cold and destruction? Bara was reminded of florist's freezer and she shivered.

There was stirring across the room—Courtney and Colin. Colin moaned. Courtney blinked to clear her vision and tried to come to her feet. She failed. Both she and Colin were covered in that fine silver dust. Bara looked at her arms. They were as silver as the rest of the room except for a streak of red where the dagger had cut.

Again laughter. This time just a sharp little chuckle. A woman was laughing. Bara didn't understand what was so funny. She scanned the study once more, stopping on an upright and rigid form. Had another lawn statue found its way inside? Tall with long slender limbs the Wisp didn't move. A highbrow sat over arched eyebrows. Cheek bones, also high, flanked a slender nose. She had a full, very red mouth but the mouth wasn't one to kiss. Lips were drawn into an odd sneer. Her eyes opened and stared. They were as silver as the room. Bara had seen those eyes before on another face. The other face remained forgotten. *Remember*! But she didn't ... not yet.

The Wisp twitched and slowly brought her arm to touch her face. The hand passed through her head as though either hand or head—both—wasn't there. She then flipped a foot and tried to kick away a stool that had fallen at her feet. Like her hand had passed through her head, her foot passed through the stool. She was free from the amber but still the Wisp had no real body. Anger transformed her beautiful face. Her eyes sparked with rage. Her teeth lengthened and sharpened. She turned to Bara.

What had Courtney called just as Bara had been about to stab the amber? *You don't know what you're doing*! In an instant Bara remembered. She knew where she'd seen those silver eyes. Only for a moment the human face of the Wisp became the bestial muzzle of the Wolf.

The Wolf was the Wisp, the Wisp the Wolf.

Looking at Bara seemed to calm the Wisp. Her face returned to normal and she smiled. Her smile grew opened mouthed and it stopped being a smile, becoming an 'O' long and narrow. It grew and grew until it threatened to overwhelm her pale face and then it did. Just like the doppelganger's had her mouth opened to consume its own face. Nose, eyes, and forehead disappeared until nothing was left but a large black hole. Specks of her silver hair were just visible over the ebony abyss.

The air sizzled with charge. Silver light streamed out of the dark chasm that was once a mouth, forming traces through the room, vapor trails of electricity … searching … searching …

It occurred to Bara that the Wisp and her doppelganger were one, just like the Wolf and the Wisp were one. In the split second she had to think about it she understood why the Wisp had disguised herself such. She'd made Bara her own worst enemy in more ways than one. But the understanding came too late. Bara understood at the very same moment the hair on her neck stood on end, just before a streak of silver made contact and entered into her. Just like in her dream she was lifted to standing and then into the air. Her toes grazed the silvery ground below. It was almost pleasant, defying gravity, but then the pain hit. Silver spread through her body like razor edges, scraping, cutting her out hollow.

There was a voice in her mind now. It was sing-song pleasant but much more ominous—bird chirping delivered on the winds of an approaching electrical storm. *I will grant you eternal life. You and I will live together forever, beautiful and powerful. You will never be lonely. I will not leave you, not like they did. I offer you a great gift. You need only share with me the one thing I need. I offer you everything. You need only share. Share with me your material form.*

Material form ... the Wisp wanted her body ... *to share?* Something told Bara it wouldn't be an even split.

Let me in little girl and you will live forever the Wisp came again.

The silver light cutting through her blood like jagged glass eroded her strength. It wouldn't be long. Bara began to drain away. She fought back but it was a losing battle.

And a new voice rang in her head—her own mutinous voice.

I should let her in. The Wisp will give what she's promised. I need only share my body. I'll never be alone, so much for so very little, and the pain—the pain will stop.

"No!" came a voice from across the room.

Courtney struggled to her feet and clasped her hands together. Bara had always known her stepmother was beautiful but Courtney's beauty had taken her father from her mother. It was an evil thing. But now with her hair flowing down her back and framing her face, Courtney resembled the closest thing to a goddess. *No, not a goddess* Bara corrected *an angel.* For Courtney wore a halo.

Courtney pulled her hands apart and a golden light spread out as the silver had from the Wisp. It grew tentacles, moving throughout the room, meeting and entwining with the silver. It also entered into Bara. Courtney spoke but her lips didn't move. The voice was in Bara's head.

Think of white light. It will protect you.

For once Bara did as her stepmother wanted. Like that which comes from a star she imagined the purest of white light. It pushed against the silver, forcing it out. A sudden sharp pain like claws had been plucked from her bones and

Bara regained control of her legs and then her torso and arms. Her mind cleared and then the silver left. Courtney's golden glow remained only a second longer and it too left. Bara fell to her knees.

The Wisp realizing she'd lost the battle drew in her silver light, back through the room and into the gaping hole that was her mouth. The electricity and its incessant hum died away. Her mouth closed and shrunk. Her eyes became visible again, a nose and then finally her face returned to its icy beauty—icy beauty and rage.

Only for the briefest moment the Wisp glared at Bara before turning to Courtney whose glow was gone. Fine bone structure remained but as though she'd aged a decade in a minute Courtney now looked worn and pale. She seemed barely able to stand.

Raising long arms the Wisp lifted tapered fingers. Silver bolts shot from the tips and connected with Courtney's torso. Courtney slammed into the wall—hard—and didn't move. But the Wisp wasn't finished. She floated closer and again shot Courtney with silver. Courtney screamed this time. Bara tried to help. She grabbed a busted lamp and threw it. The Wisp had no real body and the lamp passed clear through.

Bara came to her feet and limped across the room. The

Wisp paused in her torture and watched almost merrily. Bara reached Courtney and took hold of her shoulders. Her fingers sparked at the contact and she withdrew in pain. The Wisp laughed and sneered but still she waited, seeming to have all the patience in the world. Willing herself to ignore the burning and the smell of her own singed skin Bara took hold of her stepmother and pulled. Courtney wasn't a large woman. She should have been able to drag her to the door but Courtney seemed cemented. Her body wouldn't budge.

Courtney opened her blue eyes and stared.

"Run!" she said. "You can't save me. Save yourself."

"I can't leave you."

"I'm already dead. She can't be stopped. Run. Go to the librar …"

Her words were lost to a scream. Courtney was hit with another bolt of silver. The Wisp had tired of waiting. Another bolt sent Bara careening across the floor and into the chaise.

"Listen to your step-mommy," the Wisp taunted, "while you still have the chance."

Then she lost interest in Bara. Courtney wouldn't have long. Through it all Colin had barely moved. Bara crawled to his side. She couldn't help Courtney but maybe she could get Colin to safety. She shook him. He moaned and opened his eyes.

"We have to go!" she urged. "You need to get up!"

"What happened?" he asked groggily.

"There's no time? Can you move?"

Colin sat up. Bara slipped an arm under his and helped him to his feet. Drawn by her screams Colin looked at Courtney. Courtney lay on her stomach. She screamed once more and then her screams faded to whimpers.

"She's dying!"

Bara read the look in his eyes.

"There's nothing we can do. I tried. I don't know how to save her. You can't help either, not unless you know magic."

"We can't leave her."

"Colin, please, I don't even know if we'll be able to save ourselves."

It went against everything inside him but Colin turned from Courtney and her suffering. He and Bara hobbled to the door. Bara reached for the doorknob. Her hand disturbed the silver dust. The knob was oddly slippery and she had to struggle to get a proper handhold. Using her shirt tale she eventually gripped it. The door resisted but Colin pulled too. There was a sucking noise like the room had been under pressure, and grudgingly, it opened.

Colin and Bara remained where they were. Their path was blocked. Ms. Korey and a dark-haired boy—with deep blue eyes—rushed past, forcing them back into the room. Her body and mind froze. With all that had happened Bara was now struck, almost paralyzed, by the appearance of a boy—the boy from her dreams.

Amy was there too. She had the diary. Somehow Amy had found the dark-haired boy.

Bara regained the power to move. She turned to see the same golden light that Courtney had used come from Ms. Korey and the dark-haired boy. Ms. Korey's light settled on Courtney, bathing her in a protective glow. The Wisp continued to shoot silver but now it only glanced off the gold. The dark-haired boy aimed at the Wisp. He was pushing her, pushing her farther and farther from Courtney.

The Wisp was forced back until she stood just inside the broken window. She stopped taking aim at Courtney and turned her attention to her attacker. The dark-haired boy stood his ground. The silver bounced off him in a shower of sparks. With Courtney no longer under fire Ms. Korey also focused her light on the Wisp. The Wisp still wasn't fazed. She used a hand to aim at each of her foes. The match seemed even but then movement from the other side of the room caught her attention. She'd seen Amy. Her silver eyes widened with fear. It wasn't Amy who frightened her; it was the diary.

"Get the amber to Bara," Ms. Korey shouted.

But there would be no time. The Wisp stopped fighting. Stirring up a tremendous wind she rose several feet above the ground, turned fast, and flew out the broken window.

II

Like a blanket lifted over an unmade bed the wind the Wisp had stirred settled. Dust still hung in the air but more and more of it landed, coating everything in a two inch layer of silver. A still burning fire was the only evidence that the study had been, until recently, functional.

Bara stood among the debris, not sure what she should do. Amy was helping Colin limp to a chair. He moaned, complained, and joked. Bara almost smiled. He'd be okay. Ms. Korey and the dark-haired boy were seeing to a bleeding and bruised Courtney. Her future seemed less certain. She sat propped up against the wall, her head lolled disturbingly to one side.

"Will my stepmother be okay?" Bara asked.

The dark-haired boy turned to her. His eyes were even bluer than they had been in her dreams. Odd under the circumstance with Courtney apparently near death but he grinned and winked. He closed his eyes and put his hands together as in prayer. Slowly he pulled his palms apart. A globe of blue light formed. Beginning at her head Mathew put his hand inches away, immersing Courtney in the glow. His hands moved down to her toes, never actually making physical contact. He stepped back, leaving her awash in energy. Courtney closed her eyes. Bright flashes moved up and down her body. Silver dust lifted from her skin and clothes. Cuts closed. Bruises faded and disappeared. When the light dimmed she appeared healed. She opened eyes now free of any discomfort.

"Your powers are weakened," the dark-haired boy told her. "I don't know how much longer you have."

"Yes," she said with pained acceptance. "I expected as much."

"She is healed," he announced to the room.

Everyone then turned to look at Bara. There was a long silence. Bara looked once more at the ruined study and understood the reason why. It was clear now. Her hatred of her stepmother had blinded her to the Wisp's evil intentions. Worse yet she'd coaxed Amy and Colin along on her crazy trip. She was to blame for everything. She opened her mouth to speak but then closed it again. What could she say, really? *I'm sorry* seemed woefully inadequate. The dark-haired boy gave her a sympathetic look. He seemed to read her thoughts.

"The demon is cunning." He tilted his head in Courtney's direction. "You should have had more warning."

Ms. Korey gave an annoyed look. She helped Courtney to her feet and guided her to a chair. Courtney was greatly improved but still wobbly.

"She tried to tell me," Bara admitted. "I wouldn't listen."

"The demon knows our weaknesses and ..."

Courtney interrupted.

"You were mine."

Courtney smiled at Bara with what could only be described as tenderness. Then her smile turned suddenly sour. She looked back at the dark-haired boy.

"Mathew?"

The dark-haired boy had a name and it was Mathew. But for some reason Courtney didn't seem all that wowed to see him.

"Just how long have you been back in Windfall?"

"Long enough," he responded in kind. "I would think given my timing you'd be more pleased to see me."

"I'd have liked to have seen you a lot earlier." Courtney turned to Ms. Korey. "I suppose you knew he was here all along?"

"I keep Mathew's secrets as I do yours."

Ms. Korey spoke with that strange accent. Her real voice.

"Of course, you do," Courtney returned.

"Perhaps we could simply be grateful he is here now."

Ms. Korey nodded in Bara's direction. Bara held the arm that had been cut by the dagger. Courtney sighed and turned back to Mathew. He took a step in Bara's direction. There was a small trickle of blood on her arm. Bara was also pretty tired but otherwise she felt okay. Behind her Colin let out a gasp of pain. Amy was checking him over. He was covered in cuts and bruises. He seemed in far worse shape. Bara took a step back and placed a hand on his shoulder.

"Could you help him first?" she asked Mathew. "Please."

Mathew gave a queer smile. He seemed almost pained but then he put a hand out to Colin. Like Mathew had tried to touch him with a rattle snake Colin drew back.

"Whoa, dude! What are you doing?"

Courtney intervened.

"Maybe, Bara, you should go first."

Mathew shrugged and grabbed for her hand. He led her a few steps away to the fireplace. A warm glow danced across his face. He continued to hold her hand, staring into her eyes. Bara felt a strange rush of energy. She couldn't help herself. She blushed. He gave her hand a reassuring squeeze and then let go. Her cheeks were still aflame when the blue light came. Silver lifted from her flesh and clothing, her few cuts closed, and bruises faded. Then suddenly the light dimmed. Mathew examined her arm, tracing a finger along the cut before meeting her eyes. There was that rush of energy again.

"Your wound is from the dagger," he told her. "It won't be healed with the light."

Bara was on the verge of swooning from the feel of his fingers on her skin. Her stepmother brought her back from the edge. Courtney let out a small gasp.

"The cut isn't deep," Mathew reassured. "It will heal on its own."

Mathew turned again to Colin. Still Colin hesitated. He had that same odd look on his face Mathew'd had just a short time earlier. It was like he'd just made an ugly realization but wasn't quite ready to accept it as truth.

"Can't one of you two do it?" he asked Ms. Korey and Courtney. "I'm not sure I want the coffee guy practicing voodoo magic on me."

Coffee guy? Bara made the connection. Mathew had to be the new Tragic Sip baristo, the one the Goths had been so excited about.

"The power of healing hands is Mathew's alone. Don't worry," Ms. Korey assured. "You'll be as good as new."

Colin stood and limped over to stand next to Bara.

"If it's all the same to you, I'll heal the old-fashioned way."

He placed a gentle hand on Bara's back that found its way to her shoulder. She stiffened. The gesture was meant to be reassuring but for some reason it had the opposite effect. There seemed to be a sense of ownership in it.

Mathew looked down and rubbed the back of his neck.

"The choice is yours."

Then he crossed to the chair Colin had emptied and plopped himself down. He stared at the fire.

"You'd be better off allowing him to heal you," urged Ms. Korey. "Mathew has helped me many times. The process is quite painless."

Colin dropped his hand from Bara's shoulder.

"Process?" he echoed. "Forget it. What are you guys? And what the hell was that thing?"

III

Courtney sat in a tattered wing chair. The glow of the fire played across her face.

"Brynndalin and those like her have many names. Demon, succubus, incubus, the old hag, and the boogie man, or boogie woman as in this case. And yes, even the will o' wisp you thought she was."

"Those like her?" Bara echoed. "You mean there are more of those things?"

Courtney nodded.

"In my dreams she was a wolf. Is she a werewolf?"

"No. She wants only soul energy, not blood and flesh, and only in her world can she shape-shift. Anything the dreamer fears will do. Wolves are a common fear but wisps are not like natural wolves. They know no compassion. Werewolves, and even vampires, are capable of compassion—in small doses. And of course they were once human."

"Back up a second," Colin interrupted. "Werewolves

and vampires are real?"

"Yes," Courtney confirmed. "But Brynndalin is the most dangerous. Now that she is free of the Slip no one is safe."

"The Slip?" Amy repeated. "Like in *Slip* spirits? Sedgewick talked about Slip Spirits?"

"The Slip is a sliver of consciousness between the waking world and the dream world," Courtney told them. "There, the wisps feed on the sleeping, robbing soul energy. The contact lasts only a few moments before one wakes or falls into a normal dream. But a Clavigen can stay longer, go deeper. It is much more difficult for the wisps to feed off us. But they can sometimes create a kind of waking dream. Brynndalin was able to do this with you three."

"Sedgewick called the finder of his book Clavigen. You're saying we are *all* Clavigen.

"It would seem so, yes," Courtney confirmed.

"It's strange that all three of you are gifted." Mathew said. "But you, Bara, are especially adept."

"No one in your family has powers, unexplainable gifts?" Ms. Korey asked Colin and Amy.

They shook their heads.

"I never really had the dreams like Bara," Amy said, "or even Colin. I only ever saw her once in my bedroom."

"And I only had one dream," added Colin.

"But you've all seen her wolf form. You were in the Slip, deeply so. You're either all Clavigen or something most peculiar is going on."

"And you're very sure?" Mathew asked Bara again. "Your parents are not Clavigen?"

Courtney answered for her.

"No. They are not."

"Strange," Mathew said. "An ability as strong as yours is usually passed down. You'd have known the dangers then. You wouldn't have been alone in all this."

"She wasn't *alone*." Colin countered with a little more emphasis than needed.

"What I meant *is* she should have had a guide, someone with more knowledge of the Slip and its forces. Someone ..." Mathew paused and gave Bara a shy smile before continuing. "Someone should have used his dream time more wisely."

The last statement was cryptic to all but Bara but Colin sensed something was up.

Looking at Mathew, as if he'd just lifted his shoe and discovered something smelly and brown, he quipped. "Thanks for the info, Yoda."

Mathew said nothing for a moment and then responded

in kind.

"Not a problem *Jar Jar.*"

Mathew was referring to Colin's tall and almost impossibly thin frame. He'd taken aim and hit.

Colin took a step in Mathew's direction. Mathew looked about ready to rise. Bara was quick. She put a hand on Colin's chest. Still smarting from his injuries he let out a small yelp. Mathew chuckled and settled back into the chair. But Colin wasn't finished.

"So werewolves and vampires are humans gone bad and the Wisp is a dream demon. What about you three? Are you *human*?"

He smirked at Mathew. The question was meant to be a jab. Mathew got the point.

"Human we are, young Jedi," he volleyed back.

"Very funny, you're a funny guy. Maybe you wouldn't be so funny with a ..."

"Yes," Courtney interrupted. "We're most definitely human."

"But I've seen you fly?"

"We all have certain powers once we've captured a wisp."

Ms. Korey and Mathew held out metal lockets. They opened to reveal amber stones with what appeared to be insects inside. Mathew actually had two stones, one on each face of the locket.

"The powers of the captured wisp are transferred to the one who imprisons it and wears the amber about her neck. Observe."

Courtney raised her arms. A breeze blew through the room. Silver dust lifted and swirled around in eddies. Eddies moved to the fireplace and settled in the hearth. The fire had burned down but there were a few embers left. The mountain of silver dust smothered the last of the heat. Courtney turned to Ms. Korey. Ms. Korey's grey eyes flashed with orange sparks. The silver dust ignited and within seconds every last speck disappeared in flames.

"We are all very strong and can harness the power of light. We can move objects and even other beings without actually touching them. Only I can fly but Mathew and Martha are very fast. Martha is also a firestarter. Mathew along with the power of healing can enter into the dreams of others. Martha and I can't do this. I tried with you, Bara, but failed."

Bara remembered Courtney's face in the cottage window. Maybe Courtney had succeeded after all. She was about to share this knowledge but Mathew interrupted.

"You make too much of my ability, Courtney, and I can

never speak in the dreams of others, no matter how important the message and ..." He paused and looked intently at Bara. "I must be *connected* with the other dreamer—deeply."

All thoughts of Courtney fled. Mathew had been entering her dreams on purpose? Bara looked at him questioningly. She could almost feel the heat of his gaze in return, a silent *yes*. Then she thought about the kiss they'd shared and the heat became real. He shot her a brilliant smile and her cheeks threatened to ignite. She opened her mouth to ask just how they were *connected* but he shot her a warning glance. It suddenly occurred to her that Courtney, and even Ms. Korey, didn't know he'd been in her dreams. Courtney hadn't known he was in town, so this was most likely the case. Then there was Colin and Amy. Amy knew about the dark-haired boy but she had no way of knowing it was Mathew. And Colin ... he knew nothing, and for some reason Bara liked it that way.

No, now was not the time to ask.

"Brynndalin has escaped the Slip," Courtney said. "She has no body of her own and must find a host. Then she will begin to hunt, draining souls as she goes."

"How do we stop her?" Bara asked.

"*We*," Courtney corrected. "Won't do anything.

Mathew, Martha, and I will take care of this."

Bara went to argue but Ms. Korey spoke for her.

"She's one of us now. You knew this was the risk."

Courtney didn't look very happy but said nothing more.

"But first you have to face your father," Ms. Korey said. "He can never know. The demon power is too tempting and there are other, more perilous ways into the Slip. Staying too long makes one vulnerable to insanity and illness. Even being Clavigen is sometimes not enough to stave off madness."

"But how are we going to explain what happened to the house?" Bara asked. "The study? His books?"

Mathew winked and smiled.

"That, we can fix."

The witches stood, raising their arms to shoulder height. Their fingers shot out with light. Courtney's light came slower and was never as bright. The light darted around the room, mending furniture, returning books to shelves, reassembling broken glass, and filling holes in valuable paintings. Less than a minute later they lowered their arms and it was finished. The room looked as it had before. As on cue there was a commotion in the hall. Mr. Cavanagh was home. Courtney went to the fireplace. She ran her fingers along the mantel. The bookshelf to the left came forward and slid sideways, revealing a hole in the wall.

"Hide! I'll follow soon."

Ms. Korey ushered Amy and Colin through the passageway. Mathew followed. He paused and looked one last time at Bara before disappearing into the dark. The bookcase slid back. The passageway closed just in time.

IV

Mr. Cavanagh paced in front of the fireplace. His face puffed up and became very red. Like a clogged water fountain words sputtered from his mouth.

"And the way you've treated Courtney. Let me make this clear, once and for all. She was not to blame for the divorce. From this moment on you'll treat her with more respect, no more snide comments, no more insults—nothing!"

Bara nodded but he threw up his arms as though she'd not agreed at all.

"I'm telling you! I've had enough, quite enough, and so has your stepmother."

"We've worked out our differences," Courtney told him.

Her voice acted the chill pill and Mr. Cavanaugh took it down a notch. But he was far from finished.

"That's good. But I want to hear her apologize. Bara, apologize, right now."

"That's not necessary," Courtney insisted.

"The hell it isn't."

After all she'd done Bara was truly sorry.

"I've been rotten, really. Please forgive me."

"And?"

Bara thought for a moment what she might add.

"I hope we can be better friends …"

Mr. Cavanagh's face lightened from red to pink and his breathing slowed.

"If you want to be, I mean?" Bara added.

Mr. Cavanagh actually clapped. Courtney didn't say anything but smiled a smile that would have convinced the dead to dance at their own funeral. She picked up her tea, obviously trying to hide a rush of emotion.

Mr. Cavanaugh still had questions.

"Where were you?"

Her mind went blank. Bara couldn't tell him what had really happened and she certainly couldn't tell him about her nighttime trip into the woods. She had to lie for his sake as much as hers but had no idea what to say.

Courtney did.

"She was at the library reading when I found her," she told her husband.

"The library?"

"Yes, Bara spent the whole night there. The place is so large. She went undetected."

"Really? You weren't with Colin?"

"I talked to the head librarian, a Ms. Korey. She remembers Bara coming in last night—alone. And when I pressed her she couldn't recall Bara leaving."

"You spent the whole night at the library? Alone?"

Bara didn't dare speak. She nodded and her father accepted the lie. Letting out a sigh, a cross between relief and annoyance, he sat down beside her on the chaise.

"That's something. But really I don't know what to do with you. Grounding doesn't work. You've made that clear."

"I really think she's learned her lesson," Courtney said. "The problem was our relationship. We've fixed that now. Thinking up some new and horrible punishment isn't necessary."

"I'm sorry. I just don't agree."

He turned back to Bara. "And what you said about Courtney being a witch? Ghosts and such?"

Bara looked to Courtney for support, took a deep breath, and lied too.

"Dad, I'm sorry. I was being stupid. I made it all up."

"Well—good," he sighed, truly relieved. "I'll need to talk this over with your mother when she returns. Until then you can consider yourself grounded. And this time I'd appreciate you not leaving the house. Go to your room. I'll have a tray sent up."

Bara didn't argue. She stood. She was tired and welcomed the chance to rest. Feeling a rush of sorrow which often comes with lost sleep she hugged her father, apologized one more time, and headed for the foyer.

"Let me fix you a drink," Courtney said as Bara left.

Courtney fixing you a drink? Bara wondered if her father would find himself in a deep sleep before long. At the thought she stifled a yawn. If Courtney had offered she'd have actually accepted one of the sleeping concoctions.

Bara returned to the Pink Palace. Everything was neat and clean. There was no sign of the struggle that had occurred the night before. The window was repaired. Had Courtney done this or a workman? Bara shrugged. It hardly mattered. After drawing the drapes she slipped off her boots and climbed into bed, far too exhausted to undress.

Besides she was still wearing the pink pajamas.

Oh, the bliss. The feather quilt was warm and soft, the sheets clean and crisp. Bara wouldn't need any help from Courtney. Minutes later she was asleep. Too exhausted to dream she slept deep and well. She slept her fill. A full nine hours passed before the rain, the most gentle of alarm clocks, *pitter-pattered* her awake.

Bara stretched to rid the sleep from her limbs and feeling a little more alert looked around. A muted glow lit the room. Someone had turned on the bedside lamp. It had been early afternoon when she'd gone to bed. Now no light framed the edges of the closed curtains. It was night. She noted that the bedside table held a half-eaten sandwich, turkey, what was left of the ruined Thanksgiving feast. It was then she heard breathing, not her own. She started and then relaxed. Amy lay dozing beside her, snoring lightly. Telltale bread crumbs peppered the side of her mouth.

Amy had left with the others through the secret passage—left with Mathew. Curiosity got the better of Bara. Feeling a little guilty, assuming Amy was probably still very tired, Bara shook her gently. Uncharacteristically Amy stirred and opened her eyes.

"How did you get up here?" Bara asked her.

Amy stretched and spoke through a yawn.

"Courtney let me up once your dad fell asleep. He went to bed just after you."

Bara nodded, her suspicions about the *drink* confirmed. Amy brought herself up on her elbows and turned glossy, tired eyes on Bara, signaling she was ready to talk. Bara wanted to ask about Mathew but she didn't know how to begin. She wasn't quite ready to tell Amy that he was the dark-haired boy. But then Bara remembered another boy.

"How's Colin?"

"There's a room below the house. He's down there."

"A secret room! I guess not much is surprising after all this. How's he doing? Did he let Mathew help him?"

"Ms. Korey gave him some first aid. He seems okay."

Bara was worried about Colin, no doubt about that. But Mathew and his blue eyes continued to fill her silent thoughts

"Everyone else is still here?" she asked.

"Mathew and Ms. Korey left but they came back."

"How did you know to bring them here?"

"I went to the Tragic Sip. Mathew served me. I came back to the library and saw your stepmother and those men take you away. I didn't know what to do, follow or go back down into the stacks. I chose the stacks and found the diary and there they were. I was a little confused as to why the coffee guy was with Ms. Korey. Something didn't seem right. I tried to run but I couldn't move. I figured it out then. Ms. Korey was the other witch. I guess she told Courtney we were in the library."

Bara thought about how she'd seen Mathew's face in the cottage window. She'd figured it had been some kind of waking dream, not real, just a slip of a tired mind. And then she remembered the boy outside the library. It had to have been him. Mathew must have followed them through the woods and to the library and then filled in Ms. Korey.

"I thought they were going to kill me," Amy said. "I wanted to fight but Mathew did this weird thing with his eyes and I just gave him the diary. I thought it was all over—that they'd won and we were all going to die. But he flipped through and handed it back." Amy reached down and pulled the diary out from under the bed. She opened to the page she wanted. "Here. Read it yourself.

$\mathcal{V}$

Dawn's muted light entered. Pinks deepened to dusty rose and mauve, giving the Pink Palace a comforting, dreamlike quality. Amy and Bara had been reading for hours. They'd learned that Guenevere and Sedgewick had married.

The Wisp — Pryde Foltz

They'd spent almost a century together fighting the wisps. Sedgewick had been Clavigen.

He wrote until his final days.

The years haven't been kind. Most mistake Guenevere for my daughter, or even my granddaughter, but never my wife. I wonder how she could love such a weary old man. Still her eyes shine with love. My death will cause her much pain. She has already lost so much, felt a grief so deep I dare not describe. Yet she continues to hold out hope somehow I might join her in immortality. But as the clock inches on I know I will never capture another demon. I close my eyes, sleep and dream, but am granted only small glimpses of the Slip now.

My brain always so quick and fluid has slowed. Most of the time I move sluggishly through a thick fog of forgetfulness and confusion. My hands have grown rigid and weak. I struggle to hold the pen and so I'll choose carefully my next words. They may be my last.

About the Diary. It is most definitely a thing of magic. It appears to possess both will and at times guile. I was able to read but one story—that of one who came before. Those tales that follow have been penned by another or should I say others. They are written in unknown tongues. Perhaps one day you will be allowed to understand. I could not.

After my passing the diary will find its way to another Clavigen of my line—you. Add to these pages. The story must continue so you may help those who will come after. You have been chosen. If you don't act the demons will win and catastrophe will reign.

Use the amber, the dagger, and your dreams to fight the incubi. You know how a demon can be freed. To imprison one the blade must find its way into the demon's third chakra, the throat, and the amber to the third eye, the second chakra, just above where the eyebrows meet. Given the chance to strike do not hesitate. I'm so tired and I've no more to tell. Be careful. Death is always a possibility. I pray your story be a victorious one.

Nelson Sedgewick

Amy and Bara flipped through the remaining pages. Sure

enough everything else was written in a language they didn't understand. Bara shut the diary and placed it back in her bag. She turned to look out the window. It was a bleak day, cloudy and rainy. The air raged, throwing whatever it could into flight. Leaves, bright in their fall skin, littered the lawn and flew through the grey but did little to lift the mood. Strangely the diary had told them nothing about Mathew. It had shed some light on what would happen to Courtney now that she no longer held a wisp. Her death would be a natural one. Still the apology Bara had given her wasn't going to cut it.

"What are thinking about?" Amy asked.

"I need to talk to Courtney. You can stay here if you want."

"I should call home. They'll want to know where I am."

"There's a phone down the hall. Meet me back here when you're done. Then we should look for Colin."

Bara showed Amy the phone and then went downstairs.

Mathew, Ms. Korey, and Courtney were in the study, deep in conversation. Courtney looked up when Bara came in and threw her a brilliant smile.

"You slept well," she asked.

Ms. Korey didn't smile. She didn't greet Bara with an unfriendly face, just a slight expression of disappointment—like Bara was a relative she didn't quite get on with. Mathew smiled too. He lifted a hand to brush away a stray black lock.

"Hello!"

Bara managed a weak good morning in return and then like she was pulling peanut butter from crazy glue, on a very hot day, she turned from Mathew to Courtney.

"Can I talk with you?" she asked her stepmother.

"Of course, come in and sit down. Your father's gone to work. He has a lot of work to catch up on. Mathew, Martha, you'll excuse us."

They stood. Mathew nodded and smiled again. Bara almost forgot she'd come to talk to her stepmother and not to stare at him. Ms. Korey reminded her other, more important things were going on.

"We should check on our patient anyway," she said.

"Patient?"

"Your tall friend."

"Amy said Colin's okay."

"He's healing as only the young can. We'll leave you two alone."

Ms. Korey hit the hidden switch on the fireplace. The book shelf slid aside. She and Mathew disappeared inside. The wall closed behind them. In the silence that followed

Bara noted that the rain outside was falling harder and the wind had picked up. Things were verging on a storm.

"Did you want something to eat? You must be hungry."

Courtney motioned to a plate of croissants on the side table. Bara shook her head. Courtney misread her hesitation.

"It's not ... I mean they're just croissants. They're not drugged."

Bara chuckled.

"That's not it. I'll eat after we talk."

"Okay. You must have more questions now that you've read the rest of Nelson's story?"

"Yes but I need to say something to you first."

"I'd hoped all that was behind us."

"I'm not angry with you anymore. I hated you. I really did. I thought I was being disloyal to my mother if I let you be nice to me, never mind being nice to you. I made it so easy for the Wisp to fool me. I really am sorry."

"Brynndalin knows how to pick her victims. She's attracted to bitterness and spite. I'm sorry you were feeling that way. Divorce is always hardest on the children. We should have done more for you. You shouldn't blame yourself."

"You really do forgive me? I don't see how. I took your

immortality from you."

"Brynndalin's energy will leave me and my powers will fade. That's true. But then I'll live out my life like a normal human woman. I'll die when it's my time. You'll not be to blame. And I may still be able to recapture Brynndalin. Really all this is as much my fault as yours. We should have told you everything. Martha wanted to. I wanted to protect you. I should have known better. You can't avoid your destiny."

"But you tried to tell me before you fell out the window. *Oh God!* I pushed you out a window." Bara shook her head. "I wouldn't have believed anything you said."

"Not likely, no," Courtney chuckled and agreed. "But we're working together now."

"What about Ms. Korey? She wanted to kill Sedgewick?"

"No?"

"You know—*deal with him permanently.*"

"Martha has never killed an innocent. She wanted to erase his memory."

"You can do that?"

"With some but they forget everything, even their own name. It isn't something I readily do but Martha was scared with all the rumors of witchcraft. She was pulled from her bed and thrown into a dirty cell during the Windfall trials. She'd had the dreams and made the mistake of telling others. Mathew and I rescued her."

"Then Mathew is older than Martha?"

Courtney suppressed a knowing smile and nodded

"Is he older than you?"

"Yes."

There was an odd pause where Bara should have said something but didn't. Courtney sensed her thoughts and filled in the silence.

"Vampires also live a very long but don't believe all the romantic mushy stuff. Any older than say a hundred—stark, raving, and drooling mad. Immortality has a way of driving one crazy. Clavigen are different. A fortunate case of arrested development but we still care and love like we did when we took our wisp. Much of Mathew still remains a teenager and he still *loves* like a teenager."

It was Bara's turn to hide a smile.

"But there is also Colin to think about, isn't there?"

Bara tried to look surprised.

"Colin and I are just friends."

"Your father will be happy to hear that but I don't think that's entirely true. Colin certainly has deeper feelings for you. And with him you could still have a normal life once this wisp-business is over. That would never happen with Mathew."

Bara had to admit recently she'd felt something more than just brotherly love for Colin. She loved him—true—very deeply. They'd known each other too long for her to feel any other way. But with Mathew living and breathing?

"Whatever the case," Courtney said. "We've more important things facing us than young—or not-so-young—love. There is the matter of a loose demon. What to do about Brynndalin?"

"How will we find her?"

"Brynndalin won't go far. She must find a body. They usually bargain for one, offering the intended victim something they want more than anything."

"She said I'd live forever, be all-powerful, and never be alone."

"*The gift of the ages ... a living coffin* I believe Nelson called it. She was tempting you. She didn't count on you resisting but she'll find a more willing victim. They always do. Brynndalin will find a host and then the real fight ..."

Smash. Something crashed through the window and a twisted form landed on the floor. Bara and Courtney jumped and moments later there were footfalls behind the wall. The bookshelf slid sideways and Ms. Korey and

Mathew emerged. Amy appeared through the door. Colin was last to arrive, nursing an obvious limp. They'd all expected to see Brynndalin returned but the Wisp wasn't back. The wind had broken a branch from one of the maple trees that grew in the front yard, whipping it through the window. In a litter of red leaves and glittering glass, the dark limb lay on the carmine and gold rug.

"It's really storming out there!"

Amy was smiling with relief but the witches still looked very worried. Bara thought they might be concerned about the window which had now been smashed twice in as many a day.

"You can fix it easy, right?"

Courtney nodded and waved an arm. A small wind, almost imperceptible with the wild gusts bursting through the broken window, lifted the leaves from the floor, but the branch didn't budge and the glass shards merely shook. Courtney dropped her hand and the glass stopped shaking.

"I need help," she said to no one in particular.

Ms. Korey took over and soon the branch was back outside, the window repaired.

"The weather's picking up," Mathew said.

"It's November," Courtney returned. "There are storms in November."

"We all know it's unlikely to be just a storm."

"What's Snow White talking about?" Colin asked.

It took Bara a minute to realize *Snow White* was Mathew with his dark hair and pale skin. Mathew gave Colin a withering look in return but nobody said anything.

"Fill us in here, will you!" Colin demanded.

"Will someone tell Ichabod Crane what's going on in Sleepy Hollow?"

Colin looked about ready to murder Mathew.

"Each time a wisp gains a body," Courtney told them. "Some kind of natural disaster follows. Brynndalin may have found a host. If she has the weather will only get worse."

"The storm hit quickly," Ms. Korey added, "which means she's nearby."

"We'll see her soon," Courtney said with a sigh. "She will want her revenge, revenge against me. Brynndalin will be coming."

Colin kicked at a leaf that had escaped the cleanup.

"Great! So what? We just sit around and wait for her?"

"If we're lucky our dreams will reveal her host before she can do any real damage."

"Real damage?" Colin baulked. "She almost killed us."

"She can do worse."

Colin shook his head and threw himself down on the chaise. "Sweet dreams, then."

VI

Monday morning found Amy and Bara back in their dorm room. Outside a steady rain drummed and the wind whistled along. The sun hadn't risen, the room was still dark, and the alarm hadn't sounded. Amy lay snoring, a restful look on her face. Dark lashes grazed the skin beneath her eyes. Bara's eyes were wide open, two glossy orbs in the dim light. She'd been up for more than an hour, awakened by a strange dream. Her eyes had fluttered opened, her thoughts racing. She'd filed through her mind.

Only now was she remembering.

It was dusk, the light a misty, magical hue only the edges of day can produce. Bara sat sandwich between Mathew and Colin on a Ferries wheel. As the cart ascended Colin offered her cotton candy which she accepted. Mathew waved a candied apple under her nose. It was bright red. Aromas of sweet caramel and cinnamon wafted through the air. Bara took the apple but then turned to taste the candy.

The sugar melted in her mouth. It tasted like cotton candy should, sweet and light, but artificial. Bara then bit into the apple. It snapped satisfyingly crisp. It was as sweet as the candy but tangy too. She took another bite of the apple and tossed the cotton candy over the side of the cart. The descending cloud of sugar fell like a rock, sounding with a thud when it crashed to the ground.

The Ferris wheel car reached the top. There were the dazzling lights of the fairgrounds directly below. Bright neon bled into the subtler hues of the surrounding landscape, a patchwork of farmer's fields, spotted with gold and crimson trees. The horizon was brilliant with carmine and indigo. Bara looked at Colin. His auburn hair was as vivid as the streaks of red in the sky. She looked at Mathew. His eyes were as radiant as the dusk's young stars.

They began to descend. Bara went to take another bite of the apple. Suddenly angry Colin reached out and took it. Her teeth met with air. She tried to argue but was distracted when he offered a Teddy bear with fur the same color as his hair. Mathew held out a stuffed unicorn with eyes shockingly blue. Somehow Bara held the apple and the cotton candy again. Her hands were full. She put both treats into the same hand and went for the unicorn, enraging Colin. He reached past her and shoved Mathew.

The car was ascending again, faster than before. The lights of the park and the sky blended together. Luminescent trails traced nonsense paths through the pale blue expanse. Mathew returned Colin's shove, knocking the cotton candy out of Bara's hand in the process. The candy fell from the car. This time instead of plummeting to the ground it floated above their heads, a turquoise cloud. Angry at seeing his gift gone Colin plucked the apple from Bara's other hand and tossed it out of the car. The sound of bells rang as it fell.

The ringing stopped with the thud of contact.

The thud had been real. The wind was blowing with such a force it banged against the closed window. Gusts of air knocked on the glass, demanding to be let in. As Bara lay remembering it didn't let up, not one bit. She looked over at Amy who was managing to sleep through the noise and sighed. There'd be no more rest for her. She got out of bed and went to the window. Down below leaves, branches, and twigs performed a frantic dance. Trees stretched at what seemed painful angles and then snapped back. The wind suddenly died down but then returned stronger still. Limbs bent again. Back and forth they twisted. Bara imagined the trees bowed at such agonizing angles pleading with someone to just turn off the music so they could rest.

There was another loud thud of wind and rain. Bara flinched and Amy woke.

"Is it still storming?" she asked, not really needing an answer.

Bara watched a large branch cartwheel across the lawn. After skidding into one of the out buildings it lay motionless. She turned from the window.

"Yeah it's gotten worse. Did you have any dreams?"

Amy yawned, stretched, and came to sitting.

"The regular run-of-mill type. You?"

"The same. I dreamt I was at an amusement park. There was cotton candy and candy apples."

Bara thought about mentioning Colin and Mathew but changed her mind, quite certain her teenage, and not-so-teenage, love triangle had nothing to do with Brynndalin.

"I think I was only hungry," she said, letting it go.

"Speaking of which ..." Amy sprung from her bed, all of sudden full of energy. "Let's get dressed and get some breakfast before class."

**

Bara and Amy were seated at one of the long tables in the dining hall with two bowls of warm oatmeal. They didn't normally eat oatmeal but the day called for it. Biting air found its way through stone walls. Despite heavy cardigans they were both cold and warm oatmeal was never so appealing.

"Where is everyone?" Amy asked in between mouthfuls of the sweet goop.

Just twenty minutes before class the hall was oddly empty. Normally it was a struggle to find a couple of open seats together. The sound of near to a hundred girls eating and talking excitedly was the norm. Today there were maybe twenty students spread thinly throughout the hall. Most peculiar the Pop's table was almost empty. There were a few hangers on but no Cassandra and no Louise.

Bara was relieved. She had enough to deal with, without having to face the terrible twins.

"The storm must have kept some people from getting back," she offered with a shrug.

"We should check in with everyone before class," Amy suggested. "Maybe they had more luck than we did."

Bara didn't respond.

"Bara?"

"Yeah," she said automatically.

Bara stared intently at the door. Amy turned to see what had her attention. The headmistress, Ms. Lenton, had entered the dining hall accompanied by Professor

Chestermire and the school psychologist, Doctor Comfrey. Lenton went to the podium that was kept in the dining hall. The room often doubled as the school auditorium. Professor Chestermire and Doctor Comfrey stood on either side and exchanged looks of distress. Chestermire put a hand on Lenton's shoulder before stepping away. Comfrey nodded her support and also stepped back. Just then Den Mother slipped into the hall. She didn't join the other adults but stood just inside the door. Her usually granite-hard exterior had crumbled. Yes something definitely had happened to take the hard edge off Den Mother.

Lenton's pained voice broke through the murmur of conversation.

"Attention ladies, I need everyone's attention."

The chit chat stopped and everyone turned to listen. She cleared her throat and spoke again.

"I'm sure you've all noticed the weather. I'm afraid ..."

The sentence was lost to a sob. Lenton took a moment to regain control before continuing.

"I've horrible news. Miss Louise Bellevue and Miss Cassandra Banks lost their lives last night."

At first the hall was silent. Was it some kind of joke? Cassandra and Louise dead? It couldn't be true. Yes they were dreadful snits but they were always alive, full of themselves and full of life. They couldn't be dead? The adults continued to look out with their solemn red eyes. Den Mother looked away. It was no joke. Gasps and oh-no's were heard throughout the hall.

Somebody asked how it happened.

"It was a car accident. They were on their way back to school. We assume with the weather their driver lost control. He may also have been using his phone." Lenton choked back her tears. "I know you all must have questions but I think we need time to let this sink in and for the police to investigate further. Classes have been canceled. Those of you who can should go home. For those of you who wish to stay the dining hall will remain open. Doctor Comfrey, Professor Chestermire, Den Mother, and I will be available if anyone would like to talk."

Lenton stepped back from the podium. She and the other adults crossed the room and sat down at the Pop's table. A couple of students went to join them. Quiet murmurs and sobs were heard throughout the hall. Many girls were very upset. Bara, more shocked than upset, had often wished that something would take the terrible twins off her hands. But not like this. It was only last week they'd been giving her a hard time. She hadn't been fond of the two but she never wished them dead.

So much was happening—everything with Brynndalin, the storm, and now two of their schoolmates dead. So much distress, so close together.

"I have a funny feeling," Bara told Amy. "Brynndalin had something to do with this?"

"She's causing the bad weather. So in a way she's to blame but Lenton said the driver was talking on his phone."

"I know. Just something doesn't seem right."

Before Amy could reply another voice joined the conversation. It was Patsy Pillanger. She placed her breakfast tray on the table and sat down.

"I can't believe we'll never have the fake and bake twits lording over us again," she said.

The terrible twins had supported year round tans.

"That's an awful thing to say," Amy returned.

Amy hadn't liked Louise and Cassandra either. *But come on!*

"How was your Thanksgiving, Pats?" Bara asked, trying to change the subject.

It was a no-go. Patsy was determined to talk about Cassandra and Louise.

"Old bat Lenton says they died in a car accident but my dad says they didn't have a mark on'em."

"What do you mean?"

"The SUV was found at the bottom of a cliff. It was real banged up, alright. The driver, he was a mess, but Cassandra and Louise were untouched. Only they were a strange putrid-gray—like the life had been sucked out of them or something." Patsy paused to cram an enormous forkful of eggs into her mouth.

"But the driver was talking on his phone," Amy said. "That's why they crashed."

Patsy smirked.

"Yep! But he was calling 911 and … he was using a hands-free."

"Because of the accident?"

"Nope, he called before, talking about how he had two sleeping teenagers in the back and couldn't move to steer the car. Then there was all this screaming. The 911 operator heard the crash."

Amy and Bara exchanged frighten looks. Bara strove for a steady voice.

"That does sound strange," she agreed. "Listen Pats, I'd loved to keep talking but this whole thing's gotten to me. I think I'm going home. Are you ready, Amy?"

Bara knew she was.

"We'll see you later, 'kay."

"Yeah sure. Enjoy your time off," Patsy called after

them and then she really tucked into her breakfast—two eggs, bacon, pancakes and sausage.

One thing was for sure. Patsy hadn't lost her appetite.

VII

Bara almost called for a ride. The weather hadn't improved but then it wouldn't have been as easy to go to the Tragic Sip. After waking up early she definitely needed a coffee. Also she was honest with herself. She wanted to see Mathew. So instead she and Amy grabbed a couple umbrellas and braved the wet and the wind. They all but ran from the school to Library Square. The umbrellas didn't help much. They were already soggy and very cold when Bara suggested they stop in for coffee.

Amy was against it.

"There's coffee at your Dad's."

"It's not as good."

"I just want to get there," Amy said. "If I went into the café I'd never want to leave."

"Here, you go on ahead. I'll bring you back a croissant."

Bara tossed her newly-acquired keys. Amy was too

cold to argue. She turned and hurried away. Bara watched her go and then headed for the café.

A familiar sight greeted her.

Despite the wind and the rain Ragman was seated outside on the patio, smoking. He gave her a little nod and a smile, exposing sharp canines. Sometimes his teeth were like this and sometimes they were normal. Bara supposed he wore fake fangs like some of the Goths, an artistic affectation. His smile was meant to be friendly but something about the gesture seemed just a little menacing.

I guess it's the teeth.

"Hey Girlie," came his gravel tones. He had a slight French accent. "Anything new?"

Ragman exhaled a huge cloud of smoke. Bara stopped under the purple awning and took down her umbrella. Ragman had never spoken to her before. Did he actually want to start up a conversation? She stared at his glistening teeth. *Vampires and werewolves are real. Could he be one?* She almost laughed out loud. *Ragman's been around the café for years, sipping his coffee and smoking his dreadful cigarettes. Next I'll be seeing fairies in my latte foam.*

She batted at the smoke.

"Should there be?"

"You look different."

He took a sip of his coffee. Her green eyes grew wide. The coffee was red—blood red.

Ragman swallowed and continued, "You look a little worldlier."

"I don't know what you're talking about." she lied.

"It's in your eyes. You *know*."

"The only thing that's in my eyes is your dreadful cigarette smoke. It causes cancer, you know?"

Bara moved forward. Quicker than humanly possible Ragman was up and blocking the way.

"Oh come on, *mon coeur*," he said through a sharp smile. "Let's be honest with each other."

Bara knew one thing for sure. Those teeth weren't fake. They were the real thing and they were growing longer.

The café door opened.

"As usual, Nicolas, you're barking up the wrong tree."

It was Mathew. Even with his Tragic Sip purple apron he managed to look intimidating. His hands were on his hips and his eyes flashed with a sharp light.

"*Maintenant* there are more of you," Ragman shot back. "That wasn't the deal."

Mathew came to stand between Bara and Ragman. The moment was both long and tense. Ragman actually sniffed Bara like she might be something good to eat. A strange look came into his eyes but then he stepped back.

"It doesn't matter our number," Mathew told him. "Everything's the same. You stick to nibbling on woodland animals and we won't have you put down."

Barking ... nibbling ... put down ...

"I'm not a dog."

"No," Mathew agreed. "You only smell like one."

Ragman growled. He *really* growled.

Bara understood.

"Calm down cur," Mathew quipped.

"Then stop calling me a dog."

"You're a werewolf?" Bara asked Ragman.

"Give girlie a prize."

"But you have no hair."

"It helps control fleas," Mathew mocked. "Do you shave or wax?"

Ragman growled again. Mathew continued to poke fun.

"Electrolysis?"

Ragmen looked about ready to murder him.

"Okay, okay, down boy. Next coffee's on me."

The offer of a free coffee mollified Ragman. He glared at Mathew but sat back down.

"Make it a mocha and don't skimp on the whip cream, coffee boy."

"I'll leave room for blood," Mathew promised.

He opened the café door and ushered Bara inside. His voice intermingled with the door chimes.

"Why don't you sit down over there? I'll get his coffee and then take my break. We can talk."

Mathew didn't wait for a response but went behind the counter. The fear she felt with Ragman ebbed and uncovered just how nervous she was about what was to come. She was going to be alone with the dark-haired boy. Outside of her dreams they'd never been alone. Adding to her anxiety there were eyes on her as she crossed the room. A couple of Goths looked on agog. Bara didn't have to be a mind reader to know what they were thinking. *He could have just about anyone and he's with her! No way!*

She gave her schoolmates an unassuming smile and settled at the table. Her hands trembled as she took off her wet coat and scarf. For the first time Bara thought about what she must look like. The umbrella had prevented her hair from becoming completely plastered. She guessed the damp had instead transformed her curls into something bordering on a poodle perm. Suspicions were confirmed by her reflection in the window through which she watched Mathew deliver the promised mocha to Ragman.

Mathew came back inside and went behind the counter.

He said something to Surly Bob. Surly Bob frowned but nodded his head. Mathew went into the back room.

Bara looked out the window again. Ragman produced a small metal flask—she assumed not made of silver—and poured something thick and red into the cup. Mathew hadn't been joking. *Blood and coffee.* Bara could only hope it was animal blood. Ragman noticed her gaze. He lifted the cup in her direction and took a big gulp. When he brought it from his mouth there was a reddish-brown foam above his lip. He licked his lips and rubbed his stomach to emphasize just how much he was enjoying his blood mocha. Bara had to fight back the desire to be sick. Thankfully her attention was drawn back to the front counter. Mathew had come back out. His apron was gone. He picked up two coffees and started in her direction. His movements were both athletic and musical. Her heart literally skipped a beat.

"Black Mountain Blend, right, just cream and cinnamon?" He placed the cups down and then seemed to hesitate before choosing the chair next to and not across from her. "More privacy," he said as in way of explanation.

Sitting so close Bara could smell his scent. The aromas of sandalwood and angelica entered her nose and caused her stomach to do a strange little flip. She fought to maintain her senses, maintain her cool, so to speak. She didn't have to look to know the Goths still stared. She tried to ignore the intense feeling of being watched and thanked him for the coffee.

"How did you know I liked Black Mountain Blend?"

She took a sip. He'd gotten the cream and cinnamon just right too.

"It's what you always order."

"You've never served me."

He shrugged.

It was strange sitting there with Mathew. Technically they'd just met but Bara felt like she'd known him for a very long time. In her dreams she had. There was both a newness and a sense of familiarity being with him. She didn't quite know how to act. Mathew too seemed a little unsure. He was looking at her very intently.

"What is it? Do I have something on my face?"

"No your face is fine—better than fine."

Bara doubted if this was true. She didn't wear much makeup, only eyeliner. She wondered now if it were smudged and had to fight the urge to rub at her eyes.

"You remind me of someone. That's all. But it's not the way you look. I can see that now. Well maybe your eye shape and you have just the hint of gold to your skin."

Mathew continued to study her. She blushed under his scrutiny.

"But no, you look different. You look like yourself. It's the way you move and do things. It's very strange."

He looked down and stared into his cup.

"Who do I remind you of?" she asked.

"No one important," he told her and sipped his coffee.

His answer was an obvious lie. His pained expression gave that away clearly. Bara would have quizzed him further but he brought the cup from his mouth and artfully changed the subject.

"Did ole Nicolas scare you?"

"Is he really a werewolf?"

"Yes but we have a deal. He makes do with animals and we let him live."

"*You let him live?* You'd kill him?"

"Incubi, succubi, your wisp, comes first. But on occasion we have to hunt werewolves and the odd vampire, though they mainly stick to Europe with their need of birth soil."

"Why?"

Mathew laughed.

"Because they drink human blood."

"I thought only vampires drank blood and werewolves

ate flesh."

"If you eat raw flesh why wouldn't you also drink the blood? It's more portable. There are differences. Vampires never touch flesh and consume *live* human blood, usually killing their victims. Werewolves aren't so particular."

"If vampires and werewolves kill too, why do wisps come first?"

"Werewolves and vampires take human life, which is a tragedy, but the demons take souls, or at least the stuff that gives it its power. That's far worse. They imprison the soul, feed off its energy, and prevent it from continuing on in its journey."

"Which is?"

Mathew gave her a wry smile which softened as he continued to look at her.

"Heaven? Rebirth? Your guess is as good as mine. If you're expecting me to tell you what happens after you die, please don't. I have no idea. I just know that the purgatory the wisps throw their victims into isn't any place I'd like to spend eternity."

"Purgatory?"

"Just a metaphor."

He took another sip of coffee.

"Shouldn't you be at school?"

"They cancelled classes. A couple of girls were killed in a car accident."

He gave her a sympathetic look.

"I'm sorry. Were they friends of yours?"

"Quite the opposite. Cassandra and Louise weren't my friends."

"Still it must be upsetting."

"I guess. I never really liked them but it seems so wrong. The young aren't supposed to die."

"No," Mathew sighed. "The young aren't supposed to die but they do sometimes. And sometimes the old live way beyond what one would have thought possible."

"Oh!"

Bara realized the meaning her words would have for Mathew, the immortal teenager, but he laughed and it was loud and warm. Others turned to look. The Goths stared at him and then at her. She recognized clearly the look on their faces—piqued-eyed envy.

"Don't worry," he reassured. "You didn't hurt my feelings. I often forget how old I am."

He lowered his head and gave a sideways grin.

"I must seem like a decrepit old man to you?"

"No … I mean you don't seem all that old to me."

"Not all that old, hey? Good! I'd hate for you to think

of me as some old geezer."

His smile widened and it was infectious. Bara smiled too. Without really meaning to she looked at him from under veiled lashes. She couldn't help herself. She was flirting. He motioned to her hand.

"You've finished your coffee."

Bara looked at her empty cup. She didn't want her time alone with him to end. Even if she did only remind him of someone else he was still her dark-haired boy. And they still hadn't discussed just how it was he was able to enter her dreams—their connection. She wanted desperately to know but the whole thing with Ragman had distracted her. When would they get more time alone? In her dreams?

Mathew stood.

"I'll tell you what. I'll get us a couple more and then I'll walk you home. Nicolas is harmless but a bit of a pest."

"Sure," she said, obviously eager.

Bara had tried and failed to hide just how much she liked the idea of him walking her home.

VIII

The rain had stopped when they came out of the café but

the wind was still strong. Trails of the Tragic Sip's purple awning flapped vigorously. Mathew's hair was tousled and Bara's made for an escape on the gusts. Ragman kept up his perch on the patio. He had to no hair to blow. Looking at Mathew and Bara, he let out a loud sigh and grasped a hand to his chest. He kissed the air not once but twice.

"*Jeune amour*," he said. "How endearing!"

Bara blushed. Were her feelings so obvious?

"Keep that tongue from wagging, dog," Mathew shot back. "Or I might just have to cut it out."

Ragman chuckled but said nothing more.

Mathew and Bara made their way down the cobbles towards Library Square. They'd only gone a few meters when she felt his light touch on her shoulder.

"Can I carry your bag?" he asked. "It looks heavy."

No one had ever offered to carry her bag before. Yes seemed the obvious answer. Bara helped Mathew lift it from her shoulder. Their hands touched. Heat blazed right through her arm and up into her face. She said a quick thank you and turned away to hide the red now in her cheeks. Ragman laughed again. Bara turned back. A mocking light glinted in his green eyes. Thankfully they entered the square and escaped his attention.

They walked without talking, leaving the square and

starting down the east end of Windfall Boulevard. Mathew filled the silence by whistling a familiar tune she couldn't name. All the while her thoughts rushed. Finally she couldn't stand it anymore.

"Mathew?"

He stopped whistling. She opened her mouth to ask just how it was they were connected but he looked at her so intently; she lost her nerve.

"Just how old are you?" she asked instead—a question that carried its own weight.

"Ahh ..." he said like he'd been expecting the question. "I guess I could play coy and ask you how old I look. But then that wouldn't be fair."

Mathew grinned but didn't say anything more and then he looked away. Bara gave up expecting a straight answer. Why would he share his age with her, a girl he hardly knew, well outside of her dreams?

You're so lame! she silently scolded herself.

They passed the few remaining business on Windfall Boulevard and entered the forested parkland. Bara realized she'd been all but staring at Mathew. She turned her head and studied the trees to her right. An eye in the sky would have seen her head turn from him just before he turned to study her in return.

Bara marvelled at the blustering weather. The woods were alive. Enchanted by the singing wind, leaves flew and trees danced. There were even a few saplings that would never reach maturity, cracked in two, downed by the gusts. With the wind what it was much larger trees might soon fall too. Maybe walking home hadn't been such a good idea—a person could get brained.

Mathew's voice broke through the wind.

"I'm over sixteen hundred years old," he told her.

Bara turned back. He raised an eyebrow.

"How's that for old?"

She didn't quite know how to respond.

"It's pretty old," she finally said. "I guess."

Mathew was a hundred times her age, had life experience she could only dream of. How could he ever see her as anything but a kid? She deflated but then she remembered what Courtney had said. It didn't matter how old he was, Mathew still loved like the sixteen or seventeen-year-old he looked. Maybe there was still some hope. There really was only one way to find out. Bara took a deep breath and found her courage.

"Why have you been entering my dreams?" she asked.

With the wind blowing through his dark locks Mathew smiled and her heart ached. He held back a second longer and then opened his mouth to speak.

"I saw you in the square and I …"

Mathew stopped midsentence. His blue eyes widened. He grabbed her hand, bringing them both to a stop, and placed his body between her and the forest to the right. He was tense with alertness and power.

"What's wrong?" she asked.

"We're being watched."

An unpleasant electric current ran through her.

"What? Where?"

"There, in the trees."

Bara scanned the wood. At first her vision was overwhelmed. The trees swayed. Loose leaves soared. Her eyes slowly filtered out the unimportant and then she saw it too—one large head with a powerful jaw peering from behind an ancient oak. They were indeed being watched.

"You've been found out!" Mathew shouted.

The head continued to stare back. It didn't move. Mathew and Bara didn't move. It was like when prey confronted with a predator freezes in the slim hope that by remaining still, it might also become invisible. The question was who was the prey?

Mathew shouted again.

"Divulge yourself!"

Large deep-set eyes looked sideways, one way and then the other, before returning to stare at them. A powerful leg stepped out from behind the oak, revealing the enormous body that went with the head. It took Bara a second to make the connection. He was dressed differently. Gone was the black G-man suit and dark glasses, replaced with simple jeans and a red-checked flannel shirt—lumberjack chic. But she was certain. It was one of the men who had forced her and Colin from the library. It was one of Courtney's goons.

"It's okay," she told Mathew. "He works for my stepmother."

Mathew didn't relax. He continued to hold her behind him. He raised his other hand.

"He doesn't work for Courtney."

"He and two just like him were with her the other day."

"That may be true but he isn't under her spell now."

The goon began walking toward them. For such a large a man he moved with incredible stealth and fluidity. And he stared so intently. Bara was reminded of a stalking tiger. There was no doubt. She knew who the prey was now.

"*Under her* spell?" she asked, alarmed again. "What are you talking about?"

"He's a Conjure. Look at his eyes."

The Conjure came to the road edge and out of the

shadow of the forest. He was but ten feet away. Daylight lit up his eyes. Strangely they reflected back the light. They were silver, not silvery blue, but metallic silver. He had the eyes of the Wisp.

"He's Brynndalin minion," Mathew told her.

Bara didn't quite understand but she knew the Conjure didn't mean them well. With fist clenched he eyed them from the forest edge, a murderous glint in his cold gaze. His breath was so heavy he pulsed with the strength of it. He was ready to attack but seemed to be waiting for something. *What?* An instant later a second, identical Conjure came out of the woods and barrelled in their direction. Mathew and Bara didn't move. Danger had multiplied. Turning toward the one who came meant turning your back on the one who watched. Neither choice seemed a good one.

The second Conjure reached out a hand to take hold of Bara. He was inches away when a flash of golden light struck him in the chest, sending him reeling. He soared through the air among the falling leaves, his powerful limbs wind-milling to slow his descent. He landed hard on the dark wet road. He lay still but the respite was short.

Mathew's hand still sizzled with charge but he didn't have time to turn around. The first Conjure came out of the woods, ramming into him and knocking him down. The book bag fell from his shoulder and landed on the road as the Conjure came hurdling. Mathew took evasive measures and rolled to the side, just avoiding having his chest crushed by twice his weight. In return Mathew launched himself at his foe. He was definitely at a size disadvantage but somehow held his ground. They struggled upon the wet asphalt, one combatant gaining advantage and then losing it to the other. Brown leaves scattered in their wake.

"Run!" Mathew shouted.

Bara didn't move. She stood still, watching. The Conjure was on top but Mathew held back its head and jaw at what only could have been an excruciating angle.

"Run!" he said again, through clenched teeth. "What are you waiting for?"

"You!" Bara returned.

Frantically her eyes searched for something she might use as a weapon. Her book bag lay at her feet with the heavy diary inside. It would do just find. She picked it up, preparing to smash one massive cranium. She wound up and let the swing go. Something held her arm back. The other Conjure had recovered and returned to his feet. He held her bag in his granite grip. Bara pulled on the strap. The Conjure pulled back. She and the bag smashed into his chest. He then took her into an embrace. Unlike Mathew she was no match for his steadfast sinews. He tossed her over his shoulder and lumbered into the woods, leaving Mathew still battling with his mirror image on the leaf-littered asphalt. Bara watched through the trees until Mathew vanished from view.

IX

Bara struggled in the Conjure's grip but it didn't matter how she hit, kicked, and screamed. She might as well have been striking a brick wall because only she felt the pain. There seemed no point in fighting. She was at the monster's mercy. Worse still she was pretty certain she'd soon be at Brynndalin's. So instead she fought to make out details of the journey should she be lucking enough to retrace the trip. But the speed they traveled blurred her vision and it was still so very windy. Leaves and debris threatened to take out an eye. The Conjure seemed little bothered and actually sped up but Bara did manage to note a large fallen tree, no doubt a victim of the storm. Her staccato breath caught. Through the tempest an enormous wolf soared, clearing the log with one incredible leap.

Oh my God! The Wisp! Things began to move in slow motion then. With its claws out and teeth bared the wolf sprung once more. A deep growl rode on the wind. The Conjure turned his head at the sound but it was too late. They were hit by a tremendous force. The Conjure let go. He was falling. He was going to fall on Bara. She pushed against his shoulder and just managed to roll to safety onto the leaf-covered forest floor.

Free from the Conjure and not yet in the claws of the wolf, Bara didn't stop. Instantly she was up and running. She gave no thought to retracing her path. She could only hope she ran toward Mathew … and she did. There was a blur up ahead, weaving through the trees. At first Bara didn't understand what she was seeing but then the blur slowed into a boy. As in a dream there was the dark-haired boy running toward her. Ten more steps and she slammed into his chest. Their hearts raced, paced each other, and then slowed. It happened way too quickly to be natural but Bara was grateful for the odd calm all the same.

Unlike Courtney, Mathew couldn't fly but he could run faster than any Olympian. He'd wasted little time, not sure he'd find Bara still breathing, or worse, find her breathing but nothing but a shell for Brynndalin to fill. Too much time had passed. It had taken him too long to defeat the other Conjure. It had been strong, strong with the Wisp's power coursing through it. The light had done little but faze the damnable thing and he'd only been able to use it once. In the end several head blows with a rock had broken the connection between the Conjure and Brynndalin, broken the connection between the Conjure and life.

Mathew pulled back and looked Bara over, beginning with green eyes, green eyes without a trace of silver. Her red-gold curls were a mess, littered with leaves and twigs. She was obviously terrified but she hadn't come to any obvious harm. Reassured he smiled.

The relief was one-sided.

"Brynndalin's in the forest!" Bara told him.

"Brynndalin?" he asked, alarmed again.

"I saw her. She was in her wolf form."

Mathew cocked his head to one side and thought. He released her and started walking *far too calmly* in the direction she'd come.

"Let's go," he called over his shoulder.

"Didn't you hear me?"

"I heard you. Come on! We have to get the diary back."

Mathew hopped over a large log with ease. Bara had forgotten about the diary. It was still with the Conjure and Brynndalin. Mathew was right. They had to get it back and so she pursued, struggling with the log he'd all but soared over. She soon caught up. Mathew seemed surprisingly relaxed. Her heart was racing again.

"Don't you think we should move a little faster?" she asked as she passed him.

Mathew actually laughed. Bara stopped. Up ahead the Conjure lay across on the forest floor. The wolf straddled it, saliva dripping from its canines. It was then she saw her mistake. The wolf was as large as Brynndalin but this one looked out with green eyes and its coat was definitely grey, not silver. Mathew came up beside her. He placed a hand on the small of her back. It was instantaneous. Her heart slowed to normal again.

"You see?" he said.

Of course, Ragman. But how?

There seemed only one explanation. Ragman had followed them from the café. Bara would ask why he did this later but for now he was her hero, rescuing her from the Conjure and keeping the amber and the diary from the Wisp. She thanked him but he wasn't exactly gracious in response. He seemed to snicker through sharp canines.

Not bothering with niceties Mathew said but one word. "Change!"

Ragman growled but then grew silent. He sat down

upon his haunches and gagged like a dog that had eaten too much grass. But he didn't vomit. He vibrated and waves of movement rippled through his furry hide, small waves at first but growing to more than a foot in length. It was as though there was a separate being moving within, which as it turned out was the case.

Throwing his head back like he meant to howl Ragman opened his wolf mouth. No sound. Instead jaws opened ever wider and a hand came forth, followed by another. Fingers worked to open the muzzle. There was the sound of ripping skin and the splatter of a lot of blood. A bald head appeared and then broad shoulders. Ragman fought his way through his own werewolf jaws and a naked and very slimy human form emerged. What was left of the carcass fell away like a discarded fur coat. Then on rubbery joints and muscles, Ragman collapsed, landing on the forest floor next to his empty pelt.

Bara had never witnessed a birth and so she had no way of knowing the similarities. She watched in disgust as the infant-man writhed and wriggled upon a bed of moist leaves. His skin was raw, red, hairless, and covered in a gelatinous mucous. He let out a cry quite similar to that of a newborn. His pink eyes stared up at the sky above without focus. Ragman seemed to see nothing but pain. There were many loud groans and cracks as bones hardened and joints snapped into place. His torment went on for more than a minute but finally he stilled, closed his lids and lay as though asleep. Eyebrows grew back in seconds and when his eyes reopened they were green again.

Ragman yawned and stretched as though he'd only woken from a nap. He came to his feet. Not concerned with his nakedness he smirked when Bara looked away.

He said in response to her thank you, "You can owe me." With wry grin on his now hairless face he looked down at the dead Conjure and then regarded Mathew. "Changing works up quite an appetite, *mon frère.*"

Mathew gave a look of disgust.

"I am not your brother," he said but then nodded. "*Bon appétit* but let us clear out before you chow down."

Mathew picked up the bag from where it lay on the ground, took Bara's hand, and led her from the carnage that was to come. As they retreated there was a growl and then what could have only been the sound of tearing flesh and crunching bones. Mathew read her mind.

"Remember what I said about werewolves not being very particular. I wouldn't look back if I were you. It's not a pleasant sight."

Bara took his advice and they put some space between

themselves and Ragman—and his dinner.

X

The wind had died down with the death of the Conjure. The forest was oddly still, a mystical, magical place. The ground was soft with leaf litter, the clouds low, wrapping the trees in their filmy gauze. With Mathew by her side Bara could have easily believed she was dreaming. They didn't speak as they winded their way through the woods. He continued to hold her hand. She found herself wishing they'd walk a little slower, that they'd spend a little longer alone among the trees ... but there was the road up ahead. They came out of the forest and onto the asphalt.

Bara broke the silence.

"I thought werewolves only turned at the full moon?"

Mathew let go of her hand and looked off into the woods. "Lycanthropy affects its victims differently. Some have no control over when they change or their behaviour when under a full moon. I've seen a werewolf try to kill her own mother." He paused and then looked back at Bara. "Ragman is of the second type. He's more like a shape-shifter but can only take the shape of a wolf. His kind has much more control. If they don't to prey on humans we let them live."

They left the parkland and entered the Grande Oaks District.

"But you let him eat the Conjure."

"Conjures aren't human. I don't know if they ever were."

"What are they, then?"

"A kind of lesser demon. A wisp, or one in possession of a wisp, can raise them. They obey the desires of whoever called upon them. They appear out of mist and return to it when they're released or when the conjurer's hold is weakened for some reason. Unless they're killed and then they just rot away—or become a werewolf's lunch. They're very strong and fast and unlike most Clavigen …" Mathew paused and waved a hand over his own slim physique—which Bara had not the slightest problem with—and continued on, "… they look it.

"Conjures can be incredibly useful tools. But since only a weak mind link is maintained between the conjurer and the conjure, they don't exactly think on their feet. I don't use them but Courtney does from time to time."

Bara was listening so intently she barely noted the trees and mansions of the Grande Oaks District slip by. Far too quickly they arrived at the Lavender House. Looking through the iron gates she could see the study light. It had begun to rain again. A light drizzle misted the air. She should have been anxious to go inside but she lingered.

"Are you going to come in?" she asked Mathew.

"I can't."

Her mood plummeted but she recovered when she saw his face. Mathew didn't want to leave either.

"I haven't finished my shift at the Tragic Sip," he explained. "Although by now I'm probably fired. I'll have to think up a very good lie but I'll be back soon."

Bara smiled eagerly and then was embarrassed for seeming so keen. She looked down. She didn't know much about boys but she knew they didn't like girls to seem too eager, too clingy. But then Mathew was no ordinary boy. *No* he was a sixteen-hundred-year-old boy who hunted werewolves and vampires and imprisoned demons ... and haunted her dreams. She looked back up, not quite ready to let this chance slip by.

"You didn't answer my question, you know."

"What question?"

"Why you've been entering my dreams."

"Oh that? That's a long story." Mathew sighed and sat down on the low brick wall that formed the base to the fence. "You know Courtney and I have our differences. So I wasn't doing it for her if that's what you're thinking. I didn't even know you were her stepdaughter. I came back to Windfall and got a job at the Tragic Sip. It's important for us to blend in. People think Martha is my aunt. But I live in the cottage. She lives in town."

"That was you in the window? It wasn't a dream."

He nodded.

"You told Ms. Korey about seeing us in the maze?"

"I thought you could use the help. She told Courtney and Amy let us in on your plans to release Brynndalin. I wished we could have been a little quicker."

"Why didn't you tell me yourself about the Wisp? Let me know you were real?"

"Having your dreams suddenly come to life can be a little offsetting. I was looking for the right time and didn't want Courtney to know I was back, not yet. I should have revealed myself. I know that now. This is as much my fault as yours."

Bara gave a half-smile. At least Mathew didn't blame her for setting Brynndalin free. That was something. She read the sympathy in his eyes and felt the closeness between them. *Their connection?* She realized they'd gotten off topic, yet again.

"But how did you know about me in the first place? Did Ms. Korey tell you?"

"No. I'm enrolled at Windfall High for appearances sake. One day after school I saw you in the square and there was just something about you. I felt I knew you. Even though I was certain we'd never met." Mathew gave a shame-faced grin. "The stalker in me took over then, I guess. I followed you and ended up at Courtney's. I realized you must be her new stepdaughter. I needed to know more and so I attempted to enter your dreams."

Bara remembered again the kiss they'd shared and all the handholding. She blushed. Mathew seemed to understand the reason.

"You're a teenage girl," he said. "Teenage girls dream of kissing and stuff."

"So that was all me?"

Looking at his face she really didn't need an answer. His smile threatened to push his ears off his head. She could barely hear with all the blood rushing between hers. One thing for sure he knew all about her feelings for him.

"I wasn't sure I'd be able to do it ..." Mathew was trying and failing to suppress his laughter. "Enter your dreams, I mean. I could always with my family members and after a while with Courtney and Martha and a few others. As far as I knew you were a stranger. But I gave it a try and surprisingly I could. I realized you were Clavigen. So I decided to keep an eye on you, help you if I could but still stay out of sight of Courtney."

"Why are you both so angry?"

"It's not that we're angry. Just so much has happened. It's a long story and not entirely mine to tell. I think she needs tell you. I'm sorry but I really do."

Bara realized that if she had to wait for her stepmother to tell her yet another secret, she might have to wait awhile.

"Okay, but I have just one more question."

He raised an eyebrow.

"Just one more questions, hey? What's that?"

"You can only enter the dreams of those you have a connection?"

Mathew nodded and she asked the obvious question.

"Then how are we connected?"

He shrugged and smiled

"Honestly I don't know. Time will tell, I guess."

That was all Mathew said. He took a deep breath and came to his feet. He could have left then but it was his turn to linger. There seemed something else he wanted to say. For a long moment he said nothing and neither did she. They both just stood there. But then like someone had shoved him Mathew moved closer. Her heart raced. Bara thought he might kiss her. He didn't. He held out her bag. Of course that was why he hadn't left. She accepted it and slung it across her shoulder. She turned to the gate, punched in the code, and unlatched the lock, but didn't push the gate open. Not yet.

"Bara?" he came again.

She turned back and he gave her a shy smile.

"You should take the leaves out of your hair before you go in. You don't want your father to see you like that."

Bara hadn't given any thought to her appearance. After her run-in with earth, wind, rain, and lesser-demon, she must look a mess. Embarrassed she began to pick at her hair but without a mirror she was at a bit of a disadvantage.

"Here, let me."

Mathew stepped closer and with a gentle hand removed a leaf. Never, not if Bara lived a million years, would she understand what came over her then. Sandalwood and angelica wafted in the space between them, sandalwood, angelica, and his warmth. Like she wanted to tell him a secret she stepped in all the closer. He bent down so he might hear a whisper. She reached up and kissed him on the mouth with a passion way beyond her years. At first Mathew didn't respond. His lips might as well have been her pillow for all the desire they returned. Bara felt the most overwhelming sense of rejection. She started to pull away but then strong arms drew her closer.

The dark-haired boy kissed her in return like she'd always dreamed he would.

XI

The door wasn't locked and Bara entered without knocking. No one greeted her and she was relieved, certain her face was still flushed. Sure enough the entryway mirror revealed a few leaves tangled in her hair and cheeks hot with color. But Bara didn't care. She leaned against the wall and relived the kiss. It was a good thing Mathew had held her so tightly. Otherwise she'd have certainly crashed to the ground. Who knew going weak in the knees from a kiss was something that could really happen?

Mathew had been the one to draw back. He didn't say anything but gave her a shy look. Then he lifted her hand to his mouth and kissed it. It was a gesture out of another time, almost old-fashioned, but from a sixteen-hundred-year-old teenager it worked. He'd looked into her eyes, searchingly, and smiled. Then without a word he walked away, leaving her standing at the gate, still feeling his warmth on her lips, still smelling his scent on her clothes.

Gloria came into the foyer. Her southern tones brought Bara back to reality.

"You must've been with young Master Colin," she accused mockingly.

Shaken from her daydreaming Bara remembered her hair. She pulled frantically at the few remaining leaves.

"Don't worry," Gloria said chuckling. "You're secret's safe with me. If'ya wanna hear my opinion?"

Bara wasn't sure she did.

"Your papa is just being overprotective. That's a papa's job. But I like that boy. He'd never *d'ya* any harm."

Bara looked down, wishing the ground would open and swallow her up. She did not want to discuss Colin.

"Speaking of your papa," Gloria continued, "he's still at work and Mrs. Cavanagh went out real early this morning. Your friend, nice girl, she's in the study."

"Do you know when my stepmother will be back?"

Gloria took her coat and bag.

"I'm sorry, Miss Bara, but Madame didn't tell me when she'd return. I must've been in the kitchen when she left. I didn't even hear her leave."

Bara wondered. Had Courtney actually left the house?

"Could you make up a guest room for Amy," she said switching gears. "There's a problem at school and we'll be staying the night.

"I'll get right on it."

Gloria headed upstairs with the coat and bag. Bara waited for her to disappear and then went into the study where Amy sat under the glow of a lamp, studying. She looked up when Bara came in. A knowing smile played around her mouth.

"You took your time."

Bara played dumb.

"Did I?"

"Where's my croissant?"

Bara had completely forgotten. She shrugged. Amy wasn't bothered. There was a plate of meringue next to her. Gloria had obviously seen to her needs.

"Mathew was there," Bara said.

"*Was he?*" Amy returned like she didn't already know.

Bara picked up a sofa cushion and tossed it in her direction.

"You know he was."

"And?"

"*And* I don't want to talk about it. I *want* to go in there."

Bara pointed to the book shelf that hid the secret passage. She had more to share then the retelling of her first romantic kiss. *Which was amazing!* There was the run-in with the Conjures. Everyone needed to know they were in a lot more danger than they realized. She grabbed a meringue, went to the mantle, and felt around. She found the hidden button and pushed it. The wall opened up and light from the study spilled in to reveal a few feet of stone corridor.

"Let's go."

Bara shoved the cookie into her mouth and entered the passageway. She didn't get far. It was nothing but a dead end. Perhaps there was another secret doorway that would allow them to carry on their way. She felt around for a second trigger. Amy pushed past. She knelt down and hefted up a stone from the floor, revealing a small gold handle. She gave it a tug. As the flap of wood lifted the bookshelf slid shut again. It was dark while their eyes adjusted. A dim glow came out of the blackness. Amy was silhouetted in the light.

"It's down here," she said.

Her dark head slipped from view. Bara took a step closer and stood where Amy had been. She looked down on a spiral staircase lit by wall torches. It was very atmospheric like a scene from a Gothic movie. The dark cool earth reached up and literally gave her the chills. At the foot of the stairs there was a pool of black where no torches glowed. Amy must have disappeared into that darkness. With all that had happened one would have thought little could faze Bara, but she hesitated to go down those stairs—too much unknown ... too little light ... too much darkness.

"Amy," she called.

There was no answer.

"Amy?"

Still no answer.

She must have moved out of ear shot. Get it together, loser. Bara bolstered her courage and took the first couple of steps but then stopped. Something moved down in the darkness, shuffling just beyond the glint of the torches.

"Amy!" she shouted with a lot more alarm than she'd have wished.

A tall shadow, much too tall to belong to Amy, emerged from the black. It was unnaturally large like someone had taken a normal human and stretched her out until she was seven-foot-tall and as thin as a rake. Extending a black reach up the stairs it threatened to overwhelm Bara. She screamed, high-pitched, blood curdling as they say.

The creature asked—mockingly, "What are you hollering about?"

A second scream died away.

"Colin?"

Grinning his familiar face appeared in the dim light just a couple stairs below.

"Yeah, who'd you think it was?"

"I don't know. Just with everything that's happened ..."

His grin was infuriating. She tried to hide her embarrassment.

"I'm a little on edge. Is my stepmother down there?"

"On edge? I'll say." He chuckled. "Follow me. Everyone's here."

Everyone Bara noted didn't include Mathew. Being in Colin's presence and thinking about Mathew niggled at her. She felt oddly guilty but shrugged it off and descended the stairs to join Colin at the bottom.

They stood in a long corridor also lit by torches. Bara looked up and started. Colin stood very close. In the shadow and flicker of the torchlight his face took on an almost ominous expression. He stared at her questioningly.

"You smell weird."

Bara sniffed her sweater. There was just the faint smell

of sandalwood and angelica. *Mathew.*

"All I can smell is the gas from the torches," she lied.

"That's not it."

"Whatever."

Bara went to walk away but Colin stopped her. He leaned in and picked a twig from her hair. He held it out with a quizzical look on his face.

"Were you rolling around on the ground?" he asked teasingly.

There was that odd guilt again.

"Kind of."

He raised an eyebrow.

"Take me to Courtney and I'll fill you in."

Colin shrugged. He turned and led the way down the stone corridor. In twenty paces or so they came to a large wooden door. He pushed on the oak. It gave way reluctantly. As though they couldn't believe they were being forced to work at their age, ancient hinges complained with a loud whine.

XII

Flickering candles created areas of warm light and dim shadow. Heavy tapestries hung on the walls, keeping the cold out and the warmth in. Four wing chairs each with a foot stool surrounded a wooden mantle and a roaring fire. Amy and Courtney each sat in a chair. There were two canopy beds with filmy curtains. One bed held the resting form of Ms. Korey. She was covered with a fluffy quilt. A similar quilt covered the other bed.

"It's a bedroom!" Bara said.

"We like to think of it as more of a sleep lab."

Ms. Korey only appeared to be sleeping. She sprang out of bed with such speed she came close to bouncing off the ceiling. She stretched and yawned.

"Sleep is the only way we have of communicating with the Slip. There are times when we want to communicate and then there are times when we just want to sleep. The chamber allows us to do both. Look up."

On the ceiling were chalk markings, a series of circles. The largest circle contained a smaller. It in turn held a still smaller one. There were twelve circles in all. In the very center there was a five-pointed star like the one on the inside cover of the Clavigen Diary.

"The circles and the star help open up the Slip while protecting the dreamer from evil intent. When we just want to sleep the star is replaced with a cross."

"You've all been down here sleeping?" Bara asked.

"Us three have, yes," confirmed Courtney, referring to herself, Colin, and Ms. Korey.

"They didn't miss you at school?" Amy asked Colin.

"I said I was sick."

"They're going to check and see you're not in your room."

He shrugged.

"So what do we know? Anything new?"

"The Slip has revealed little," Courtney told them. "But one thing is certain. Brynndalin's found a host."

"What about my dream?" Colin asked.

"We're not even certain your dreams matter."

Mathew stood at the door. No one had heard him come in. Even in the dim light of the chamber his eyes shone.

"Mathew," came Ms. Korey's crisp voice. "You have a stick in your hair … and a leaf."

Mathew reached up and removed a red maple leave. He shared a smile with Bara. Like lightening it was only for a second and then they looked quickly from one another. But not quick enough. Because just like lightening it was impossible to miss. Courtney had seen the look—so had Colin. Seeming physically pained Colin let out an audible gasp, stiffened, and then looked away, mumbling something about the return of Prince Charming.

"Shouldn't you be at work?" Courtney asked Mathew.

"Something else came up. I made an excuse."

Mathew closed the door. He didn't struggle with the weight the way Colin had.

"You should sit, Bara."

He crossed the room and placed a hand on the small of her back, guiding her to one of the armchairs. She felt his warm breath on her neck and smelled his scent.

Just before she sat, he whispered, "Next time—I'll kiss you."

Bara didn't need a mirror to know she'd gone bright red. Colin's angry voice broke in.

"It's the new millennium, Harry Potter. Bara's perfectly capable of sitting by herself if she actually wants to sit."

He strode across the room, plopped down in the last empty chair, the chair next to Bara, and glared.

"You were in the Slip?" Amy asked him. "What happened?"

Colin was forced to come out of his funk.

"I dreamt I was at the base of a cliff. I think it was the one off the highway into Windfall. There were two girls. At first I thought they might be you two. They were wearing St. Cat uniforms. It was two other girls though. They weren't familiar but then I don't really pay much attention to your schoolmates. They were out of it. Their faces were zombie-like and they were a greenish-grey. They just kept saying the same thing over and over again. Give us back our source. We want to move on. Give us back our source."

"It could have just been a dream," Courtney said.

"You know that's not true," Bara returned.

Courtney's face revealed the truth. She knew the dream was very significant.

"You're trying to protect us again. Those two girls were our schoolmates. They died last night. It happened just like in your dream, Colin, at the base of the cliff. Patsy, she's the Sheriff's daughter, she said they were grey when they were found." Bara turned back to Courtney. "Brynndalin took their souls, right? That's what they meant by source."

Courtney sighed and relented.

"She took the energy that allows one to travel between the material world and wherever one goes when they die. They are in limbo. They are trapped in the Slip."

"Purgatory?" Bara said, looking at Mathew.

He nodded.

"How can we help them?" Amy asked.

Ms. Korey was performing a series of stretches. She was standing with her head between her legs, one arm to her ankle and one hand to the sky.

"When Brynndalin is back in the amber they may be released."

"They'll be alive again?"

"No, it's too late. Their bodies are dead. There's no bringing them back to life but they may be able to move on. We never know for sure. Finding Brynndalin and recapturing her is their only hope.

"Brynndalin is also using Conjures," Mathew told everyone. "Bara and I had a nasty run-in with a pair this afternoon. She came pretty close to getting Bara and the amber. We'll have to be a lot more careful. The sooner the Wisp is captured the better."

"But we don't know where to find her," Amy pointed out.

"The Messengers will lead us," Mathew reassured. "They've never let us down before."

"So what? We all take turns sleeping down here?" Colin shot back. He was thinking *there's no way I'm leaving you down here with Bara, so think again buddy boy.* But he kept his thoughts to himself.

"Those of us who can, yes," Courtney confirmed. "But Bara, you will not."

"You can't stop me from being involved."

"That's not what I'm doing. Your mother's back.

You'll have to go home."

XIII

Before a silver tea service the Cavanaghs sat. The Earl Grey had been poured but the four steaming cups were all but untouched. Everyone had taken but one sip. The conversation was polite, if uncomfortable. No harsh words had yet to be spoken. Bara had expected to have to sit silently while her father told her mother about her running away, twice, but all seemed not just forgiven but forgotten. How much Courtney had to do with his choice to remain silent Bara could only guess.

Mrs. Cavanagh wore a pink cardigan set, *Ms.* Cavanagh a blue-grey Chanel suit. With the amber destroyed Courtney wore pearls, as did Ms. Cavanagh. Twenty pounds seemed to have melted off Ms. Cavanagh's once plump frame. Now she could have been Courtney's younger and slightly slimmer sister.

"The diet they had me on was amazing," she raved.

A strand of gray-free blonde hair fell onto her lap. She looked at it as though it was something far more unpleasant and then a diamond-encrusted hand swept it away. The jewel glinted, far too large for her thin fingers. No Ms. Cavanagh hadn't just gone to a spa; she'd had plastic surgery. There was no doubt. Nor did she deny it. Rather she called her doctor a *real* miracle-worker. Smiling with white teeth that belonged in a toothpaste commercial she did her less-than-subtle best to insult Courtney.

"I should give you her number. We could all use a little nip and tuck, here and there."

Bara interrupted

"Mom, do you need some time to settle in? I could stay here a little longer."

Bara had to draw back to escape the smell of perfume—jasmine and orange blossoms. It should have been pleasant but her mother was wearing way too much.

"We'd love to have her stay a little longer," Courtney added. "You still must need rest after your procedure."

Ms. Cavanagh reached across the chaise and took Bara's hand.

"Haven't you missed me? I've missed you."

Bara *had* missed her mother. A few days ago she'd have given anything for her to have come home. But that was when she'd thought Courtney was evil. What Bara wanted now was to keep Brynndalin from harming anyone else. She could do this best where she was, with the others.

"I want you home with me," Ms. Cavanagh said.

Her eyes glistened with tears. What daughter could deny her mother after that?

"I'll go get my stuff."

Bara left the adults and went up to the Pink Palace. She didn't need to take much, just the essentials—coat, cell phone, and book bag, which she checked contained the Clavigen Diary. They'd all debated whether she should keep it. Courtney and Ms. Korey had said no. She, Colin, Amy, and, surprisingly, Mathew had argued that Bara had found it; it should stay with her. Courtney and Ms. Korey eventually gave in but they'd insisted that the dagger be kept at the house.

When Bara came back down the hall she could hear her parents at the door. They were arguing. *Nothing new.* It was obvious they were trying not to yell but their voices easily carried to the second floor. Bara stopped before she came into view and listened in.

"You're not fooling anyone with that perfume, Beth."

"I don't know what you're talking about."

Courtney's voice was absent from the conversation.

"You just be sure that Bara doesn't suffer. You understand me. I won't have it."

"Oh Richard, you make so much of it. I'm fine and so is

Bara. I would never hurt her. Unlike someone else I know, I have *never* hurt her."

It was a very thinly-veiled accusation and Mr. Cavanagh lost it.

"Just the same!" he bellowed. "You watch your temper!"

Bara couldn't see her mother's face but she sensed her smirk all the same.

"Oh yes. I'll watch my temper because you are always so calm and controlled."

"You know what you get like when you've had too much."

Things were getting hot. There was only one way to cool the situation down. Bara made her presence known.

She came out from hiding and chirped as cheerfully as she could, "I'm ready!"

Ms. Cavanagh bit back whatever nasty remark she'd had on the tip of her tongue and smiled up at Bara. She did a very good job at pretending everything was just fine.

"We should go then," she almost sang.

Bara came down the stairs and stopped next to her father. They hugged and he ruffled her strawberry curls before letting her go.

"Hey kiddo," he whispered into her ear. "See you next

weekend."

There was the *clip-clop* of approaching pumps. Courtney rushed into the foyer.

"Sorry an emergency trip to the little girl's room. I'm glad you haven't left. I did want to see you off."

Courtney came to stand next to her husband. Then she did what would have been unthinkable just a few short days ago. She hugged Bara. Bara hugged her back. Courtney didn't let go right away.

"Be careful," she whispered.

Bara felt something heavy slip into her coat pocket and then Courtney released her.

"Call me if you need anything," she said.

"What would she need that her mother couldn't give?" Ms. Cavanagh snapped.

"Courtney was just being gracious," Mr. Cavanagh returned. "Let's not have a scene." He too then did the unthinkable. He embraced his ex-wife. "You look great. Take care of yourself, Beth"

Mr. Cavanagh opened the door and ushered her out. A dark car waited. The driver lounged against the side. When the door opened he sprang into action. He came around and opened the rear passenger side. Ms. Cavanagh descended the stairs and disappeared into the dark depths of the car.

Bara kissed her father again and then joined her mother. The driver closed them in, went around the other side of the sedan, and climbed into the front seat.

"Home, Miles."

Ms. Cavanagh smiled and patted Bara's knee. Then as though she'd just endured a terrible trial she lay her head back and closed her eyes. The car began its journey to the front gates. Past the marble statues they drove. Bara fought the desire to wave goodbye to the lifeless observers. She'd hated the small stone army. Now she'd almost miss them.

As they waited for the gates to open Bara looked back at the house expecting to see a closed door. She was surprised to see Courtney standing under the cupola. With a worried face Courtney watched the car pull away. Bara remembered Courtney had placed something into her pocket. She slid her hand into her coat and fingered the heavy object. It was unmistakable—a long thin blade and a cold metal hilt—the dagger.

XIV

Ms. Cavanagh had begun a makeover of her life and everything in it. It shouldn't have been a complete surprise.

She'd mentioned she might give the house a *freshening up* ... a new coat of paint or some drapery. *But not this!* Bara stood in the foyer she'd left a warm shade of vanilla with gold trim. It was now repainted a light blue. Wooden floors had been replaced with marble and it appeared her mother had gone shopping in Courtney's front yard. A large statue of a half-naked woman embracing a swan now held court in the center of the foyer. Bara felt she was stepping into a palace and not her once-familiar home.

Ms. Cavanagh looked around as if she were expecting someone else to be there. Seconds later, almost running, a uniformed maid entered. They often got temporary maids when Betty had time off. Bara smiled and said hello. The maid remained expressionless, nodding a greeting in return.

Ms. Cavanagh handed over her coat.

"Bara," she said, "give Sonya your things."

Sonya still said nothing but stepped in her direction. Bara clutched at her bag.

"I can do that myself."

"Nonsense!"

"I need the bag. It has my homework."

Ms. Cavanagh ignored Bara and spoke again to Sonya. "Hang up the coat and take the bag to her room."

Her word was final. Sonya took the bag and helped

Bara ease out of her coat. She hung the coat on a stainless-steel tree that had replaced an antique rack. It would have seemed silly to argue over such a small thing. The bag would no doubt end up in her room. And the coat? *I'll get it back first chance I get,* Bara silently promised. She waited for Sonya to leave and then asked the burning question.

"Mom, what have you done to the house?"

Ms. Cavanagh said nothing but went into the sitting room. Bara looked past a set of open French doors. Shocked she followed her mother in to get a closer look. The sitting room like the foyer had been transformed. All the furniture had been changed. Gone was the overstuffed ease Bara had grown up with, replaced with modern furniture, all sleek lines and shiny surfaces.

"Mom," she asked again, "what have you done to the house?"

Ms. Cavanagh continued to ignore her. She tossed aside a pile of mail, picked up a little silver bell, and rang it. In answer to the summons *silent* Sonya—as Bara was coming to think of her—entered the room and stood beside her.

"Yes madam?"

It appeared Sonya could talk after all.

"I'll have tea in the conservatory in twenty minutes."

Bara waited for Sonya to leave and then in that

judgmental tone only a teenage girl can obtain when speaking to her mother, echoed, "*Conservatory?* Since when do we have a conservatory? Seriously Mom, what—have—you—done?"

Ms. Cavanagh let out a bothered sigh.

"Your father certainly doesn't need an office here anymore, now does he? Really you're making too much of this. I thought the house was looking tired. It will be nice to live in something a little more modern."

"I liked the house the way it was."

"You'll get used to it."

Ms. Cavanagh crossed to the bar. She brought her hand to her brow and as though her diamond ring were ice to soothe an aching head, held it there. She lowered her hand and took the lid off a silver ice bucket and dropped actual ice into a martini shaker. She poured a generous portion of gin from a blue glass bottle and waved the shaker in the air with vigor.

"You said you were thinking of changing a few things," Bara said. "Not the *whole* house. Don't you think you should have asked my opinion?"

"No," her mother returned. "I don't think I have to run my decisions by my teenage daughter."

"It's my house too ..."

Bara had to step suddenly aside. Something whizzed by her head, inches from contact. There was the sound of breaking glass. A martini goblet had smashed against one of the French doors and now lay in shatters upon the marble floor. It was amazing the door hadn't broken too. Ice slid down the lead pane.

"I will do what I want to my own house!" Ms. Cavanagh hollered. "You silly, stupid girl! Get out! Leave me alone!"

Despite her real desire to do exactly that Bara stood rooted. It occurred to her that her mother had been drinking even before she'd come to get her. That was why her parents had been arguing and that was why her mother had chosen to wear so much perfume—to hide the smell of gin. Her mother was drunk. Bara looked now at Ms. Cavanagh's beautiful face bent in an ugly rage and slowly common sense took over. Her legs came to life and she fled the room, making it to the foot of the stairs before a pleading voice stopped her.

"I'm so sorry," Ms. Cavanagh called. "Don't go."

What else could she do? It was her mother after all. Bara retraced her steps and returned to the sitting room.

Teetering on her knees Ms. Cavanagh attempted to clean up the broken crystal. She looked up with her tear-filled eyes and held out the broken glass like it were a peace offering. There seemed a real danger of her passing out among the broken shards. Bara went to her side, placed a hand on her arm, and helped her stand. She guided her to the sofa and they both sat.

Ms. Cavanagh buried her face in her hands.

"I promised myself I'd never be this way with you. *Never.* I'm so sorry. I don't know what came over me."

The answer to that question seemed obvious. Bara took a deep breath and ran full on in where angels fear to tread

"Maybe if you hadn't been drinking …"

Ms. Cavanagh stiffened and looked up with an expression that stopped Bara midsentence. She'd stopped crying. When she spoke her tone was harsh and mocking.

"I didn't get your permission to redecorate but that doesn't mean I'm an alcoholic. How dare you? You little …" She finished her statement with a queer laugh and then rose from the sofa. She was back at the bar. "Run along and let Mommy have some peace. I have a horrible headache."

That was it. The subject was closed. With a crystal glass to her lips Ms. Cavanagh swallowed gin like a thirsty desert dweller. Bara watched her down the martini and felt as though that desert sand was filling her own stomach, creating a heaviness that threatened to drop through to her feet. But there was nothing she could do, at least not now. Bara left the sitting room and headed upstairs.

XV

Her mother was certainly thorough in her desire for change. Bara walked down a hallway under reconstruction. Walls were being repainted and dust covers hung over unfamiliar furniture shapes. Reaching her room, apprehensively, she opened the door and breathed a sigh of relief. It was as she'd left it, exactly as she'd left it, almost a month ago. A trail of clothes led to an open closet. Her green comforter lay across the bed, half covering her teddy bear. The only addition was the book bag, hanging on the arm of an easy chair. Bara went inside and closed the door. She crossed the room, plopped herself down on the bed, and pulled the teddy bear to her chest. *Disappear* was her only thought.

She was just about to plunge beneath the blankets when there was a tap on the window. No doubt it was Colin preparing to scale the house and invade her room. She really didn't want to be alone with him again. *Not after the Kiss with Mathew.* It had changed things. It had changed her and somehow it had changed her relationship with

Colin. She needed time to process.

There was another tap. He wasn't going away.

Bara let out a surrendering sigh, wiped the wet from her cheeks, and went to the window. She pulled back the drapes and smiled with surprise. Mathew was perched—a little precariously—on her stone window ledge.

She opened the window.

"Can I come in?" he asked.

She stepped back and let him climb through.

They stood for a moment, looking at each other, not speaking. It felt somehow right having him in her room—in the flesh. After all he'd been there many times, always in her dreams, but many times. And just like in her dreams he filled the space with energy. Of course there was another current flowing through the room, from boy to girl and girl to boy, and it made his presence not only comfortable, but exciting too.

Finally he spoke.

"I wanted to make sure you were okay. How's your mother?"

"Changed."

"How so?"

"She's had plastic surgery and redone the whole house. I guess it has to do with getting over my dad."

Bara sat down on the bed. She was still trying to come to terms with her mother's drinking problem and wasn't ready to discuss it, even with Mathew, but he sensed something was up.

"Don't worry," she reassured. "I'll get used to it."

"No sign of Brynndalin?"

"Not a one."

There was another silence.

"I guess I'll go."

Mathew went for the window.

"Stay!"

Mathew turned back. He seemed uncertain. Realizing she'd probably sounded just a little desperate Bara strove for some nonchalance.

"Unless you have somewhere else to be, I mean."

He grinned and raised an eyebrow.

"I have nowhere else to be. I could stay for a while. What did you want to do?"

"We could talk."

"Oh," he said teasingly. "You have *more* questions."

"You know just about everything about me. I mean, you've been in my dreams. Don't you think it's only fair I know something about you?"

He sat down on the bed next to her.

"Okay what do you want to know?"

There was so much she wanted to know. But he was sitting so close she found it hard to concentrate.

Finally her mind settled on a question.

"When *exactly* were you born?"

"355 AD."

"That makes you …"

He interrupted, giving her a bashful grin.

"Please don't do the Math. Let's just leave it at I'm very, very old. Next question."

"Where were you born? It couldn't have been here, not in the fourth century."

"I was born in Ireland." He paused and gave her a measuring look before asking a question of his own. "But why don't you ask me what you really want to know?"

If it was at all possible he leaned in closer. She shot him an innocent look. He laughed.

"What's so funny?"

"I don't know but I guess if I were you, I'd want to talk more about our *connection* and that kiss you gave me."

Bara lowered her gaze.

"Yeah, that."

Mathew took her chin, forcing her to look back up.

"Yeah that," he mocked good-naturedly. "I've been

giving it some thought and ..."

There was a sound in the hallway.

"My mother!"

It wouldn't do to have Ms. Cavanagh meet Mathew for the first time this way. Not to mention *Mr. Cavanagh* would most certainly die of apoplexy when he found out Bara had been alone in a bedroom with yet another boy.

"You have to leave!" she urged.

Mathew didn't need coaxing. They both leapt from the bed and headed for window. She threw open the pane. He put one leg out. She was holding the curtains back so they wouldn't block his escape, standing just close enough. He looked at the door to make sure no one was coming through and then leaned down. The fingers of both hands grazed her neck before taking hold of her nape.

"I don't know how we're connected," he whispered, "but I have a pretty good idea."

Softly but insistently he kissed her. Despite the very real threat of being discovered it wasn't hurried, but long and sweet. They'd all but forgotten her mother anyways.

None too quickly and far too soon, he pulled away.

"I told you I'd be the one to kiss you the next time."

Mathew smiled again, now a little abashed. Bara said nothing in return, still not capable of speech, but she blushed the most adorable, if insipid shade of red. Really she'd have been a perfect match to the Pink Palace. Mathew climbed through the window and crouched on the stone ledge.

"One more thing. Don't be alarmed if you see a couple of Conjures out in the yard."

Bara was alarmed.

"Courtney's idea," he explained. "She summoned a couple to watch out for you."

Mathew jumped from the sill. Bara leaned out the window to see him land with the agility of a cat on the slate patio below. He looked back up and smiled and then with his incredible speed ran across the lawn. Dry leaves scattered in his wake. Bara watched him until he disappeared over the stone wall which he also scaled with feline grace. She continued to stare out at the yard, hoping he might reappear. He didn't.

Bara shuddered. Someone was watching in return. She scanned the yard but saw no one. No doubt, somewhere shielded from view in the shadow of a tree, was a Conjure or two looking out for her safety. Funny thing, the idea of a couple Conjures outside the house, even if they were on her side, made her feel not one iota safer. She closed the window and the drapes. Her mother had failed to materialize and Bara wished Mathew hadn't left. She sat down on the window seat and thought about the kiss, their second kiss, comparing it to the first, reliving every wonderful moment. She sat there for a good long while.

***

What time was it? Bara looked at the clock. It was well after 7:00pm. There'd been no call for dinner. She could go down for a snack ... no sleep was a better idea. She headed for the bed but had a sudden thought and re-crossed the room. She took the diary from her bag, returned to the bed, and put it under her pillow and then climbed under the covers and placed her head on the pillow. The sleeping chamber was off limits. But if she slept with the diary it might help her enter the Slip. It was worth a try. And so Bara pulled her teddy bear into an embrace and slept.

XVI

A Dream

The wind struck her face and Bara shook with a shiver. She scolded herself for not making sure her bedroom window was closed. But she kept her eyes closed tight as though with enough determination on her part the cold might just go away. Another gust shook her further from rest. She reached down for the warm softness of her comforter and felt something wet and cold instead. And then something sharp and thin scraped her face. With flaying arms she did battle with the many fingers of her foe but she faced no human. Windborne branches from a leafless willow tree whipped against her cheek and cut through her hair, grabbing hold and refusing to let go.

None too easily Bara tore out of the willow's reach. She found herself in a late-autumn meadow upon a bed of moss. Red light filtered through the forest. The sun was either rising or just about to set. No doubt it was setting. The wind was harsh and she wore only a light sweater and jeans. It may only be a dream but the cold seemed pretty real. And of course she wore no shoes. Bara looked down at her stocking feet and swore from now on she'd sleep dressed for a blizzard. But despite the cold her mood lifted. She'd found her way into the Slip. She'd have her chance to make things right. A challenge to her boldness rode on the wind. Somewhere a wolf howled. She wasn't alone.

Bara swallowed her fear and scanned the meadow and its edges. Her eyes settled on a small break in the bush—a trail. She took a step forward and left the mossy mound with a splash. Thick grass hid the true nature of the clearing. Here wool socks could do little. She was shin-deep in water. *Not a meadow ... a marsh. Wonderful! What's next?* One thing for certain the Slip seemed to insist on suffering feet.

There was no point going back onto the moss. It would take forever for her socks to dry and waiting would accomplish nothing. So ignoring her discomfort Bara waded through the wet to the meadow edge and peered down the path. The way was narrow and slowly being invaded by ferns and bush but there seemed no other choice. She lifted her feet onto the trail. It at least was dry. Somewhere a bird trilled its support. Other than the howling wolf it was the only sign of animal life. Taking it as a good omen she gathered what little she wore around her exposed neck and entered the forest.

She battled her way through the underbrush and a setting sun darkened from red to mauve and then violet, casting the forest in an eerie glow. The trail widened as darkness fell. The light left and the wind grew stronger still. Trees swayed violently. Small tornadoes whipped up fallen leaves and swung them in a circular fury. Whirligigs of debris cut across the path. The wind reached deep into the forest with its rough grip, rattling through the dense canopy and twisting through the bushes and saplings. Such was the strength of the oncoming storm; giants would find themselves uprooted before dawn.

Brynndalin was at work here too.

No bird sang for Bara now. There were no sounds but those of her footfalls and the whining wind echoing through the night. She wished that Mathew might appear and guide the way. He didn't. The air grew colder still. She pulled her sleeves over her hands and wrapped her arms around her waist. But her sweater and jeans were no match for remorseless wind and the dropping temperatures.

It's only a dream she reminded herself.

Tell that to my chattering teeth another part of her mind returned.

The night wore on and the stars were hidden. The clouds warmed things a little but they took on a pinkish hue, a sure sign of coming snow. The first impish sliver fell, brandishing icy blades. Soon it was joined by an abundance of its little thug friends. This would be no light and fluffy fall of Christmas carols. Small hard pellets stung her face and hands. The wind sliced at her ears. Bara pulled her sweater over her mouth and nose, burying frostbitten ears further in woolen folds and kept going.

***

Time passes differently in the Slip. Like in any normal dream a second can feel like an hour, a minute a lifetime. Bara didn't know how long she walked. Well at first she walked and then she trudged, through ever-deepening snow, ankle-deep, shin-deep, and finally knee-deep. Her wet socks had frozen solid. It was like being shod in ice trays. But she no longer thought about her feet because blessedly she couldn't feel them. The snow did eventually stop which should have been a relief but the wind persisted, stirring up icy pellets.

Focusing on putting one foot in front of the other Bara watched one frozen pink argyle sock sink into the snow until it ... then her ankle ... and then her shin, disappeared. She lifted her foot from where it lay in the snow and ice, replaced it with the other, and repeated the process. Bara watched her feet as though they weren't part of her. She watched them as though they were some cog-operated machine pulling her along. She had to. She couldn't let herself think of the cold—one foot and then the other—one foot sinks and then the other.

Pulled along by icy feet she watched her dark shadowy head bob up and down in front of her. A meditative process, it allowed her to continue. Her shadowy head went up and then it went down—up and down, up and down.

Over time her shadow transformed, growing additional heads—one, then two, and now three heads. Her shadow had three heads! Bara was so tired. She almost accepted the additional heads as some new reality. But these heads were shaped differently. They were thinner and longer. She stopped and her shadows stopped too. She turned in profile. The shadows did likewise. Long sharp snouts revealed themselves, long sharp snouts that couldn't possibly belong to her. She turned around. She knew what she'd find and there they were—not just one wolf, but a pack.

One, two, three, four, five, she counted silently.

There was a white, two black, one much larger than the other, a red, and one brown. The silver wolf—Brynndalin—wasn't there. Bara didn't know whether to be relieved or disappointed. Then only one emotion seemed right. These wolves were every bit as big as Brynndalin, their claws and teeth as sharp, their eyes just as hard. Fear rose up and out of her gut. She ran. The wolves followed.

XVII

A Dream

Bara fought to take in enough air. She ran with more power than she thought possible, getting nowhere. Deep snow prevented any real progress. Black shadows rose in front of her on the white snow. She waited to feel sharp canines bite through the denim of her pants, slice open the tender flesh of her ankle. Her only hope—her numb skin wouldn't feel the pain. Heavy paws would crash into her back and propel her forward, too quickly. She'd fall. She imagined her small body, dark against the white, lying helplessly as the wolves tore her to shreds, her red blood black in the night.

But the wolves didn't pounce even when her pace slowed to a stumbling crawl. Any wolf used to living in the wild and chasing down its prey could have easily caught her. These wolves did not. Bara stopped and collapsed to her knees. Gasping she fought to catch her breath. Still no attack occurred. She looked back over her shoulder. The wolves showing no sign of tiring were still there, pacing, waiting. She came to her feet slowly this time and backed away. They matched her pace, always keeping a distance of a few feet. They weren't going to kill her, at least not now.

At a loss Bara spoke.

"Why are you following me? What do you want?"

Her voice echoed through the forest. She didn't really expect an answer but she got one. The wolves did not speak but the wind whined with voices.

Free us too!

We will reward you beyond your wildest dreams.

Bara faced not just a pack of wolves but five wisps, incubi Mathew had called them. They would give her anything if she'd only do for them what she'd done for Brynndalin. *Get away!* her silent thoughts screamed. *Get away now!* Ignoring her fatigue Bara turned and again fled, moving as fast as she might in the thick snow. Unperturbed the wolves kept pace, all the time cajoling and coaxing.

Money!

Fame!

Power over all!

Eternal youth and beauty!

Love!

The larger of the black wolves came astride.

We know who you love. We can make him yours.

The red wolf joined him on the other side.

Maybe make it so you can have both.

Bara slowed. Why keep running? It wasn't as though

she'd be able to outrun the pack. She slowed and walked, promising to find whatever it was that awaited her even if they shadowed her every step. And they did, matching each tread. Sensing her growing resistance the wolves increased their efforts. They overtook her, no longer choosing just to follow. Bara thought for a moment she'd assumed wrong. She hadn't accepted their offer and they were going to kill her. No. Instead they behaved like house cats, weaving back and forth across her path, getting so close they brushed her legs. Death was still not on offer. And now the voices of suffering children spoke on the wind.

Free me!

Free me!

Free me!

We are suffering!

You are the only one who can help.

Please help us.

Bara put her hands to her ears and kept moving forward. She told herself their cries of pain were only a ploy to get her to do the unthinkable and shivering, she continued. The wolves noticed her discomfort.

You are cold.

We can make you warm.

We can make it so you are never cold again.

No more cold.

No more hunger.

No more pain.

No more pain.

No more pain.

Bara kept moving. The pack continued to follow. Persisting in their temptation she persevered in her resistance.

Even the walls of Jericho fell. In time the Great Wall of China will crumble to dust and so must your resolve.

Bara didn't know how much longer she could hold out. She promised herself she'd never give over. These demons would never gain their freedom, at least not from her. After what she'd already done she swore she'd remain true even if it killed her. But she began to worry for her sanity. Ms. Korey had said that sometimes even being Clavigen wasn't enough. With each taunt, each temptation, Bara felt her mind lose its grip on reality.

Such as it was in the Slip.

XVIII

A Dream

The trees thinned and they came to the lake. Instantly the wind stilled and the wolves quieted. Choosing to settle underneath a tree whose evergreen offered shelter they stretched out, seeming more like a pride of cats than a pack of dogs. The white wolf yawned, giving a memorable view of sharp canines. He wrapped himself around the already sleeping brown wolf. The brown wolf scratched her haunches and nuzzled her snout under a hind leg. She snickered in her sleep. Only the larger of the black wolves kept a keen eye. There was something familiar about this one. Bara was reminded of the man from her dream, the tall man with the top hat. If Brynndalin could change shape then certainly he could. Were the tall man and this black wolf one and the same? As though he could read her mind he lifted an eyebrow. It was him.

Bara forced herself to ignore her watcher and turned her attention to the lake. Winter had done its savage best. Ice covered unknown depths. She looked to the sky for a falling star and the arrival of the Messenger. Thick clouds blocked out any stars and they were pink again.

Great! More snow!

Bara continued to stare out onto the lake and before long an idea took hold. There might be some answers somewhere out on the frozen surface. Maybe someplace where the ice was thin and the Messenger could come to her. It was worth a try. She stepped onto the ice. Frost-encrusted socks didn't offer much grip. She slipped but maintained her balance. The black wolf tilted his head and stared curiously at her. Ignoring the predatory glow of his eyes she took another step. Not concerned he sniffed and laid his head down.

She half-walked, half-slid her way across the ice and before long arrived at the lake's center. *No luck.* The lake was frozen solid from shore to shore and seemingly from top to bottom. There'd be no answers here either.

Frustrated and disappointed Bara turned back to the shore. She'd taken no more than a couple steps when her feet slid out from beneath and she hit the icy lake—hard.

When her sensed returned she took stock of her bones. Arms and legs moved okay. Her rear-end would certainly have a nasty bruise but nothing seemed broken. She came to her knees and placed her hands down to heft herself up. Her face was inches from the surface. *No!* The Messenger stared back from beneath the ice, her face frozen and silent, a mouth opened in an eternal scream never to be heard. Yet Bara heard screaming ... in her head ... no, not in her head. It was her voice, howling in horror.

The wolves stirred. They stood, ears pointed and alert. Her screams turned to hysterical tears. The pack exchanged knowing glances. As though it were a game to be played at they howled along. Ravenous saliva slid past their greedy canines. They left the beach and took to the ice. With sharp claws they gripped the surface, making rapid progress towards their intended prey. Bara looked up and saw their approach. There was little time. She still knelt on the ice. She tried to stand but fell again. A question rose in her mind, something she hadn't thought of before. *I'm going to die. If I die here, will I die in my world too?*

The pack was now but a few feet away. Bara heard their rasping breath, the *clip-clip* of their claws on the ice ... and another sound—a high pitched laughter and *swoosh*. She assumed it was coming from the wolves but they stopped suddenly. Rather they stopped running and slid across the ice out-of-control. Two wolves fell, continuing forward snout first. Bara almost laughed at the comical way they came but she was more concerned about why they'd stopped. The sight of something had brought their pursuit to a not-so-sudden end.

She turned her head and there it was.

A formless blur of silver and white glided across the ice. As it neared the blur took shape. White robes were a whirlwind and flashes of silver sparked like lightening. Strands of silver hair weaved in the wind. Laughter sounded like thunder. Clouds released the promised snow and it hailed through the torrent. Gusts were hurricane force. Closer the twisting figure came.

In wafts of red-gold her hair blew as though trying to convince her to run. But Bara stayed firm. She wanted to run but the words of Shakespeare came to mind. *Screw your courage to the sticking post.* Lady Macbeth had been browbeating her husband to commit murder but the words worked here too. And so Bara stood, screwed her courage to the sticking post, and waited.

The wind stopped when Brynndalin did. Brynndalin had been spinning so fast that when she ceased to move Bara felt she was now revolving. It took a moment for the world to settle and for her eyes to focus.

Hands upon her hips and well over six-foot-tall even without her powers Brynndalin would have been intimidating, intimidating and beautiful. Her skin and bone structure were as flawless, her lips still full and red. But she'd changed somehow. There was something different, yet familiar about her—the way she tilted her head at just a certain angle. She took a couple of steps forward. The way she moved was changed too, less gliding, more ... *human.* Bara feared Brynndalin, was repulsed to her very core. Yet she had such an urge to fall in those icy arms, to embrace her enemy and tormentor? *Why?*

Brynndalin spoke and Bara knew.

"I told you," she said to the wolves. "She is not for you. She is mine. Bara will do my bidding."

She is stubborn returned the wolves.

Brynndalin turned to Bara

"Is she now? She will do my bidding or she will die."

The wolves grumbled but retraced their steps. Brynndalin watched their retreat with satisfaction. She returned her attention to Bara. She smiled a familiar smile.

"Join me," she said. "Don't be foolish."

Bara cringed at the sound of that voice. It hadn't been the drink that had caused her mother to strike out. No because Brynndalin had smiled her mother's smile, just as she'd spoken with her mother's voice.

"Oh Mom!"

"We are one," Brynndalin confirmed, her voice chiming with two tones. "Join us."

Welcomingly she opened her arms.

Again that desire to run into Brynndalin's arms—her mother's arms. Her inner voice screamed *No! No! No!* Bara knew what was happening, what had happened to the terrible twins, but she didn't care. Her warm hand reached out to touch the cold hand of the Wisp. *Thunk!* She heard the impact before she felt its pain. Something heavy and hard had knocked her hand out of reach. Pain seared through her arm as a second rock hit, cracking the ice. A slender form dressed in pink stood on the shore. Courtney had somehow found her way into Bara's dream. She'd thrown the rock. Unlike Mathew she was able to speak.

"Don't listen to her!" she called. "She's not your mother, not anymore."

"Ignore her," Brynndalin countered. "Come. It's what you want, what you've always wanted, to be with me."

Courtney raised an arm. Another rock hurdled through the air, this time hitting Bara in the head. *Why?* As Bara left the Slip she understood.

XIX

The smell of gin and perfume reached into the Slip and yanked Bara back. Her eyes flew open. She was back in her room. She bolted upright and brought her knees to her chest. Ms. Cavanagh sat beside her on the bed, watching her sleep. Her one hand was wrapped around a martini glass, the other drummed long, elegant fingers upon an empty book bag.

"Did I scare you?" she asked. "You were having a nightmare. I thought you might be dreaming about your *poor, unfortunate* schoolmates."

Cold silver glinted in her possessed blue eyes. *The Wisp*. Ms. Cavanagh—fatally foolish Ms. Cavanagh—was in there too, somewhere, but it was obvious Brynndalin was in control. She lifted her hand from the bag and wiped away a stray lock from Bara's forehead.

Bara took a deep breath and spoke.

"I know who you are."

Brynndalin smiled, almost gently.

"Of course you do. I'm your mother. I haven't changed that much. We really should do something about this room. It could use a makeover."

The Wisp rose and began to tidy, something the real Ms. Cavanagh had never done. Gin from her martini glass spilled as she went. She grabbed a sweater from the floor and went into the closet, disappearing inside. Bara didn't hesitate. She sprang from the bed and out of the room. If she were only quick enough she might get to the dagger before Brynndalin got to her. Cursing herself for not remembering to grab it before going to sleep, she made a dash for the stairs on her still defrosting feet. She was halfway down before she heard the pursuing footsteps. Brynndalin wasn't running, still intent on enjoying her martini.

"You are such a naughty girl," she called. "Come back to mommy, this instance."

It was the same multi-toned voice she'd used in the Slip. She'd dropped the mask.

"You're not my mother!" Bara hollered back.

Brynndalin laughed.

"That is not entirely true."

Bara reached the bottom of the stairs. The new stainless steel coat tree stood bare. Her coat and the dagger within were gone. Without the blade she was powerless. *Think!* Betty often took overflow items to the back closet. Maybe Sonya had done the same.

Please, please, please ...

There was a flash of movement on the stairs that could only be the Wisp. Bara ran for the back of the house. She prayed that her mother hadn't relocated the rear closet. She entered the windowed hall that spanned half the length of the house. The closet should be at the end, next to the back door. There were footfalls in the foyer. *Faster! Faster! Faster!* Bara ordered her straining muscles.

At the end of the hall was the closet. It was still there. She reached for the knob and turned. The door opened. Something large and heavy fell to the floor.

Oh Mom! What have you done?

Bara knelt, praying there might be life left in the body.

"Betty!" she cried. "Betty wake up!"

Betty didn't wake up. Bara rolled her over and gasped. She understood now why Pillanger had been so shocked at finding the terrible twins. Betty's skin was putrid grey and flaking. But Patsy hadn't mentioned the eyes. Betty's open eyes were the worse. They'd been drained of color. The brown that twinkled when she'd smiled was gone. Only black pupils remained enlarged lid from lid—black eyes like the doppelganger. Bara reached out and touched a dry cheek. Along with soft fingers a tear fell. From touch and tears a once feathery smooth skin turned to an oozing mud. Betty was quickly rotting away. Bara pulled back just as Brynndalin entered the hallway.

The Wisp drained the last of her drink and threw the glass aside. It smashed against the wall. She put her hands on her hips and raised an eyebrow.

"She means nothing as will you if you continue to behave so dreadfully."

Bara stood and dashed inside the closet. Brynndalin moved faster but Bara reached her coat first and plunged her hand into the pocket.

The Wisp didn't know what Bara was after. Perhaps the *brat* was going for a phone and so she moved with no great panic, toying with the child. *My child* she thought with a sense of possession and no real love. Bara would be in her grasp before she made any call. Almost with merry amusement she watched her re-emerge from the closet. She glimpsed the green and instantly her predatory glee dissipated.

It all happened so fast. The dagger flew from Bara's grip and skidded across the floor, coming to a stop a good ten feet away. She went to retrieve it, taking no more than a step before she lost all forward momentum and her legs gave way. She'd have fallen but Brynndalin grabbed hold and hoisted her off the ground.

"I have had enough of you!" she snarled.

Bara struggled but she was no match for Brynndalin. Fingers tightened around her throat. She couldn't breathe and her eyes felt they might actually leap from her head. Her senses were leaving her so she barely heard the sounds coming from the front of the house—a loud thud and heavy footfalls. Startled by the noise Brynndalin loosened her hold, not so Bara could escape but enough for her to breathe again.

Into the hall barreled two Conjures. Their eyes weren't shielded by dark glasses and they weren't silver. They were as blue as a midday sky. These were the Conjures Courtney had summoned. Brynndalin loosened her grip yet again. Bara squirmed. She sensed freedom was close at hand. The Conjures were still coming. The Wisp would surely have to let go and do battle. But Brynndalin didn't let go. She actually chuckled.

"Stupid witch!" she said to an absent Courtney. "You are too weak to maintain these petty demons."

She lifted her free hand and it shot out with silver. The Conjures rammed into the light and stopped. They froze.

Brynndalin spoke again.

"Go back from whence you came!"

Seemingly electrified the Conjures began to vibrate and sparks ignited throughout their massive bodies. They struggled but the vibrating only grew faster. Violently they were jarred side to side while their feet remain rooted. Fissures formed from the strain, starting down low and working up pillar-like legs and into larger still torsos, until finally square jaws and granite cheekbones were riddled with cracks. Fissure became cracks and cracks opened to chasms. And then they were an inferno. There was an awful smell of scorched meat. Their borrowed blue eyes were engulfed in red fire just before purple flames burst through the top of their heads. What was left of their skin flaked away to ash. Finally with nothing left to burn the flames became smoke, not mist, but smoke.

Mathew had said Conjures turned to mist but he'd spoken euphemistically. Bara had never witnessed anything so horrific. If this was what happened to them when they were no longer needed she understood why he chose not to use them. In comparison the death Ragman had given the one in the woods seemed gentle and humane.

Smoke hovered where the giants had been. There was a growl and the ground opened up to consume the offering. Turning in on itself the smoke whirled into a funnel. Like a volcano in reverse the earth drank up what was left of Bara's would-be defenders. The floor closed once again and the Conjures were gone.

Brynndalin turned back to Bara with a victorious smirk.

"So that's that," she said.

She still held Bara at a full arm's length but now lowered her so they were eye-to-eye. It was the position one might have held a baby to babble kind nonsense. Brynndalin did begin to murmur but it held no meaning to Bara. It might as well of been baby talk but her voice held no gentleness and there was no love in her eyes.

Icy silver eyes locked onto her watery green. Bara went limp. She tried to fight but her limbs wouldn't move. She willed her eyes to shut, to sever the deadly connection. Paralyzed like the rest of her they just wouldn't close.

A sudden sharp pain and Bara forget about her eyes. Had her heart been plucked from her chest? No there was still too much pain. It was as if she were being turned inside out, her skin pulled from the muscle, the muscle from the bone, the bone from the joints. *Please just let it end* ... the last thing she heard before dropping to the floor was a loud shout. Then there was the thud of her body and then—blissfully—nothing.

XX

Bara gave in and fell from her body. She'd tried, done her best to make things right, given her life and possibly her soul. Still Brynndalin had won. There was nothing to do but give in. *I'm part of her now?* An indeed for a mere second that held all the pain and hate of more than a thousand years, Bara felt what Brynndalin felt, thought what Brynndalin thought—an abyss of dark horrors and absolute cruelty. Into a razor-sharp black she plummeted …

But then as though attached to an invisible string Bara fell only so far and was yanked back the way she'd come, out of the darkness and into a hazy fog. Now if this was limbo, purgatory, she could deal. Like floating around on a cloud or a fluffy blanket—a flying blanket. Flying carpet, why not a flying blanket? There was no pain, no want, just being. She looked for a bright light but saw none, only a dull haze. But a bright light was only a small missing detail. She closed her eyes and surrendered to the painless miasma of death or so she thought.

Sharps sounds broke through the low hum of her supposed eternity. She tried to ignore it. She turned her head away but it only grew louder. There was arguing. Two voices … two women. She heard her name.

Sounding a long way off someone shouted, "You can't have her."

"She's mine," countered the other voice.

Bara put faces to the voices, her mother and Courtney. In an instant the flying blanket was pulled away. Bara fell, she landed, and the pain came roaring back. Muscles tensed and then went limp. This happened many times, over and over again, adding to her pain and then lessening it. Her young body was wringing out ancient anguish.

Bara lay on the hardwood of the back hall, Betty's dead body inches away, her arm slung across the corpse's bloated belly. She bolted upright, far too fast and her stomach threatened to empty. She swallowed hard and looked around. Brynndalin and Courtney were struggling a few feet away. Bara figured why she'd come back. Courtney had interrupted Brynndalin's attack. There was also a loud banging but it wasn't coming from the struggle. *No* it wasn't banging. It was knocking. It was coming from the closed door leading to the foyer.

And there were other voices calling her name through the back door. *Colin and Amy.*

Bara crawled to the door closing off the foyer. If Amy and Colin were at the back chances were it was Ms. Korey and Mathew in the foyer. She turned the knob and pulled— and pulled. Obviously under some kind of spell the door wouldn't budge. Brynndalin and Courtney blocked her way to the back door. Bara watched their struggle. Courtney was losing. Brynndalin held her by the neck and there was a stream of silver passing between their pupils. Courtney's feet dangled a couple of feet off the ground. She was still fighting but just barely.

There was no other way. Bara came to her feet and made a wild dash. With her free hand Brynndalin stopped her with ease. Bara skidded onto her backside, smashing into the dead Betty. Her hand slid beneath the body.

Brynndalin took a moment to glare at Bara.

"I will get to you later," she promised and turned back to Courtney.

Bara went to remove her hand from beneath the body. She stopped, feeling something hard and cold. The dagger. It had been lying at the other end of the hallway before she'd fallen unconscious. Courtney and Brynndalin must have moved it in their struggle. Bara pulled it from beneath the lifeless weight and held it aloft. Emerald green and iron flashed in the dim light of the hall. She looked back at the flagging figure of her stepmother and the frenzied, powerful creature that was the Wisp. Courtney suddenly stopped struggling and hung limp.

Oh God, no!

There'd been no time to think about what using the dagger on Brynndalin would mean. Bara closed her eyes, wishing like in a dream it would all just go away when she reopened them. Her lids lifted and she swallowed a sob.

Nothing had changed. She was faced with a horror even in her worst nightmares she'd never imagined.

"In the nape of the neck!" came a muffled voice.

Mathew called through one of the windows. He was with Amy and Colin at the back of the house. The glass was beveled and almost opaque. His face was distorted into ill-fitting angles but his blue eyes shone clear.

"You have to do it!"

Bara hesitated. A dagger through the neck would kill.

"Do it or Courtney will die!" Mathew shouted.

Somewhere inside her Bara found the strength to do what was most painful, the right thing. She launched herself down the hallway at Brynndalin—at her mother.

Brynndalin heard her coming but she wasn't concerned. Bara would never have the speed or strength to get past her. *Let the silly thing try to save the witch.* It would do her no good. She didn't realize Bara had the dagger. Even if she had she still wouldn't have been overly worried. Bara would never aim to kill her, *not in this body*! The Wisp had worked out her revenge perfectly ... or so she thought. She put out one arm to stop Bara, maintaining her eye-lock with Courtney, and so she saw the glint of the dagger a second too late. There was no time to turn her body aside and block the coming blow. Her throat was all but grazed. But once the metal made contact with skin it took on a force of its own. The flesh absorbed the blade, bringing it deeper and deeper. It disappeared to its hilt into the nape of her soft white throat.

The gash was brutal and complete.

XXI

There was no blinding light, no waves of sound. Brynndalin's chin merely lifted like a lily petal in a summer wind. Blood trickled from her wound, tracing rivers of red down an ivory throat. Still she held Bara in her stare and Courtney in her grip. Maybe the dagger hadn't worked … but then the first wave of pain hit and her torso bent like a flower stem in a winter gale. Brynndalin let go and Courtney fell to floor. Brynndalin's hands flew to her throat to stop the blood. Diamonds rings glittered. Next to the white throat and brilliant red it was sight of horrific beauty.

Bara stared at this being who would have easily taken her life. Just about everything was the same. It was the same chin, the same mouth, the same nose. *Mom*! But the eyes were different. Although only a horrid gurgling sound escaped her mouth, silver-glinted eyes delivered the message loud and clear. *How could you?*

Courtney struggled to her feet. Bara reached for her mother. Brynndalin snapped out. Courtney pulled Bara away just in time. Sharp white teeth bit into empty air.

"She'll take you with her!" Courtney warned. "Don't touch her!"

Brynndalin fell to the floor and both the foyer and back door flew open. The others piled into the hall as the Wisp let out a different sort of sound. It was a scream which should have been impossible. Her vocal chords were severed. But this scream didn't come from the throat. Sounding like the cry of a cat or an infant it came from the gut. Bara pulled from Courtney. Again she was stopped before making physical contact with the suffering Brynndalin. Mathew got to her first. He held her back.

"She's not your mother, not really," reasoned Ms. Korey. "Not now!"

Brynndalin's blood had turned silver. Streams of molten metal spilled from her neck and puddled about her. She hissed and convulsed. Sparks flew from her finger tips, denting walls and breaking windows.

"We need the amber!" Mathew shouted. "Where's the diary?"

Bara didn't seem to hear him. He repeated himself,

shaking her this time.

"Upstairs, in my room," she told him. "It must still be on my bed, under my pillow."

"Take her!" Mathew said to Ms. Korey and Courtney. "You," he directed Colin, "come with me."

Mathew released Bara and he and Colin ran from the hall. Ms. Korey and Courtney came to Bara's side to keep her from Brynndalin. They needn't have. The being that now lay in spasms no longer looked anything like Beth Cavanagh. Brynndalin had turned silver from head to toe. Like indoor lightening sparks shot from her fingertips, colliding with the walls and ricocheting around the hall. There was no aim but the danger was still very real. The group had no choice but to take cover on the other side of the hall door. Leaving it slightly ajar they watched the last living moments of the Wisp.

A pearl necklace broke loose. Pearls flew violently around the hallway. A vicious wind found its way indoors and re-launched them as they fell. The windows lining the hallway broke one after the other. Shards of glass joined the pearls in flight. Wooden boards peeled from the floor and slammed into the wall. The melee increased. It raged for what seemed like forever but couldn't have been more than a few moments. And then without warning the wind and destruction ceased and the hall was quiet.

Brynndalin lay motionless but a silvery mist lifted from her body. At first it had no form and then it took on human shape. Long thin arms and legs revealed themselves, attached to a slender torso. Tentacles of metallic hair searched through the air, sending out charges that hissed and cracked. Silver eyes opened and glared. Looking fully herself now the Wisp floated above the body she'd once possessed. She turned to the door. Her cold, beautiful face was aflame with rage. The storm returned suddenly, matching her ire.

"Run!"

The group fled. At the foot of the stairs they collided with Mathew and Colin. Mathew had the diary. He clutched at the front cover and pulled. A piece of amber came off in his hand. He thrust it at Bara.

"You have to do it!"

"No!" Courtney protested. "I don't want this for her."

She went for the amber. Ms. Korey held her back.

"Bara used the dagger!" Ms. Korey said. "She has to finish the task!"

Courtney dropped her arm. Mathew held the amber in his open palm but as all the new renovations were torn apart around her, Bara didn't move. Through the debris flew Brynndalin. She stopped only a few feet away, hovering near the ceiling, and eyed each of them. She looked at Ms. Korey and then Mathew.

"Not the witches!"

She looked at Bara.

"You had your chance but you, my dear, you look like a good choice."

Her stare had settled on Amy. Amy panicked and fled up the stairs. A cold wind struck Bara in the face. In the split second it took for her to look at the stairs Brynndalin was already on Amy. Amy had fallen halfway up. A black mouth was opening to the chasm that foreshadowed the act of possession.

"Now! Press it against her forehead!"

Mathew forced the amber into her hand. Still Bara hesitated.

"Do it or your friend is lost!" Ms. Korey barked.

Not Amy! Brynndalin couldn't have Amy. Bara ran up the stairs to where Amy lay with the Wisp floating above. Silver eyes and a high forehead were just visible. Bara reached out with the amber but the Wisp wasn't to be caught off guard. She turned her attention to Bara.

Through a large black mouth that moved in waves and sparked with silver, she spoke.

"Since you refuse to leave me alone I will oblige you."

Bara felt the familiar paralysis take over. The others rushed to help but Brynndalin was strong from all the energy she'd consumed. She shot silver from both her hands and everyone flew back. There was the sickening thud of flesh hitting marble. Even the witches were no match for Brynndalin now. There'd be no more help. Bara had little fight left. It was all she could do to maintain her grasp on the amber. She was moments away from losing herself to Brynndalin and Brynndalin knew it.

The Wisp let out a victorious howl.

"You are even more stupid than your mother," she taunted from somewhere inside her black hole of a face.

At the mention of her mother Bara felt something rise above the pain—anger. For a small instant rage overcame pain and terror, giving her the strength to dig for strength. She thought about all Brynndalin had done. The demon had played her a fool, used her to accomplish so much evil. Killed Louise and Cassandra, killed Betty, and destroyed her mother. And her rage grew to match Brynndalin's.

Somehow Bara lifted her arm. It was like moving splintered bone through raw flesh and she howled along with Brynndalin—pain versus delight—but she didn't stop. The black chasm engulfed silver eyes. Bara had but a second. She forced her hand and the palmed piece of amber against the energy field that was Brynndalin's brow and held fast. Sparks and flames licked at her fingers but Brynndalin seemed little bothered. The current traveled up her arm and still the Wisp held her. Then the charge moved over her heart and her hand threatened to let go.

"Hold it there!" Mathew hollered from below.

Bara looked for him in the rubble. He was at the foot of the stairs with Courtney. She was trying to get to her but Mathew held her back. And Colin was there too. Ms. Korey restrained him. They were all still alive and Bara didn't let go ... a sudden flash of light. Had she exploded? No. Her eyes cleared and she found herself lying on the stairs next to Amy. *Blessed heart* ... Brynndalin was gone.

Her hand burned. The pain mingled with other hurts. Bara opened her palm to reveal the amber and brought it to her face. Her vision was blurry. She had to squint to make it out but there was what appeared to be a little insect trapped within. She'd done it. Brynndalin was back in the amber, back in the Slip. Courtney and then Mathew loomed above. Someone took her other hand. Filled with relief and overwhelming fatigue Bara passed out.

XXII

Above was the kind of winter sky that usually signals a cold night. Yet Bara lay on something soft and felt warm and sheltered. She breathed out, expecting a stream of what her mother called dragon's breath. *Mom!* Bara sat up, realizing she wasn't outside but in the sleeping chamber. The starry sky was nothing but the glint of quartz in the stone ceiling above, the something soft one of the beds.

Amy lay beside her. Amy was pale but breathed steadily. As if sensing she was being watched she stirred and rolled over. She'd be alright.

Someone slept in the other bed but Bara couldn't tell who. Colin lay sprawled in one of the big wing chairs, his spidery long legs up on a foot stool, a blanket pulled up to his chin. A fire crackled reassuringly, shielding out the cold earth. Mathew and Courtney sat in the chairs closest to the heat. They were in deep conversation. Courtney looked okay. Mathew must have done his magic, healing all wounds. Maybe there was still hope.

Bara went to get out of bed. Mathew and Courtney turned their heads and Courtney came to her side.

"You need rest," she said

"Courtney's right." Mathew agreed. "I couldn't fix the

damage done by the amber."

Bara waved them off. She ached and felt a little warm. Her hand was wrapped in gauze but she'd live.

"My mother?" she asked, expressing her real concern.

Courtney and Mathew said nothing.

It was a good thing she was sitting because Bara would have collapsed. Blood drained from her head and there was that heavy feeling in her gut. She breathed deeply.

"You couldn't save her! She's dead."

"Beth isn't dead," Courtney reassured.

Her tone was uneasy but the weight in Bara's stomach lifted some. Courtney gestured to the other bed. Bara pushed past and went to her mother. Ms. Cavanagh was just visible above the blankets. She looked as she had before. Middle-aged skin wasn't as tight and now lightly-lined. Her hair was again streaked with grey. She was still thin but that was all that remained of the transformation. No doubt the weight loss hadn't been part of the demon deal. But what mattered was she breathed steady and strong and Brynndalin was gone. Bara shook her gently.

Courtney placed a hand on Bara's arm.

"She won't wake up," she told her.

"What do you mean?"

"Do you remember what we said about the wisps?"

Mathew asked. "What happens to those they possess? What happens to their souls?"

"They are drained of energy ..." The realization hit. "Are you trying to tell me my mother is soulless?"

Silence was the answer.

"We captured Brynndalin. She's back in the amber. You said that would free those she'd enslaved."

"It frees what's left of the soul. No one ... no one's body has ever survived possession. Somehow I was able to heal her flesh. There seems to be enough energy left to keep the body alive but not enough for her to wake up and be who she was."

"But she's breathing on her own," Bara insisted. "She's fine. She's alive"

Bara shook her mother again, this time more forcibly.

"Mom! Wakeup!"

Amy and Colin had been awake for a while but they'd chosen to remain silent. When Bara called out Amy sat upright; Colin bolted from his chair and came to her side. Mathew had pulled Bara away from her mother. She struggled in his arms. Colin shoved Mathew. Mathew stepped back but an inch. A look came into his face, a look Bara had never seen before—rage. He shoved Colin in return. All arms and legs Colin took flight and landed on the bed next to Amy. His hands balled into fists Mathew charged the bed.

"Mathew!" Courtney sharp voice broke through. "You'll kill him!"

His rage left him as suddenly as it had come. Mathew stopped mid-room and unclenched his fist. He went to the fireplace and stared into the flames. Colin returned to his feet. It looked for a moment he might retaliate. He turned to Bara. She was looking from him to Mathew with a worried, pleading face. He shrugged off his anger and went to her side. Confident that the threat of violence had passed Bara knelt next to her mother again.

"They're trying to tell me that she has no soul," she told Colin. "That she's just an empty sack of bones."

Mathew spoke without looking up from the fire

"Feel for a second, Bara, you'll know."

Bara was silent, thinking about what he'd asked her to do. Tentatively she took her mother's hand and felt for the sense of something, for the sense of a soul. She held that hand for what seemed like forever and felt nothing. She placed a hand on her mother's forehead. It was warm but that was it. There was no real life, just flesh and bones. Her mother was gone. The first tear fell.

Courtney knelt and tried to embrace her.

"This is your fault!" Bara said, shirking the touch. "You brought this to us." On some level she knew this wasn't true. If it was anyone's fault it was hers. But her grief was talking and grief will look for someone else to blame, often the one we love the most.

"And you ..." She turned to Mathew and sobbed, "you should have stayed out of my dreams!"

Courtney looked down but remained kneeling. Mathew only nodded. Colin brought Bara to standing and ushered her to Amy. She sat between her two friends and wept. At some point Ms. Korey had come into the chamber. No one had noticed. She helped Courtney to her feet.

"Tell her now," she whispered.

Courtney shook her head.

Mathew looked at Bara, the tears streaming down her face. She had her head on Colin's shoulder and Colin held her hand, his other hand stroked her hair. The muscle in his lean cheek twitched but Mathew said nothing. He turned and left. Bara looked up and caught one last glimpse of the dark-haired boy before the heavy door closed behind him.

XXIII

A Dream

The Slip was sunlit and cheery. Gone was the snow and blustery wind of her last visit. Warm moist air had coaxed the world to life. Green shoots and purple crocuses stood daringly bare of any white. Birds sang and the sounds of small mammals could be heard rummaging in the understory. Yes winter was gone. It was spring.

Trees loomed overhead. Green leaves rustled in the wind and glinted in the sun. They seemed to be waving her on. With the thick-soled slippers Bara had taken to wearing to bed, just in case, the going was easy. But even if she had been barefoot it wouldn't have mattered. The path was covered in that lovely moss. All other trips into the Slip had been full of danger, evil hanging thick above, ready to fall upon those unaware. Bara looked up, only leaves, leaves and the clear blue sky. Just then a cardinal shot across the sky, a red lipstick smile.

A sound that couldn't possibly belong to a bird broke through the chatter of sparrows and wrens. It was laughter, giggles actually. Bara shivered when she thought of the last laughter she'd heard in this forest—Brynndalin's evil howl of triumph. But this laughter was joyous if also mischievous. The rustle of leaves and the snap of breaking twigs joined in. Something was approaching. Whatever it was, it was close, coming from only few feet off the path. Bara peered into the forest. At first she saw only the colors and shapes expected of a wood and then blonde hair and black. Shinning manes caught the sun rays and glinted. Like camouflage uncovered two familiar faces took shape below. Cassandra and Louise stared back.

The terrible twins stepped from the woods and stood blocking the path, arms on hips. They were clothed in leaves and bark miniskirts. For once Bara was happy to see the duo. They were still dead but here in the Slip springtime forest, among the flowers and chirping birds, they lived on. It may not be heaven—if heaven even existed—but it wasn't some horrendous purgatory where good did not.

And they were together. *Cas-Cas and Lou-Lou.*

They continued to stare. They were mocking Bara. *Nothing new!* But their look held more meaning. They were daring her. They were daring her to speak.

There was only one thing for her to say.

"I'm sorry," Bara whispered.

Just a little phrase *I'm sorry.* It seemed pathetic. No words could bring back their lives. The terrible twins seemed to agree. Their youthful faces took on the look of dour old ladies, stern from jowl to brow. But then their girlish faces returned, carefree and whimsical. They stuck out their tongues and blew raspberries. Their tongues sputtered out in unison and this brought on more giggles which quickly grew in intensity. Overcome they fell to their knees and onto their backs. Bara laughed too. Cassandra and Louise immediately stopped and glared.

No Bara wasn't forgiven. A chuckle stuck in her throat, burning like a dry aspirin.

The terrible twins helped each other to their feet. Even though they were already clad in the forest floor they dusted each other off. Louise gestured to the east and stared intently and then without a word she and Cassandra grabbed hands and slipped into the forest. Bara was left behind, an unpopular child not allowed to join in on the play. But Louise had pointed the way.

Bara left the path and headed east.

She soon came to a very different part of the Slip. Trees were down, ripped from their roots. Those that still stood had been stripped bare of any spring green. The forest floor was littered with the young sprouts. With no shade the sun shone unheeded, shining a blaring light on the destruction. What had caused the ruin? Other than an unassuming wind that couldn't have broken a twig from a branch there seemed no likely suspect. Even the strongest of winds couldn't have uprooted the giant that now lay across the forest floor. It was by far the largest tree Bara had ever seen. It would have taken centuries, if not a millennium, for it to have grown. How long she wondered would it take for it to rot away to nothing?

Bara crossed to the fallen goliath and stood at its base. She rounded the trunk and was among its exposed root system. Like the snakes of medusa dark brown tresses searched the air for earth they'd never find. But some had found water. Down below a small pond had formed. Its reflection doubled the destruction. Bara scanned the watery mirror and jumped. Someone was standing at her shoulder.

She spun around and then relaxed.

A life-size statue stood on the edge of the pond. Why had she not noticed it before? No forest greenery yet grew to mar the white marble. With time ivy and moss would find a root and erode it to dust but for now it was beautiful and perfect. There was something oddly familiar about the figure, something about the curve of the neck and long hands that held up thick hair. Bara looked at the pond again. There was her reflection and that of the statue which should have been lifeless. But the vision returning her gaze was one of flesh and vitality. Beth Cavanagh's face reflected back.

Mom! Bara fell to her knees and plunged her hands into the water. Grasping for flesh and bone she met with nothing solid but the slime of the pond floor. Frantically she felt around for anything and found nothing. She wetted herself to her shoulders before giving up on trying to recover her mother from the water. She sat back on her knees and waited for the surface to still. When it did her mother's reflection returned as lifelike as before.

Bara turned to the statue.

"Mom, is that you?"

No answer. Even in this world stone did not speak.

Bara reached out and touched the cold white marble. There was no sign of life. It was only a statue, ever immovable. It held no more of a soul than the body resting in the sleeping chamber below her father's house. Still it had to mean something? She looked at the pond once again and gasped. A mouth moved beneath the surface. Beth Cavanagh said but two words, over and over again. No sound reached her ears but Bara understood.

Save me.

About Author

Pryde was born in Winnipeg where she learned to walk on hard pack snow and deal with the inevitable fall through. Don't panic! You aren't going to die. Take your foot out of the boot, then dig out the boot, and they won't find your melting corpse in the spring. She attended high school in Calgary, Alberta. Pryde later moved to Vancouver where she obtained a B.A. in theatre and a B.Ed at the University of British Columbia. She has taught both in Vancouver and Japan and traveled extensively. Currently she is a mom and a frequent denizen of Vancouver coffee shops.

Book two of Dream Treaders is currently in the works. Also available is the collection of short stories and poems, **Strays**, and a poetic brevity collection, **Tattoo, Calling All Soldiers Home**. Soon to be released is another mixed works of short stories and poetry, **Monsters, the Tragic, Frightening, Funny, and Sometimes Brief.** All titles available in print and digital on amazon.com. Many recorded versions available on Pryde's Youtube channel. www.youtube.com/user/zendallalways

Acknowledgements

A special thank you to all the individuals who were gracious enough to read the Wisp at various times throughout its development. To those who offered encouragement and suggestions you helped make this book what it is. And thank you to my family and friends, your patience and kindness is always appreciated.

© Pryde Foltz 2014

All Rights Reserved

Made in the USA
San Bernardino, CA
22 February 2017